Separate Ways

Ryan Coull

DEDICATION

To my mum and dad, and my brother Allan.

ABOUT THE AUTHOR

Ryan Coull has published stories in the The New Writer, Firstwriter, Scribble magazine, and Storgy magazine. His story 'Garage 54' won the Swansea & District Writer's Circle competition in 2015.

PROLOGUE

Dorothy Hawthorn – Dottie, to those close to her – paced the kitchen floor, checking the clock above the cooker every few seconds, worrying at a thumbnail with her front teeth. Beneath her woollen jumper, her hand moved back and forth over her abdomen as if seeking some new development there.

Where was he?

Don't be so naïve, Dottie, she told herself. You know exactly where he is – out getting drunk, as usual. It only took someone – anyone – to suggest a session in the Admiral, and he would linger there indefinitely. She had learned to bear this side of his character, to endure it, but lately, it seemed drinking was all he wanted to do in life. He showed no interest in their marriage anymore, and this hurt, as they had been wed only three years. At twenty-eight, Dottie already suspected she'd made a mistake in marrying him, although she wasn't one to wave the white flag of defeat.

This morning, she had specifically told Billy she needed to talk to him tonight. It was important, she'd emphasised, and he had mumbled agreement before getting in his work van and driving off.

It had gone eleven o'clock now, and she knew that whatever state of dishevelment he turned up in, talking to him would be a waste of time. She could just picture him, staggering from the pub doorway, abandoning his van, and zigzagging his way home on foot. He had been stripped of his driving licence once before, in his teens, and had promised never to drink and drive again, but she knew the day would

5

come when he would risk it. Drunks never learned a lesson. His promises, she had come to know, had about as much substance as smoke.

Dottie's mind had been preoccupied throughout the afternoon. Trying to control her class of excitable eight-year-olds had done nothing to assuage her anxiety. All day, she had thought only of how Billy would react. What would he say? It had haunted her throughout, to the point where she couldn't concentrate on anything else.

Sometimes, when she expected Billy to explode, he did nothing. Sometimes, when she expected violence, he gave her the silent treatment, which in a way was worse. The man she had married was now almost gone completely, taken over by the *new* Billy. He often acted as if she wasn't even there, so convincingly that she sometimes doubted her own existence. The hardest part was admitting that she didn't know the person he'd become. The fairy tale, for Dottie, had long since ended. The man to whom she had betrothed her love would never drink himself to sleep in an armchair and suddenly vomit everywhere, oblivious to his actions.

Dottie touched her abdomen again. She knew her own body, and when her period had not happened this month, it could only mean she was pregnant. Her menstrual cycle was as regular as dusk and dawn. A subsequent urine test confirmed her suspicions. And nausea and throwing-up had begun already. She could even link the pregnancy to the last time she and Billy had made love.

Made love. She would have slapped her thigh and laughed had the whole situation not been so dire. On the night in question, he had been inebriated again, and begun tediously pawing at her under the bedcovers. "I'm tired," she had complained. "C'mon, Billy, you're drunk."

"I want you," was his impatient reply. In all-out drunken, horny-fool mode, he slid over her, pinning her arms to the bed, manoeuvring himself gracelessly inside her. One. Two. Three. Wham bam. After a few frantic thrusts, as she tried to escape the stench of his alcohol-laden breath, their 'lovemaking' was over, quick as it had started. For Dottie, the rest of the night had been spent listening to his hacking and snoring and being constantly roused by his fidgeting and flailing legs.

She stopped pacing and listened. A scraping sound came from outside: Billy was trying to get his key in the lock, a simple task that could take anything from five seconds to five minutes, a time even a blind man could beat.

Dottie tensed as the door slammed, the noise reverberating throughout the house. When he finally made it to the kitchen, Billy looked as bad as she had ever seen him look. His beady eyes were stewed and unfocused. His cheeks were mottled with pinkish patches, and his white T-shirt was randomly spotted with beer stains. Billy's fly was half open and one of his bootlaces undone. Judging by the wet patch at the crotch of his jeans, he had stopped somewhere to relieve himself and mistimed the whole thing.

"I told you I wanted to talk to you tonight, Billy," she said. "I asked you to come straight home after work because I had something to say to you."

His weight canted unsteadily to one side. "What's for dinner?"

"Dinner? Billy, it's after eleven o'clock."

He checked his watch and staggered. "So what? I'm starving here."

"It's in the microwave."

Billy winced, trying to focus on the machine's buttons. He started the process without even looking inside. "So, what's so important you've to tell me, huh?"

"We're going to have a baby, Billy." She folded her arms and looked at the floor. "I didn't want to tell you like this, but you don't give me any choice."

His back straightened, his slouch suddenly gone. "A baby?" He looked confused, then wary. "What about the – the pill? You're supposed to be taking the pill."

"I *have* been taking it." She shrugged her shoulders. "Somehow, it didn't work. There's always a chance it won't."

"I thought we were gonna wait? That's what we decided, right? What're you trying to pull here?"

Pull? Was he serious? Did he think she was that desperate to have a child? "I said I'm still taking the pill. It hasn't worked, Billy. I didn't decide to get pregnant, but it's happened."

"Can't you even use contraception properly, you silly cow?"

Dottie, having sworn to herself she wouldn't cry, felt tears brimming. She had hoped he might be pleased, that a baby might narrow the chasm burgeoning between them. "Don't say that to me, Billy. I wanted us to use condoms, remember? You wouldn't have it. Like wearing socks in a bath, you said. It was your idea to use the pill."

"Don't try to make this out to be my fault."

"It's no one's fault. We're married, Billy. I thought you might be happy ..."

He stared at her, the stench of spirits lingering between them. "Well, what you wanna do with it?"

"Do with it? What's that supposed to mean?"

"You're the teacher. What the hell d'you think it means?"

"I'm not having an abortion, Billy. I won't kill my baby. Not for you, not for anyone."

The microwave ended its cycle with a *ping*. Billy tugged open the small door and removed the plate of steaming chicken and potatoes. He crossed in front of Dottie and stamped open the pedal bin. She swallowed as he tipped his dinner away – half of it landing on the linoleum – and flinched as he tossed the plate noisily into the sink.

"Going to bed," he muttered, eyeing Dottie with a bloodshot glare. For a moment, she thought he might strike her. It wouldn't be the first time. But he just shook his head, trudged past, and said, "Clean away that mess."

She listened to his footfalls climbing the stairs and to the rush of urine hitting the toilet – another mess she'd have to clear up, as it would be sprayed all over the bowl and floor. More thumping steps followed as he reached the bedroom and then silence.

Dottie tore some kitchen towels from the roll and began clearing the food by the bin, weeping quietly on her hands and knees.

PART ONE

TRIMESTERS

CHAPTER 1

"Set in Rhodes? That sounds interesting," Dottie said, smoothing her long floral dress. "So, how's the story coming along?"

Lynette Hobin, Aradale's one and only romantic novelist, Dottie's best friend in the world, looked doubtful. "Not too well, if I'm being honest."

"Really? Writer's block?"

"I'm not sure. It's just not coming as easily as the other books." Lynette was filing her painted nails with an emery board, extending her fingers every now and then, appraising them at arm's length. "Could be the lead character, but I think I've started in the wrong place."

"Don't you always work at home?" Dottie asked.

Lynette smiled. "I mean, I picked the wrong point in the story, to begin with."

"Oh." Dottie felt her cheeks redden and gave herself a playful slap on the forehead. She loved teaching but knew she could never do what Lynette did, writing those romance novels, juggling characters, dialogue, and everything else. "Ignore me, I'm not with it today."

"Ah, I'll work it out. Enough about me, anyway. I dropped by to talk about you and the bump there. Have you dreamed up any names yet?"

Dottie readjusted herself on the settee and placed a hand on her swollen belly. In her second trimester, she was seventeen weeks gone and felt fat and horrible – but at least she wasn't sick anymore. "There's a couple I've been thinking about. Emma for a girl. Maybe

David for a boy. I think we're going to wait till after the birth and then decide."

"The big day will be here before you know it, Dottie."

"Lynette ... how did you feel going into labour? Were you afraid?"

"Too right, I was afraid. Terrified. But that's normal. You'll be just fine. Once you've got that little bundle in your arms, it'll be worth it, I promise."

Dottie knew this to be true, although she would still be relieved when the birth was over. The winter had been long and arduous, during which she'd suffered every symptom of pregnancy in the book and a few more to boot. From dizziness to faintness, to chronic heartburn, from enlarged breasts to passing water every ten minutes, she had endured it all. She'd even found herself bursting into tears without warning and not knowing why. And the amount of ice cream she'd wolfed down lately, well, that was just ludicrous.

"God, I look at you and feel so jealous," Dottie said, setting her feet up on the little pouffe. Lynette was always so well turned out. Today she looked radiant in a navy outfit, which seemed tailored to accentuate her hourglass curves. Her lengthy black hair shone with health, touched by the April sun coming through the blind. And her unblemished face reminded Dottie of those flawless girls in skincare commercials.

"I can't wait to shrink down to a normal size – if I ever do. I've been doing my shoulder and leg stretches as often as I can. They're supposed to give you more energy, but sometimes I wonder."

"Are you still going to the health centre?"

Dottie nodded. "I walk there and back every week. The water workouts aren't too strenuous, and I do feel better about it afterward. Sometimes I have to push myself to leave the house, though."

"We all go through it. I was the same before I had Mark. I felt bloated and useless, and depressed, but it was temporary. I also had carpal tunnel syndrome – brought about by repetitive movements of the hand." Lynette wiggled her fingers. "Too much typing. We lasses just have to tough it out. We certainly can't rely on males to repopulate the earth."

"C'est la vie," Dottie said, looking down at her flip-flops. "I'll be glad to get proper shoes on, too. Never worn flat heels for so long in my life."

"You'll be back in style before you know it," Lynette assured her, forking her fingers through her hair. "So, did you have the scan this morning?"

"Yeah. Dr Cassidy's such a nice man. Really patient."

From the outset, her doctor had constantly allayed any fears that Dottie voiced when visiting him, and she trusted him implicitly. He had performed the first scan after ten weeks and calculated the baby's forecast date for delivery.

Today, she and Dr Cassidy had indulged in a prolonged talk following her second scan. He assured her there were no problems, which Dottie was elated to hear, because she'd been secretly worried the baby could be born malformed, or with an affliction. Common fears, Nick Cassidy told her. Everything would be fine.

"Handsome devil, too," Lynette was saying. "I wouldn't say no to a roll in the hayloft with him, huh? And what about that tush?"

"Lynette," Dottie said, although she knew her friend wasn't being serious. "What would Graham say if he could hear you?"

Lynette waved a hand. "Aw, who cares? Only pretending, right?"

"Well, so long as it's pretending. He is very dishy."

"Dishy?" Lynette repeated, laughing. "That's a very lah-di-dah term. I didn't think anyone still said that."

Dottie laughed and tried to sit forward, feeling like a stranded whale. "Well, what would you call him, then, smarty-pants?"

"I'd call him hot – hot as Lucifer's poker."

Dottie was glad of Lynette's company. She had thus far found the pregnancy a lonely experience, even after Billy had eventually come around to the idea. With both her parents living in Spain, Dottie felt a gaping space in her life. Her mother and father had promised to visit when the baby was born, and she looked forward to that time immensely. Having bought their stunning colonial-style manor house six years ago, her parents now woke each morning to the flower-decorated vista of Mojácar. Their home offered tremendous views of the coast and the inland plain. Dottie had flown out there only once, but the area's beauty had remained with her. What could be unappealing about three hundred days of sunshine every year?

Still, Lynette was always there for her. They had remained close since their schooldays and valued each other's friendship like no other.

"So, how's it going with himself?" Lynette asked, more seriously.

"Billy? Aw, he's trying, Lynette, you know. Sometimes, I think he just doesn't know what to do. Typical man."

"Is he staying off the booze?"

Dottie nodded, although she wasn't being entirely honest. Billy had promised to cut back on his drinking – which he had – but he still consumed too much. "He's been pretty good about it all."

"He's supposed to be there for you. Don't let him forget that. Get him doing everything you can, Dottie. Running for an extra pillow, cooking meals – anything you can think of."

Dottie could just imagine Billy's reaction if she told him to fetch pillows. That sort of thing wouldn't fly for long. But Lynette was right: he should be helping her more now that she became quite breathless after the slightest effort and suffered palpitations when merely climbing the stairs.

"He gets me everything I ask for," Dottie went on. "I've been trying to live healthily – apart from the buckets of ice cream, that is. Dr Cassidy outlined what I should be eating, and I've tried to stick to it. Fish, cheese, eggs, fruit and veg – all the good stuff."

"Billy'll have to change after the birth as well, Dottie," Lynette told her. "That's the most important time, when you'll need even more support than you do now, having the little one to care for."

"I worry about that, sometimes. What he'll be like with a new baby in the house. Will we cope? Will Billy change into the man I need him to be?"

"You think he can?"

Dottie's hands roamed across the plump globe of her stomach. "He's certainly changed since I married him."

Lynette crossed the room and sat beside her on the couch. "I'm here if you want to talk about it."

For the millionth time during the pregnancy, Dottie's eyes were welled with tears. And she hated herself for displaying weakness. "Oh, I don't know, he's so different from the man I married, from the guy who proposed out on that lake. Some days, it's like he doesn't even want to be with me anymore. He can be so ... so *cold*."

"Is it really that bad, Dottie?" Lynette handed her a tissue from the coffee table.

"No, he's better now. Really, he is. And I think that when Junior here comes along, well, it'll bridge the gap between us. It'll be the making of Billy, I'm sure."

Lynette gave Dottie's hand a supportive squeeze. "Definitely. Once he sees that little face, his heart will just melt, you mark my words."

Dottie nodded. "I hope so. Because if that doesn't work, I don't know what I'll do."

CHAPTER 2

Billy slowed the high-top van, joining the line of traffic that snaked down Prince Street, Aradale's busiest thoroughfare. "Jesus Christ," he muttered, tugging the gearshift into neutral and letting up the clutch. The rain-slick paths were teeming with shoppers in long coats, many of them toting closed umbrellas and coloured shopping bags, walking hand in hand, peering in shop windows, yakking into mobile phones.

Billy was on his last run of the day for Green Arrow Carriers, the delivery and collection company he had been slaving for over the last eight years. He had three remaining parcels to drop at Chalky's newsagents, about two hundred yards along the street, but judging by the stagnant line of cars ahead, it might be Christmas before he got there.

"Come on, come on, come on," he mouthed, jabbing his closed fist on the wheel. "Bloody slugs."

He glanced over at the cinema, where a group of youths loitered outside the main entrance. Me and the boys eighteen years ago, he thought. Most of his old buddies had fled Aradale long ago, and it smarted a little that he was still mired here. "You'll swap this dump for warmer shores one of these days, Billy boy," he promised himself.

Slumming it for Green Arrow was a shit job. He was wasted driving vans, but everyone kept holding him back. It had been the same his whole life. Dottie was the one doing it now. He was sure she had stopped taking the pill in order to conceive – after they had both agreed to wait. She thought he was dumb, but he knew what was going on. Dottie could scheme and connive all she wanted; he wouldn't forget something like this, no sir. She had tried to trick him. But he would not be tricked, not by anyone, and especially not by a female. He was a free spirit, capable of much more than running dumb parcels around town like a rat in a maze.

Wincing in the sun's glare, Billy leaned out of the van's window, feeling the cool April breeze licking over the shaven crown of his head. The sun was warm on his face, although the day had been one heavy shower after another. Deep pools of rainwater had gathered by the roadside, the drains swollen and clogged. In the distance, the ghost of a rainbow could be seen, and Billy found himself thinking of that stupid programme he had watched as a kid. The one with the man-bear and the hippo and the mustard thing with a zip for a mouth.

"Damned weather doesn't know what it's doing," he said as the stream of cars crawled forward, and the lights switched to red again.

Yes, Dottie was holding him back, just as his father had throughout Billy's childhood and adolescence. Billy had always resented being raised by his father. One morning, when he was six years old, Billy found his mother facedown on the bathroom floor. She had come out of the shower and dropped dead, killed by an aneurysm. Billy had rushed to the phone and called an ambulance, but his mother never moved so much as a finger again. He had never been the same after that.

From then, life with the old man had been a waking nightmare for Billy, and his little brother, both of them dragged up by an alcoholic whose favourite pastime – second to getting blasted – was throwing them around like rag dolls. Or coming at them with a belt. Or burning them with cigarettes. It depended on what mood he was in. Billy could pinpoint no less than eight places on his body where his father had branded a permanent reminder of his temper. Cuts, burns, scars – take your pick. He had all kinds. When Grady Alasdair Hawthorn hadn't been getting pissed or working on his sons, he had spent his time writhing on top of slappers he lured home from the pubs and clubs. Billy suspected his father had paid those women for sex but never knew for sure. Certainly, there was never any spare money for things like food or clothes.

Billy's younger brother had taken off to live in London years ago, where he had become entangled with drugs and unsavoury types, and Billy rarely heard from him anymore. It was hardly surprising.

Billy wound up the window as fat spots of rain hit the windscreen.

He had never come to terms with his mother being taken away. And he really couldn't believe his father was still alive today – if you could call the old man's current state living. Billy's memories of his mother were fond ones, and those of his father undoubtedly sour. His father – ravaged mentally and physically from a lifetime of drinking and chasing harlots – now festered up in the Mosgrove Residential Care Home. Billy didn't venture near there, despite Dottie's ongoing insistence that he should. He hated the old man, despised him, and would gladly pop a bottle of bubbly when his rancid black heart finally packed in. It gave Billy a twisted pleasure, knowing that his father was now debilitated, being fed and cared for by strangers, unable to inflict pain on anyone or anything.

"Sod this," he said, steering the van to the roadside and yanking on the handbrake. He would walk the remaining distance and carry the damned parcels.

Billy set off down Prince Street on foot, past the war memorial, weaving lithely between dithering shoppers, resisting the urge to steamroller old women and kids blocking his path.

Inside the newsagents, he dropped the parcels on the counter and flexed his shoulders. The round-eyed Asian gentleman by the till took the delivery slip from Billy and went over it, item by item. Billy grabbed a Coke from the fridge, idling there a little longer than necessary, eyeing the top-shelf glossies. Had he not been itching to get going, he might have taken the time to browse through them. At the counter, he placed the Coke and some coins in front of the Asian man and folded the delivery slip into his pocket. The Asian man nodded, rang through the sale, and completed their dealings without a single word.

"Much obliged, friend," Billy said and stepped back to the street, glad to finally be finished for the day. He sparked open his drink, setting off towards the parked Green Arrow van. Typically, the traffic had begun flowing again.

Suddenly, a red Saab bucketed through one of the pools gathered by the roadside, throwing up rainwater over Billy's body and face, drenching his jeans and T-shirt. He stopped walking, spitting out dirty-tasting liquid, and peered down at himself.

"You prick!" he called, drawing instant stares from passers-by. Billy gripped the Coke can, crumpling it slightly. With a rushed aim, he launched it at the Saab's back end. The can connected squarely with the car's rear window with a thud, its contents spraying out over the glass. Two young girls in the back seat turned to look at him, their faces set in amazement. Red brake lights flared, and the Saab screeched to a halt.

"Here we go."

Billy's eyes narrowed as he watched the driver's door open and a man get out. Adrenaline began coursing through his blood as he readied himself for a fight. Out of the Saab now, the driver was considerably smaller than Billy, both in height and build. He was dressed in a patterned mint-green sweater and pleated golf trousers. He went about inspecting his rear window for damage, running his fingers over the glass, and finally set off in Billy's direction.

Billy scrutinised the man's body language for signs of weakness. Hesitancy hindered the guy's step, and nervousness was evident in the way he wiped his hands on his sweater. This dude was afraid, but with his wife and kids in the car, he had no choice other than to react. Didn't want to be seen as a pussy. Billy could imagine him hosing down his precious car on a Sunday afternoon, dressed in shorts and sandals, while his missus prepared a roast in the kitchen. Maggots.

"What in the blazes do you think you're doing?" the man said. "You've cracked my window."

"Well, you soaked me, chief," Billy told him, amused by the little guy's false bravado. "Look at me. Wet as a whore's pussy here."

"It was an accident, for God's sake." He pointed at his Saab, his mouth agape. "You cannot go around ... throwing things at cars. Don't you know how irresponsible that is? You could've seriously hurt someone!"

"I might seriously hurt *you*, mister, you keep shoutin' at me."

21

The man lowered his arm and shifted warily back. He looked around at his wife and two children, watching from the car about thirty feet away. "Are you threatening me?" he asked. "What you just did – is against the law."

"Listen, you little turd." Billy leaned down into the man's eyeline and laid hold of his sweater. "I'll make you a deal, okay? You shut your face right now, scurry off to your mobile over there, and I won't beat the shit out of you in front of your family. How's that sound, huh?"

He stared into the little man's eyes long enough to let his words sink in before releasing his sweater with a gentle shove. The guy stumbled awkwardly back, his cheeks reddening. Then, as instructed, he obediently returned to his car without another word.

CHAPTER 3

"Home sweet home," Lynette Hobin said as she closed the front door of Netherwood House.

Her home was a five-bedroom sandstone structure built near the beginning of the twentieth century, although Lynette and her husband had modernised every aspect of the interior since moving in. It stood proudly on Aradale's north periphery, and, as the unambiguous title intimated, it was shielded from the town by acres of dense woodland, thereby affording Lynette the privacy and tranquillity she craved.

After leaving Dottie and returning home that afternoon, Lynette found her husband, Graham, preparing sandwiches in the kitchen for his night shift as a security guard. Mark, her little future scholar, was engrossed in homework. The ten-year-old sat slouched at the living-room coffee table with textbooks spread around him, bouncing a pencil against his lip.

"Hey, Einstein," she said. "You look snowed under, my boy. What are you doing?"

"Sums," Mark replied without looking up.

"Great. Which kind?"

"The boring kind."

"Right." She went to Tara. The four-year-old was kneeling by the television, cupping a glass of orange juice in both hands. Lynette touched her daughter's plaited hair. "Hey, sweet pea. You okay?"

Tara slurped her orange and nodded, giggling at the cartoons.

"Hey there." Graham sauntered in and kissed her cheek, bringing a hand over the small of her back.

23

"Did I ever tell you how good you look in black?" Lynette said quietly.

"Digging my work threads, huh?" Graham grinned, vainly admiring himself in the mirror. "Irresistible, huh? Just like James Bond."

"Get real."

"Hey, here's one for you," he said. "There's a little boy standing crying in a store, so a woman walks over and says, What's wrong? I can't find my dad, says the boy. Well, what's he like? asks the woman. Big boobs and blonde hair, says the boy."

"Been reading lollipop sticks again?"

"That hurts. My jokes are pure class."

"They're pure something, I'll give you that."

"So, how's Dorothy coping with the woes of pregnancy?" Graham asked.

"Hmm. I don't think her excuse for a husband is doing much to help out."

"She looking forward to motherhood?"

"I think she'd feel better if Billy showed more support."

Graham shrugged. "We've been through this before, Lyne. You've got to let them sort out their own problems. They're a married couple, grown-ups."

"She thinks the baby might bring them closer together."

"Uh-huh. You don't agree?"

"No, but I hope I'm wrong."

Graham picked up his jacket from the sofa. "Well, be sure to give her my love when you see her."

"I will – we're going out for lunch on Saturday."

 "Gotta go, guys. Catch you in the morning."

"Bye-bye, Daddy!" Tara called, and Mark raised a hand in farewell.

"Take care," Lynette told him. "Be safe."

Graham kissed her cheek again. "Happy writing."

With her husband gone, Lynette began preparing dinner for her and the children. She drained the blood from cuts of lamb's liver and fried them, and heated nuggets and beans for Tara. She sautéed onion and wedged open the window to expel the tangy whiff. Rex, their corgi, padded at her feet, chuffing, and she opened the back door for him. "Out you go, Rex, there's a good doggy."

As she worked, Lynette worried about Dottie, recalling how miserable her friend had looked that afternoon. Lynette knew Dottie better than anyone and could tell when she was in the doldrums. But even a dispirited Dottie didn't often moan, which made it difficult to gauge the true extent of her problems. It beggared belief that Billy wasn't a better husband to her – that he didn't *want* to be a better husband. At barely five feet, Dottie was a little sweetheart, and her innocent, almost childish smile always made Lynette think of a brown-haired Goldie Hawn.

Lynette could not understand anyone willingly making Dottie's life difficult. Billy didn't deserve her. Like so many other men, he took his spouse for granted. Dottie could do so much better. Lynette had had her reservations before Dottie married Billy. He had been renowned for trouble throughout his younger days, but Dottie had opined this was merely a passing phase, something she could rectify with time, love, and tenderness. Lynette had always doubted this. Billy wasn't just the Bad Boy in need of taming; he was inherently callous and often cruel. He'd been caught driving under the influence a year before Dottie had begun seeing him. A year prior to that, he had punched a girl in the face in a nightclub because she refused to dance with him. With witnesses aplenty, Billy was arrested, and, luckily for him, the girl bizarrely decided to forget the whole thing. Lynette had heard other stories, too, all of them as bad as the next. Billy Hawthorn – especially when drunk – didn't think twice about lashing out at a woman. Were Dottie and a new baby safe with a man like that?

Dottie was the polar opposite of her husband. She always toiled to find the good in others and lived her life conscientiously. Only last week, Lynette and Dottie had been walking through town when Dottie spotted a wad of money protruding from a cash machine.

"Wow, Lynette, look at this," she said, taking the money and fanning it out. "There must be two hundred pounds here."

"Well, stick it in your bag before anyone claims it," Lynette told her.

"What? Oh, I couldn't do that."

"Why not? The damned bank won't miss it. They're the ones who've caused this bloody recession, Dottie. Go on, take it and buy the baby something nice."

"No, no. Maybe an old lady's gone off without it or something. She might need it to pay her bills, don't you think?"

Lynette had to smile, recalling Dottie barging into the bank to hand over the money: her friend was probably in the one percent of today's society still capable of such altruism.

Yet, Dottie was stronger than her appearance might suggest. She came across as meek as a rabbit, but Lynette had witnessed firsthand the courage her friend harboured inside that petite form. Four years ago, when Mark was six, Graham had taken the family for a picnic, and Lynette suggested it would be fun if Dottie came along. Billy was invited, too, although he thankfully had better things to do.

The five of them – Graham, Lynette, Tara, Mark, and Dottie – set off under a July sun and eventually stopped by a loch Graham had been searching everywhere for. Lynette couldn't now remember the loch's name for the life of her, but Graham had been told that the fishing was good. The grey-blue water was surrounded by tall, craggy rocks. They found a perfect spot five minutes from the car. Lynette and Dottie arranged the food and blankets, and Mark was quickly jumping from the high rocks into the water, time and again. As soon as he had completed one cold plunge, he made his way straight up for another. "Careful there, Mark," she'd told him more than once, although Mark was a strong swimmer for his age, and she hadn't really been worried.

Graham, after assembling his rod, started back to the car with Tara for a forgotten tub of bait, leaving Lynette and Dottie sizzling in the sun. After a short time, Lynette became aware that she couldn't hear her son in the water anymore. With no splashing sounds, no jubilant calls for them to watch his jumps, Lynette had presumed Mark was making his way back to them. She sat up and looked around – and saw him slumped in the water. Blood covered his face, and he was, as far as she could tell, unconscious.

Lynette screamed her son's name and frantically ran down to the loch's edge. She scanned nearby for her husband, and her heart plummeted: Graham was at the car with Tara, little more than a speck in the distance. Lynette had never learned to swim, and the water was deep out there where Mark bobbed lifelessly.

Dottie dived in, front-crawling out to Mark. Lynette was beside herself, and in tears, by the time Dottie pulled the boy from the loch. There was so much blood. Dottie was magnificent, though. She fixed a clean cloth to Mark's head, staunching the blood, and fashioned a towel into a makeshift bandage, securing it around the wound in a kind of reef knot. All this was recalled from a first-aid course she had taken more than two years before.

Lynette had never felt so helpless. Hell, she couldn't even remember what day she was due at the hairdresser's, let alone recall life-saving techniques.

"Come and get some fuel for that brain of yours, Mark," she called now, laying out the plates. "Tara, dinner's ready!"

Mark trudged into the kitchen and sat down, and Lynette couldn't help feeling a lump in her throat. She had nearly lost him that day when he'd struck something in the water. Mark regained consciousness more than an hour later on the way to the hospital. But if it hadn't been for Dottie's courage and action, her son would quite possibly be dead today.

CHAPTER 4

"I'm fine, Ma. Really. Dr Cassidy's been a real help. I've another scan in a couple of months, but he says there's nothing to be concerned about. Both of us are doing great."

"That's so good to hear, Dottie. As long as everything's as it should be, and you're taking care of yourself."

"I am Ma. Promise. These maternity bras take a bit of getting used to, though. So does look like a human Space-hopper. Otherwise, I'm okay."

"How many weeks along are you now?"

"Twenty-three, give or take. I've felt every one of them, too, with Junior making his Bruce Lee impressions half the time."

Dottie's mother made a tiny squeal of delight. "Really? He's kicking?"

"Oh yeah, a little bruiser." Dottie slipped her foot from its flip-flop, brushing her sole lightly against the oak floor. She was standing in the kitchen in a turquoise maternity dress, the scalloped hem draping around her shins.

"Twenty-three weeks," her mother echoed proudly. "It won't be long, Dottie. Have the side effects been bearable?"

"I've had a lot of swelling and backache and constipation, but the exercises help. I've got relaxation techniques to do and movements that are supposed to help with pelvic toning – whatever that is."

"That's good, sweetheart. And how's Billy? He took care of you?"

"Course, Ma."

"Is he excited?"

Dottie bit her lip. "Yeah, he is. He's upstairs painting the spare room right now. He assembled the baby's cot yesterday, and we picked up nice green paint for it. It's all falling into place."

"That's good, Dottie. So what colour is the nursery?"

"We're using magnolia for the minute to freshen the place, but I'll pick something proper after the baby comes. Maybe pink, maybe blue. Listen, Ma, how's Dad doing?"

"You know him, Dottie. So long as he's got a drink in his hand and the sun's shining, he's happy."

"You better put him on, so I can say a quick hello."

"Okay, love. We can't wait to get over there and see you. Love you, sweetie."

"Love you too, Ma." Dottie heard brief clunking sounds and distant exchanged words before her father spoke.

"Hey, how's my favourite girl?" His was a deep, venerable voice, roughened from years of puffing on stinky cigars. Dottie felt instant warmth and love upon hearing it, whisked back to her childhood when he'd regale her with tales by the fireplace. She closed her eyes, savouring the cadence of every syllable, picturing him, swarthy and happy and surrounded by a panorama of Mediterranean bliss.

"How're you keeping, Dad?"

"Never mind the old man, Dottie. You just concentrate on yourself and that little fella you're carrying, hear?"

"Mother and child both in top condition."

"That's good. I hear the wee mite's been laying into you. That's a positive sign, love. Means he's healthy and wanting outta there."

"He? We don't know the sex, Dad."

30

"It'll be a boy, I'm sure."

"We'll have to just wait and see."

"What will be, will be. As long as the toes and fingers are in the correct places." A pause. "And how's Billy?"

"Oh, he's okay."

"You tell him to treat you right, or he'll be dealing with me."

Dottie laughed. "I will, Dad."

"Okay, sweetheart. We'll be across to see you soon. Take care of yourself now. And the nipper."

When Dottie dropped the receiver back in its mount, she wanted to cry – again – momentarily taken off-guard by the myriad emotional nuances stirring inside her. "Hold it together, Dorothy," she said and set off upstairs, clutching the banister for balance.

Slightly breathless, she found Billy in one of the two spare bedrooms. The Rolling Stones played "Emotional Rescue" on the portable CD player. The room, which shared a dividing wall with their bedroom, was bathed in warm early-evening sunlight. The window was pinned open, although the paint's cloying fumes still assaulted Dottie's nose. Billy had removed the curtains and draped them across the bed. He was working diligently around the window in white overalls, clutching a paint-roller, flecks of magnolia emulsion on his hands and face.

"Hey, you're getting some paint on the walls," Dottie said happily.

Billy stopped what he was doing and scowled at her. "That supposed to be funny?"

"I was joking, grumpy chops."

"Uh-huh. That what I am to you – a joke?"

31

Dottie ignored him and crossed the threshold, walking over to the cot. She drew a hand across one side. "This is all really nice," she said, looking around the room. "It looks great, Billy. You've done a wonderful job here. Really nice."

Billy set the roller down in the drip tray and tossed an old rag at her. "Take that stuff off your face."

Dottie reflexively caught the rag, which was dappled with smears of magnolia paint. She stared at him, seeking an explanation.

"The lipstick. Take it off."

"What's the matter—?"

"You're pregnant, Dottie. With my baby. I don't want you walking about looking like a ... boated slag. Wipe it off."

Dottie said nothing – she felt certain she must have misheard. She glanced at the baby's crib in the corner. A glass-eyed pink bear with a white ribbon – a gift from Lynette – sat peering out through the bars like a captive in Toyland. "Billy, you can't be serious. It's just lipstick."

Switching off the CD player, he said, "Either you wipe it off, or I'll do it for you."

Dottie watched him studying her, waiting for her to make a decision, and suddenly she was back in school, being admonished for chewing gum in class. She placed a hand subconsciously on her belly; with her other hand, she brought the rag across her lips slowly. Once. Twice. Last time. The light-pink shade stained the rag, mixed with magnolia spots. Something shrivelled and died inside her, and she received a hearty kick from the baby as if chastening her for the display of cowardice.

"Good," he said and continued painting the last section of the wall.

Dottie regarded the rag with disbelief, unsure which part of the humiliating fiasco cut her the most – his description of her as a bloated slag, his insistence that she remove almost colourless make-up, or her unwillingness to stand her ground.

"There was… a call from the residential home earlier," she said. "Your father's unwell, Billy. They wanted me to let you know about it. He has Alzheimer's, they said, and he's deteriorating."

Billy's roller arm ceased moving. "Fine, now I know."

"Billy, I think—"

"Don't harp on at me about going to see him, Dottie. I don't wanna hear it again."

She took a deep breath, crossed the wooden floor, and touched his back. It was clammy with perspiration. "I told them you would go there and see him."

He froze as if someone had paused him by remote control.

"They say he's very sick," Dottie went on. "If anything happens, you might regret not taking the time to at least visit. He's an old man, and you're his son… I really think it would be beneficial for you to see him." Dottie waited, her hand still on his back, her heart pumping.

After a long silence, tempered only by sparrows beyond the open window, Billy said, "Okay. You win. I'll go see him."

"Really? Oh, that's fantastic. You'll—"

"Now run on down and bring me up a Miller, Dottie. Good girl."

Dottie waited a moment, shocked and a mite suspicious that he'd agreed to her request with such ease. Then she laid the lipstick-stained rag on the trestle beside her and waddled from the room.

33

CHAPTER 5

Later, after showering and shaving and making a short journey across town, Billy stood adjacent to the rise of tawdry tenement flats in King Edward Court. The blocks of squalid apartments were unquestionably Aradale's finest example of deprivation. Before leaving the house, he had told Dottie he was assisting his boss at Green Arrow with moving furniture, and she had nodded her gullible-Dottie nod, saying, "Okay, Billy." It was a bloody mystery how she made the grade as a teacher.

The calm May evening was ruined by cries and shouts from a group of scraggy youngsters down the road. Billy watched them kicking a football around by a call box. They swore, seemingly for the sake of swearing, and looked like trouble waiting to happen. Another bunch of wasters going nowhere fast. Across the street, the local shop's windows were secured behind protective wire mesh, its brickwork painted in slashes of crude aerosol graffiti.

Billy shaded his eyes, squinting at the flats. Grime-clouded windows jutted open here and there, all the way up, like a dilapidated Advent calendar – only nothing pleasing was revealed inside: dingy curtains, dulled lighting, and sets of crooked blinds. He saw a woman washing dishes, an old rug draped over her windowsill.

He locked the van and began along the walkway, stepping into the cool shadow of the building. The way was peppered with dogshit and weeds.

He was surprised to find the elevator operational – a new and somewhat pleasant experience for him. It had always been faulty in the past, necessitating a hike up the stone stairs to the fifth floor, the journey usually blighted by slamming doors and mothers screaming at kids.

In the elevator, Billy leaned on the side and felt the old rumbling mechanism begin its ascent. Like the store outside, the closed-in walls were marred with graffiti, and Billy could not help but read it. Jasper woz ere. For a great blow job, call Winston. Wendy loves question marks. Johnny W is a faggot.

Billy grunted as the doors parted again, revealing a long, cement-floored hall littered with bin bags. He strode down there, the ground peppered with squashed fag-ends and stained with God alone knew what. A baby was screaming loud enough to make a mother's ears bleed. A dog barked, keening mournfully, and Billy empathised with the poor beast, wherever it was. *Get me outta here*, he imagined it was saying in doggy lingo. The rank smell of stale piss pervaded the hall, and he held his breath as he went.

He reached the third-last door and knocked twice, adjusting his crotch as he waited. After a few seconds, he heard the sound of a key turning. The door inched open a crack, and a sleepy almond eye found him.

"Surprise," he said flatly.

The door backed open all the way, and Billy studied the young woman standing before him. She was barefoot, twenty years old. Platinum blonde this month, although her roots testified to the dye job. Pert titties pushed against her white T-shirt. Her legs were bare and shapely if a touch sticklike for his taste. Pink panties. Lacy. Dark crescents shadowed her eyes. She was repeatedly sniffing and touching her nose, and he could see she was high.

35

"You haven't been around for a while," she said once he had stepped inside and closed the door.

"Well, I've been busy, Angela. But I'm here now. Got a damned kid on the way and everything."

"Oh? I didn't know."

"Well, now you do, don't you?"

Billy glanced distastefully at the strewn clothing and towels, at skirts and socks drying wherever convenient. The tarnished wooden table was cluttered with dirty plates and mugs and lots of glossy magazines. The kind of magazines with nonentity celebrities on the cover, people famous because the paparazzi managed to get a shot of their underwear. Or because they were pregnant. Or maybe they had just been starving themselves for the last six months on the latest diet. Depends on the edition. Billy shook his head. He thought he smelled a hound, but as far as he knew, Angela didn't keep one.

"I didn't know you were coming," she said. Her eyes were heavy and half closed.

"So I see. Don't you ever clean this joint? Can't you put the clothes in the drawers? Can't you wash up your dishes?"

"I've just fallen behind with the housework." She sat in the room's only armchair. "I can clear it away if you like."

"No, don't bother. Not as if I come around here for your domestic talents, is it?"

"I'm not long back from the restaurant," she said. "It's hard to find the time."

"Plenty time to get high, though, huh?"

He went to the window and inched aside the yellowed net curtain. Below, the kids were still kicking the ball around by the call box, taunting each other. Even from up here he could hear them turning the air blue.

"Don't those noisy runts drive you crazy?"

"No one can do anything with them," she said. "The police only take them home to their parents, and the parents don't care. It's not like I live here by choice, Billy. You know where I can rent somewhere swanky, working as a waitress?"

"Don't get smart, I just asked you a question."

"Sorry." She stood. "When did you—"

"Let's get going," he told her, cutting her off. "Lead the way, Mademoiselle."

In the bedroom, Billy tossed a small packet on the mattress. Angela sat and began arranging two lines of cocaine on the bedside table, expertly cutting and preparing the white powder with an ATM card.

Billy paced. The bedroom was painted in shocking pink, like something a five-year-old would choose. The walls were decorated with tacky pictures. Cute kittens in a basket; an orang-utan swinging in a tyre; a picture of Sean Connery as Bond.

Finished preparing the cocaine, she looked up at him, and he nodded consent, handing her a rolled ten-pound note. "Go ahead," he said. "Get stuck in." Angela bent over and inhaled the drug; then, she leaned back, eyes closed, sniffing, and teasing her nose.

Billy plucked the note from her and squatted by the little table, inhaling the second line with rehearsed familiarity. When he

37

straightened, a rush of supercharged adrenaline overcame him. She smiled at him shyly from the bed. He turned and peeled off her T-shirt, her arms raised to assist him. Billy took a second, appraising her as the drug tweaked pleasantly at his mind. She was bare now, save for the skimpy pink underwear. The two peaks of her breasts seemed to beckon him, call to him. He became aroused, enjoying the pleasurable assortment of sensations firing in his brain.

"Let your hair down," he said.

Angela Dunbar did as she was told. Her tress opened around her shoulders, and Billy ran his fingers through it before drawing his palm over her soft cheek. She began tugging at the buttons of his jeans, freeing him.

"That's my girl," he said and closed his eyes.

CHAPTER 6

I don't want you walking around looking like a bloated slag.

Had he really said that to her?

Broken-hearted, Dottie finished the dishes and ran a dishcloth over the kitchen counters; then, she made a brief stab at the living room. Billy moaned and complained all the time about the mess, regardless that he made most of it, but he seldom raised a finger to help maintain the place. His idea of contributing to the housework was dropping his empty Millers into the waste bin rather than leaving their crumpled remains wherever he was standing at the time. And the only reason he did this was that she asked him to.

She lifted his bomber jacket from the couch. With a small groan, she gathered his tatty work boots from the floor, keeping those bad boys away from her nose. She cleared Billy's DVDs from around the television. *The World at War. Black Hawk Down. Platoon.* War, war, war. Sometimes Dottie was surprised he had never signed up for the forces. He owned some of the gear, though he hardly ever used any of it. Only last year, he had spent a pretty penny on a pair of field glasses, claiming they would be handy when he went camping, although she could not think how. Furthermore, his five-man tent was used even less than the binoculars. He seemed to like the idea of playing soldier – but *just* playing. The reality was something very different, because he hadn't the discipline to be in the forces. He would struggle to take orders from a superior. Billy did not like to think of himself as a subordinate.

She stored his things and returned to the living room, placing a steadying hand on the couch as another dizzy sensation came and went. Standing there, Dottie weighed the tired surroundings and wished Billy would take the initiative, and decorate. The rest of the house aside, the living room was begging for a new carpet, as the present one had been down since they'd moved in. It wasn't yet threadbare, but its beige shade couldn't conceal the accumulated stains, nor could it hide the inevitability of wear and tear.

The sofa and chairs were faring slightly better, but only by a nose. They, too, needed updating into this decade. The wallpaper was discoloured in places, tinged by age, and corners had begun to curl away from the wall. She could probably do the papering herself, after the baby was born. Then they could make a start at replacing the furniture and carpets. Billy claimed that buying new things was a waste of money, and this irritated her more than anything. He hadn't been tight with money when they had met, for that was something she would have regarded as a red light. His refusal to spend on their home – their future – was yet another factor that didn't bode well.

Why fork out for carpets when there's one on the floor? Why get new sofas when we have two already? We're just sitting on them, right? You women are all the same, wanting things changed on a whim, just 'cause you get bored of the colour. Well, we ain't got the cash just now, Dottie.

It was much wiser to spend the money on tents and binoculars that sat collecting dust in the garage, the year round. Funny how there was enough money to buy a new television only last week. He'd been quite sure they could afford *that*, so he could "get the best from his films".

40

Funny, too, how the food and energy bills always seemed to come from her wage rather than his.

Well, he *was* doing work in the nursery. She should be thankful for that.

Bloated slag.

Dottie sat down carefully and touched her belly. She couldn't think where the cash for decorating would come from, once the baby arrived. If anything, the problem would worsen. Junior would be all the excuse he needed. Can't afford new things now that the baby's here, he'd say. Make up your mind, Dottie. Do you want to raise a family, or spend money on lampshades and carpets?

She shook her head. His logic was laughable, so much so that she often wondered whether he even gave thought to what he said. If he saved the money he wasted on packs of Miller, they would have the place looking like a show house. Too much of their income was frittered away on alcohol, tipped over his throat. Drinking made Billy irascible. She would ask him to cut down, to spend the money on necessities, and he would become enraged, claiming she was depriving him of his few comforts in life. He would get madder and drink more, and on it went, round and round.

He was so touchy that broaching his contribution to the marriage always backfired. Nothing was his fault. He did his best. He went out to work every morning. What did she want from him? The truth was, he had done nothing to the house since they'd bought it, and she felt embarrassed when Lynette or a colleague from the school paid a visit.

Dottie looked out at the darkening evening and wondered where he'd got to. He had said he was helping his boss move furniture, that

41

he would not be long. That had been more than two hours ago, and he still hadn't returned. She didn't know if he was telling the truth or not. She had the feeling that he lied constantly, and that he thought she was too stupid to realise. But she didn't make a scene about it. What good would it do? Besides, if she were being honest, she liked having the time to herself.

The baby would mellow him. It would make them a proper family, bring them together. Maybe he would even stop drinking, once he found what fatherhood had to offer. If he was going to stop, it would have to be of his own accord.

She felt the baby kick, and smiled sadly.

"Life has to get better than this," she said to the empty room.

*****

She was almost asleep when he finally came home. From the bedroom, she heard the engine rumbling up outside and the van's door closing. Dottie looked at her watch and saw it was ten thirty. His key slid into the front-door lock without farce, a fairly reliable sign that he was sober. Sounds of him knocking around in the kitchen soon followed: he was heating something in the microwave.

Dottie lay there on her back, wide awake now, crunching her toes beneath the bedcovers, drumming her fingertips on her big belly. What kind of mood would he be in? she wondered.

After a few minutes, the landing floorboards creaked outside the airing cupboard, and he stepped into the room. Dottie flicked on the lamp by the bed.

"I thought you weren't going to be long," she said, ensuring her tone was light.

"So did I." He shucked off his jacket, not looking at her, and dumped it on the ottoman. He sniffed and wiped at his nose. "Ten thirty's not so late. It took longer than we thought, that's all."

"That happens sometimes," she said, smiling. "What were you helping him with?"

"Just moving stuff, as I told you already."

"Oh, well. I hope he's paying you overtime for this."

"He'll see me right for it." Billy walked to the window and parted the curtains a little. "I'm gonna grab a quick shower. Bit ripe with all that luggin' around."

"Okay."

He turned and paused, as if about to say something. But then he carried on out of the bedroom, closing the door behind him.

She listened to the water spray in the bathroom. He never usually showered at night, even when he needed one – which was most of the time. He always showered in the morning. And Billy was a creature of habit, rarely deviating from routine.

Truth be told, she hadn't a clue whether Billy had really been helping his boss tonight. She wouldn't say that, of course; she knew better than to light to the fuse. She could quite easily call his boss tomorrow. His work phone number was in the little red book downstairs. That would put her mind at rest, one way or another. That said, he could always be in cahoots with his boss, too. Dottie didn't know anyone at Billy's work, and the likelihood was that they would be allied to him rather than her.

She slipped from the bed and lifted Billy's jacket from the ottoman, bringing it to her nose. She held the collar, sniffing carefully

43

in two or three places, but couldn't detect anything, perfume or otherwise. The pockets were empty, save for his van keys.

She felt terrible rummaging through his jacket, smelling his clothes like a paranoid old nag, but she was unsure whether to trust him anymore. He was so cold and distant these days, that it didn't seem impossible he would betray her with other women. If he was seeing someone behind her back, then he would clearly be careful to cover his tracks. He barely said two words to her lately, so it wasn't as if he would let anything slip in conversation. Chance would be a fine thing.

The water went off in the bathroom.

Dottie dropped his jacket and scampered under the covers again.

CHAPTER 7

On Saturday afternoon, Dottie and Lynette entered the Corner House Bistro on Buchanan Street, an establishment for which they shared a mutual liking. The food was traditional Scottish produce, and, more importantly, the restaurant's standards of cleanliness were high. The square tables were covered in starched white napery, the staff sufficiently groomed and polite, and the waiting time kept to a minimum.

Having spent the last hour trudging around stores for baby clothes, Dottie was exhausted, her feet sore. She groaned as she shuffled into the booth, pushing her shopping bags ahead of her. In Lynette's daily writing routine, she worked until two o'clock, making late afternoon their earliest chance to eat.

"God, my feet have *had* it," Dottie said, slipping off her flip-flops and scrunching her toes beneath the table. "I feel like I've walked a million miles since morning."

"That's pregnancy for you," Lynette told her.

"So, has baby shopping made you broody for another kid?"

Lynette raised a palm, as if halting traffic. "No way. Two's quite enough for me, thank you very much."

"Really?"

"I'm not saying it'll never happen again, but God, I'm content with two. Besides, one more, and I'll be kissing goodbye to my figure for good."

"What about Graham?" Dottie wanted to know. "Does he ever mention having more children?"

"No, but he'd happily perform *his* part all day long, believe me. If there's any control in our household, it's down to yours truly." She tapped her breastbone. "You know what men are like, Dottie – act first and deal with consequences later. By which time, of course, it's too late, and we're laid up for the next nine months."

"You've done well, though, haven't you? I mean, Mark and Tara are great kids."

"Yeah, they can be a handful, but I wouldn't be without them. And you've got it all to come."

The waitress arrived, and they ordered. Afterwards, Dottie was quiet, poking a saltshaker around with her finger.

"You want to talk about it?" Lynette prompted, fingering the glass bauble dangling from her ear.

Dottie looked up. "About what?"

"Whatever's on your mind. You've been on a different planet all day."

"It's nothing."

"Are you worried about the baby? Motherhood?"

"No, it's nothing. Just tired, that's all."

"Is it Billy?"

Dottie glanced away. "I don't want to discuss it."

Lynette sipped her wine, the deep red of which almost matched her fingernails. "Talk to me, Dottie. I'm here to help, remember?"

Dottie wanted to tell her about the lipstick incident, but was too embarrassed to even begin. She still couldn't believe it had come to pass. And just what did it spell for the future? That she wasn't allowed to wear make-up anymore? What came next – Billy dictating her wardrobe for her? That wasn't a marriage; it was a prison camp. No matter what angle she viewed it from, it didn't look promising.

"He was painting the baby's room," she began, drawing Lynette's attention. "When I walked in, he tossed a rag at me ... and told me to wipe off my lipstick."

Lynette's eyes widened, an expression somewhere between shock and disbelief. "He *what*? He can't tell you that."

"I know, it's ridiculous. It made me feel like I was five years old. I won't tell you what he called me."

"What did you do?"

Dottie recalled how pathetic she had felt and shrugged. "I wiped it off. He said *he'd* do it if I didn't."

Lynette shook her head and closed her fingers around Dottie's. "That's not acceptable. He's trying to control you; can't you see that? You can't lie down to intimidation. If you do, it'll only get worse, believe me."

Dottie knew her friend was right. "It will get worse. Somehow I know that."

"God, who the hell does he think he is? It takes a damned small man to threaten a pregnant woman, Dottie. Sorry, but treating you like that over make-up is ... is *abuse*. That kind of thing makes my blood boil, you can't let it go on."

"I've got the baby to consider now. What can I do? I didn't make a contingency plan for this."

"Don't ever think you're stuck there with him, Dottie," Lynette said. "You're welcome at our place, any time you want. For as long as you want. There's always room, okay? I'll never forget what you did for Mark, and I promise I'll be there for you, if you ever need me."

Dottie smiled sadly. "Don't. You'll have me welling up again. Roll up, roll up, see the amazing crying lady."

"I mean it, Dottie. You can't stand for this."

"He's supposed to be seeing his father at the care home today."

"I thought they didn't get on."

"They don't. Billy never talks about his father. I'm glad he's agreed to go, but I'm surprised he did. He even *promised* me this morning." Dottie considered this. "Still, he's promised me things before ..."

"Listen, I'm bursting for the loo, but we're not through talking about this."

Lynette clutched her little handbag and stalked off towards the ladies' room. Dottie's attention veered to the street. Why couldn't she be more like Lynette? she thought. Why couldn't she be more headstrong and take problems in her stride? That was how her friend had finally found success as a writer. Throughout her teens and twenties, Lynette had written story after story, sending them out to editors and agents with an almost religious tenacity. Every rejection slip had only bolstered her conviction, making her more determined. Dottie had to admire her.

Through the bistro window, in the distance, she saw the town church's spire above the rooftops, and her mind reluctantly skipped back to her wedding day. She remembered herself and Billy beneath the ornate building's archway, Billy in a kilt, she in white. He had been so different then. They had actually *talked*. He had taken her out,

48

and they had laughed, and she had loved him. And she had married him, despite the concerns voiced by those closest to her. She hadn't listened, because she had known her own mind.

Over the last three years, the fuel that sustained their marriage, whatever that fuel was, had begun to dwindle, and now Dottie felt she was running on faith alone. Faith that things would improve. Faith that she was a good person, a virtue that would win through in any crisis. But faith, she knew, was no more inexhaustible than any of life's provisions, and when it finally ran out, she would be lost. What she wanted more than anything in the world was for the three of them to be a normal happy family. Should baby Hawthorn be born to separated parents, Dottie would never forgive herself. She had to make it work with Billy.

"Dottie?"

She jumped, and looked around, finding a handsome gentleman with dark hair standing by the table. "Oh, Dr Cassidy. How are you?"

"It's Saturday," he said. "Just plain old Nick, today."

Dottie nodded and smiled. "Nick."

"How is everything? You and the baby are both keeping well, I trust?"

"We're both fine, thank you."

Behind the veil of her feigned smile, Dottie racked her mind for something to say. She touched her hair, and tapped a fingernail on the table. Today, for the first time, his presence made her uneasy – but not in a negative sense. Her unease was manifest due to plain old physical attraction, and the more she endeavoured to hide it, the more her traitorous body betrayed her feelings. Perhaps it was seeing him outside of the hospital that made her feel this way.

"Are you coming in, or going out?" she asked, weaving her fingers together in a bid to stop fidgeting.

"Just leaving," he said, patting his flat stomach.

Yet, Nick Cassidy remained where he was, a hand casually hidden in the pocket of his black slacks, his pound-perfect weight distributed to one leg. This relaxed posture, coupled with his open-neck shirt and a glimpse of chest hair, made Dottie ponder briefly what it might be like to be Mrs Cassidy. She couldn't imagine this man of medicine demanding that she wipe off her makeup. He wore no wedding band – this she had deduced from their hospital sessions – but she knew not whether he was single. Not that she was in any position to do anything about it, in any case.

"I'll see you for the last scan in a few weeks, then," he said and turned to move off.

Dottie suddenly found her mouth acting of its own accord. "Dr Cassidy?"

He glanced back at her. "Nick, remember?"

"Nick, right. Well, I just wanted to say ... how much I appreciate everything you've done to help me." *Don't go red, Dottie. Stay in control.* "It's nice to have someone there who genuinely cares. It's made the pregnancy that much easier to bear."

"It's my place to care, Dottie." He held her eyes for a moment, and she felt something pass between them, something that fluttered magically, deep inside her heart. "You'll make a great mother," he said. "Any child beginning its life with you for a parent is getting the best possible start."

She tried to laugh away the compliment, touching her cheeks. "Hey, you're embarrassing me," she said, still aware of that flutter. Oh yes.

"That's truly not my intention, but I mean it. I like to think I'm a fairly sound judge of character, and as far as I see, people don't come any more genuine than you, Dottie." He ceased talking, as if aware he'd perhaps said too much, perhaps overstepped a professional boundary into more personal ground. Another smile created little crow's tracks by his eyes. "I'll see you in a few weeks," he repeated.

He descended the short flight of stairs and slipped out through the revolving glass doors. Outside, on the sun-baked street, he passed by her booth and nodded at her, and that simple gesture seemed to say: everything's going to be fine, Dottie. The flutter inside her then blossomed into a glow, and it spread through her body, a sensation she had thought lost forever.

CHAPTER 8

"Sorry I ain't been by in a while, Ma. I thought I should let you know, I'm going to see *him*. Dottie's been houndin' me to go and, well, I guess I owe him a visit. He wasn't any kind of husband to you, and he was even less of a father to me, but I suppose it's time. He's sick, see, and I might not get another chance to say my piece. His mind's failing, so I've been told."

Billy threaded the last of the plastic roses into the pot at the base of the headstone. They lasted longer than real ones, and sat better, too. Real flowers just withered and died and ended up making the grave untidy. He straightened and looked at his mother's engraved name and the dates below it. The letters and numbers shone in bright gold. He'd had them repainted only last month, after they had begun to fade.

The cemetery was quiet. A few rows down, an elderly guy was collecting rubbish from around the stones. Otherwise, Billy was alone.

"Well, I better make tracks, Ma," he said, placing a hand on the stone's top. He remained like that for a minute and shook his head. "It should've been him that died. Not you."

Ten minutes later, Billy manoeuvred the Green Arrow van up the steep incline of Mosgrove Way, crunching down the gears, the engine whining in protest as he neared the long road's summit. Below, off to his right, he saw Aradale in the distance. The town's grey buildings and peaks looked just as depressing from here as they did close up.

At first, the idea of seeing his father had set Billy on edge, but now he was almost giddy with excitement, eager to see what had become of his childhood tormentor. So many incidents of fear had been seared into his mind. Seared, like when the old man had pressed cigarettes into Billy's young flesh. Sometimes, Billy had come between his father and Billy's little brother, taking a double dose of Daddy's fury, because that was the brotherly thing to do.

When the road finally levelled again, he bore left through two stone lions flanking the entrance. The grounds were impressive, even to Billy – who considered himself the least green-fingered man on earth. His elbow resting out the open window, Billy took in the sprawling golfing-green lawns and thick chestnut trees. Fancy flower beds were carved into the grass along the roadsides, all very flash.

He parked and got out, feeling dwarfed beneath the mammoth building, which was much larger than he'd imagined it would be. Huge sun-brightened bay windows protruded along the face, while dormers jutted out high above.

Billy scooped a litre bottle of water from the passenger seat and swigged down the last of its contents. The liquid drained steadily, trickling over his cheeks, until he wiped his mouth, belched, and sauntered towards the main entrance.

It was typical of the old man's luck, ending his days in a place like this. Two years before Grady Hawthorn had retired as a steelworker, he and a syndicate of four work cronies had scooped just shy of two million notes on the lottery. At the time, Billy had thought – hoped – the old man might kill himself with the money, and was continually surprised that his father was still alive. Having fathered Billy and Billy's brother in his forties, Grady Hawthorn had to be closing in on eighty now, although Billy didn't even know when the old man's birthday was. Didn't much care, either.

"Good afternoon, sir."

"I'm here to see Grady Hawthorn," Billy informed the young man behind the desk. "I'm his son. I was told he wanted to see me."

"His son? Oh, that's great. Poor Grady doesn't receive many visitors these days."

The effeminate man dusted something from his waistcoat, lifted a nearby phone, and spoke to someone briefly. Billy watched the way he moved. The cocked hip. The loose wrist. Queer boy. Even spoke in that tell-tale way they all had. He could spot them a mile off.

"Mrs Granger will be along to assist you shortly," the man said after ending the call. "She'll just be a minute."

"No rush, friend."

Billy waited a few paces from reception, just in case the guy wanted to keep chatting. He'd no desire to make small talk and so made a pretence of looking around.

The vestibule was vast, the ceiling high enough to give vertigo sufferers a twinge. The floor space was overcrowded with wide-leaf potted plants, which seemed positioned at random, here, there, and everywhere. The polished floor gleamed like the chrome on a new Harley, almost blinding where the sun fell on it. Down the hall, a black guy worked one of those mechanical buffer things, sweeping left and right, left and right, tracking a length of cable behind him. Through a large window, out in the gardens, an elderly woman gestured to a man in a wheelchair, pointing at something with her walking stick.

"Mr Hawthorn?"

Billy spun around to see a middle-aged woman extending a hand. He shook it, holding on a couple of seconds longer than necessary. "That's me."

"I'm Mrs Granger, the duty manager here today. I'm very glad you could find the time to come up and visit your father. He's been deteriorating these past weeks appreciably. He's said your name often, so we thought it only right that we contact you."

Billy liked the look of Mrs Granger. Somewhere in her forties, she was dressed in a black skirt and tights, and black shoes with that sexy shine to them. A cheeky swell of cleavage peeped through her frilly blouse. Firm of body, plenty to take hold of. Her streaked hair was overly coiffed, her eyes lined in black. Billy suspected that she spent her time preening and posturing, waiting to be noticed. She was a case of mutton and lamb, but he would gladly slip her one.

"We're currently attending to his needs," she was saying, leading him down a side corridor. "Should his condition worsen, however, we might move him to more suitable accommodation."

"What's wrong with him, exactly?"

"Alzheimer's. Do you know anything of the disease?"

"Not much."

"Well, basically it's a disorder that involves the deterioration of mental functions. A patient has impaired memory and thinking. He may have trouble memorising familiar places, or following directions. He might venture out on a cold day without appropriate clothing. Misplacing personal belongings, such as glasses and keys, say, can also be common. In short, Mr Hawthorn, your father's intellect and personality have begun to fail."

Old bastard never had much of either, Billy thought. "Aren't there drugs he can take?"

"Drugs can alleviate a few of the symptoms, but that's about all. We've noticed lots of confusion in him lately, which comes and goes. Some days he's fine, others not so good. He's also lost interest in most things, and occasionally forgets faces and names, and who his carers are. Therefore, we have to be careful with him."

"Is he violent?"

They turned down another corridor with doors on either side. An orderly passed them, pushing a trolley of laundry.

"On occasion, he can be short with people, but mood swings are really to be expected. Someone with the disease can experience dramatic changes in personality, and go from being quiet to angry, to even being afraid. Mostly a sufferer is happy spending time alone, displaying little interest in usual activities, and needs to be encouraged to participate. In your father's case, he's much too weak to be classed as a threat. We just have to be careful not to upset him."

"Uh huh. And the outlook?"

"The disease proceeds in stages and attacks everything that makes the patient function, including memory, judgement, language, and even the ability to perform everyday tasks. This is us."

They stopped outside a closed oak door.

"Thanks for the information," Billy said.

"It helps if you know what he's been going through. May I ask why you haven't been to see him before? You do live in town, don't you?"

"We aren't close. My mother passed when my brother and I were young. It pushed the old man and me apart."

"That's a pity," she said, giving him a sympathetic smile. "Some things cannot be helped. I'll be happy to come in with you, just to reassure him, if you'd like me to."

"Thanks, but it won't be necessary. I just want to say a quick hello and be on my way."

"Very well, Mr Hawthorn. Again, many thanks for taking the time."

Billy watched her head off back down the corridor at a clip, her arse swaying nicely inside the tight skirt. Her heels echoed around the high walls until she turned the corner and was gone.

"Very tasty."

Billy stepped inside.

His father occupied an armchair by the room's large bay window. He was bathed in sunlight, hidden inside cardigan and grey trousers. Blue tartan slippers covered his feet. His hair had gone grey-white and begun to fall out, revealing a skull dappled with freckly brown spots. His former musculature had wasted away, the bony physique now barely filling his clothes. His head shook in an ongoing rhythm, his shoulders twitching every few seconds. The jowly face was shrunken and shrivelled, the hands disfigured by ridges and lumps and knots, ailments that Billy guessed were evidence of arthritis. Old age had clearly played its part in his demise, no question, but the booze had likely been a greater factor. After all, there were plenty of people of a similar age in full charge of their faculties.

"Greetings, Dad," Billy said, lifting a wooden chair from the side and jamming it under the door handle. He forced it into place, providing a sturdy deterrent against anyone trying to enter.

The old man's head twitched, as if Billy had tugged an invisible lead. He looked around, his rheumy brown eyes wincing suspiciously. "Who is it there? This is *my* room."

Frail and decrepit, ravaged by time, his father's face still exuded the same sense of menace that Billy had grown up with. Clearly, his spell here had not softened his view of the world; if anything, it had probably made his outlook worse, with old age added to his list of miseries. All that remained now was a sour and spoiled soul, staring at the world through a window, waiting for death.

"It's Billy, Dad." He adjusted his crotch, crossed the oriental maroon carpet, and stepped close to the old man. "Your son, remember?"

"I just had my dinner," his father said, with an assuredness that made Billy frown.

"That's good, Dad. What did you have?"

The old man's face, deathly white in the glare of the sun, became confused, as if he were trying to fathom a complicated puzzle. "I ... I don't remember. No, wait now. It ... it was Wendy, this morning. She was here. She had balloons."

Balloons? Shit, he was really out there.

Billy walked to the window and drew the curtains. He turned around and took the old man's hand in his. It was soft as putty, gnarled, and lined with veins. "It's Billy, Dad. The boy you beat and burned, remember?"

Something akin to recognition flickered in his faraway eyes. "Billy ..."

"That's right."

Billy began squeezing the weak hand, adding more and more pressure, until his own bicep was bulging inside his T-shirt. The old man's eyes tightened in pain. His mouth opened wide, revealing a slimy pink tongue. "Aaaahhhh."

Billy kept squeezing, clenching his teeth, until a tear escaped down the folds of his father's cheek. His dad's puckered mouth opened, and to Billy's surprise, his false teeth popped out about an inch.

"Hey, your head's falling apart, old man."

Grady Hawthorn's grimace morphed into an expression of agony, and he doubled over, trying to get out of the chair.

"Sit down." Billy applied more pressure, refusing to let him up. "I just wanted to tell you that I hate you, you miserable bastard. How does it feel to be on the receiving end, huh? You like it, you withered cretin?"

"Aaaahhhh. Please ..."

"You're gonna meet the man with the horns before long. You hear me, Daddy?"

Billy finally let go of his hand, and the old man curled himself into the high-backed chair, his face contorted in a silent world of pain. "The man with the horns," Billy repeated. He unzipped his fly, fished out his manhood, and after a moment's concentration, began urinating on his father.

CHAPTER 9

It was dark outside, and there was still no sign of Billy. Keeping busy, Dottie had put on three loads of washing, all the time wondering where he'd got to. She hoped he had gone up to Mosgrove to see his father, but something told her he probably hadn't. He was likely sitting in the Admiral now, getting drunk again. It was a shame for a parent and child to be so far apart emotionally. Whatever had happened between them in years past, it had surely left its mark on Billy. Sometimes, she thought his past may even be responsible for the way he was today and for the ugly manner in which he could treat her.

Now, as the washing machine whined through its last spin, Dottie was having toast and hot chocolate, sitting on the sofa, scanning through two books she'd borrowed from the library the previous day. Books about caring for a new baby. Initially, she had brought a different book to the checkout desk, and the woman there had suggested two others instead, explaining that the information in them was more useful. She had read them herself when pregnant a year prior, the woman had said. Dottie had thanked her and exchanged her original choice.

The sheer wealth of information in the books was overwhelming, and she now felt more apprehensive than before she'd opened them. Could she really learn this stuff in time?

How to pick up the baby properly. How to hold the baby. How to lay down and wrap the baby. Topping and tailing. Bathing the baby. Bonding with the baby. Breastfeeding versus bottle-feeding. How often to feed the baby? How to monitor the infant's weight. Nappy choice. How warm should the baby be? Baby walker or bouncer?

All this and she had barely scratched the surface. The baby would be loved and cared for to the best of her ability, and nothing was more important than that. As for everything else, she would just have to do her best. It would fall into place, she was sure, and she probably wouldn't start the *real* learning process until after the birth, anyway. She was nervous, yes, but she could not wait to hold her own child. Just thinking of it made her smile.

One thing that did worry her – that was a constant worry – was Billy. She had read about how a father's reaction to a new baby can vary widely. The book said a father might be excited by the birth and happy to be there with the mother. That didn't sound much like Billy. On the other hand, he might be irritated or angry, especially if he is unhappy about the pregnancy. Fathers, the book explained, often feel jealous or rejected because the mother devotes all her time to the child. Dottie would have to ensure that did not happen, although she had accepted this would be problematic. These days, it didn't require much of a spark to ignite Billy's temper.

Dottie finished her toast and hot chocolate and put the dishes in the kitchen. She paused by the sink after feeling a twinge in her stomach. Then she took a couple of slow breaths and began removing towels from the washer, draping them over the counter. When she returned to the living room, she heard Billy's diesel van pulling into the drive, so she put her books away and sat down as he opened the front door.

"I thought you'd got lost," she said.

61

Billy dropped his keys on the table. "I went for a drive."

Dottie smiled and reached around behind her. "Look what I found today," she said, rummaging excitedly in a carrier bag. She withdrew a tiny white baby suit, an all-in-one with a hood, booties, and mittens attached together. She giggled and made the little suit dance in mid-air. "Isn't it cute? Zero to eighteen months! Can you imagine someone small enough to fit in here?"

"It's nice, Dottie."

I picked up some other bits and pieces too. I got a musical gym and a Moses basket, but I'll show you them later." She folded the baby suit away and slipped it into the bag. "Do you fancy watching a DVD, or something?" she asked. "It's not that late yet."

"I think I'll pass."

"Okay."

Billy went into the kitchen. She heard him crack open a can before he came back. At the window, he lifted a slat from the blind, peering outside.

"Did you see your dad today?"

He took a long swallow and wiped his mouth. "I saw him."

She waited, but he didn't say anything else.

"And? Did everything go okay?"

"Swimmingly. He's nuttier than a fruitcake. He didn't know I was there. He just sits and stares through a big window. Probably doesn't know his own name. Waste of time."

Dottie lowered her gaze. "I'm sorry to hear that, Billy. He's still your dad, though, even if he's not well. Alzheimer's is a terrible disease, and there's no real help for it. You know, sometimes people do things that they later regret. People make mistakes. You shouldn't write your father off like that. You never talk to me about what happened with him. I think maybe it would help if you discuss what went on when you were younger."

"Discuss?"

Dottie shrugged and offered a weak smile. "It might do some good."

"Discuss it with who – you?"

"If you'd like to. Sometimes it helps to get things off your chest. I am your wife."

"You're an expert all of a sudden, are you?"

Dottie looked down. "I just don't like to see you unhappy. Lots of people have childhoods that were hard."

"Oh, well, that's okay, then. If *lots* of people had bad childhoods, what the hell am I making all the fuss about?"

"Billy—"

"I'm just being unreasonable, obviously. Tell me, Dottie, were you raised by an alcoholic? A piss-artist who was never around for you? Did your father turn *your* life into a nightmare?"

Dottie shook her head. "I've seen the marks on your body. I know it must've been hard for you."

Billy stared, and she knew what was coming before he even spoke.

"Listen to me, Dottie, because I don't intend to go through this again with you. Understand?"

She nodded, looking away.

"You asked me to go see him, so that's what I did. I drove up there and saw him. But it hasn't changed a thing. I still want nothing to do with him, and I'll still be glad when his scrambled brain finally shuts down for good. I don't want you mentioning him to me anymore, you hear? Not ever. Far as I'm concerned, he's on borrowed time, and all I'm interested in, is the call that tells me he's dead."

CHAPTER 10

During her sixth month, when not doing housework, Dottie spent a lot of time taking the weight off her feet, lying on the bed or couch, or sitting in a chair. She did her Kegel exercises, and she did stretches where she stood with her hands on the wall, leaning forward and keeping her heels on the ground. This movement worked her calves and helped ward off cramps.

As well as countless other symptoms, she'd been suffering from an itchy belly – something she found particularly irritating. She rubbed calamine lotion on the affected area, thereby reducing the itchiness, but this didn't solve the problem entirely. Moreover, the baby had got noticeably stronger over recent weeks, and now she felt more than simple *movements*. In fact, if she didn't know better, she'd have thought Junior was trying to do her physical harm. So much so that being poked and kicked was slowly becoming second nature.

She was performing her wall exercises one morning, as Billy readied himself for work.

"When you're doing that, you look like you're trying to keep the walls from falling down," he said, sitting on the bed and tying his boots.

"Stop teasing me," she replied. "I know it looks daft, but it helps."

"If you say so."

Dottie finished up and came away from the wall. She was wearing only a large white T-shirt with Winnie the Pooh on the front, underwear, and white socks. Her hair was pinned back with a band.

"Billy," she said, "can we talk about something before you go downstairs?"

He finished tying his boots and looked at her. "I don't think I like the sound of that. Make it quick, then. I've not much time."

"Well, I got a DVD from the hospital yesterday."

"Didn't know they were renting movies. Did you get something good? Action one, was it?"

She didn't rise to it.

"It shows the labour and delivery areas there. I thought maybe we could watch it tonight, give us a chance to see what's what? It wouldn't take long. I think it'd be worth it just to—"

"I dunno about tonight, Dottie. We'll get to it sometime, though."

Dottie placed a hand on her belly. "That's what you keep saying about everything. But the baby's coming soon, Billy. I wish you'd show more interest in what's going on. I can't do this by myself."

"Show more interest? I'm running around picking up stuff for you every day. Do you think this is a laugh ride for me? You think I'm not feeling the strain too?"

Dottie stared down at her abdomen. "Dr Cassidy said we can stop by the hospital for a look at those areas during visiting hours. He'd be happy to show us. That would be nice, don't you think? We can be shown about, see the nursery and the newborns there. We can get a feel for the place. I think it'd be really beneficial."

"What good do you think that'll do?" Billy paced over to the window and looked out at the wet and windy morning. "We'll see all that stuff when the time comes anyway. It won't help us to stand around gawking at someone else's kid."

66

Guardedly, Dottie eased herself onto the bed, hanging her head. She straightened her legs, looking at her little white socks. Neither of them said anything for a short spell, during which rain whispered against the windowpane.

"I'm worried we're not prepared," she eventually went on. "Everything's happening so fast now, and we're not ready, and the baby will soon be here and—"

"Hey, take a breath, or you'll be dropping the little tyke right there on the damned bed."

"Dr Cassidy also said there's a good childbirth class every week. We could meet and mix with other expectant couples. It would be beneficial for us both. I mean, I'm stuck here in the house all the time, and there are so many things we could be doing, things to get us prepared for what's coming."

Billy came away from the window, his hands jammed in the pockets of his jeans.

"Look," he said, "I can't sit around holding hands and breathing with a bunch of weirdo strangers, okay?"

"You make it sound like a *cult* or something."

"It's not necessary to do that stuff, Dottie."

"They have special sessions for fathers only," she continued regardless. "Dr Cassidy said they'll familiarise you with the process of labour and the delivery. You can ask questions about anything you're unsure of. He said—"

"Cassidy this, Cassidy that. I'm tired of hearing that guy's name, Dottie. What is he, an expert on every-bloody thing?"

"There's an antenatal class run by the hospital, too. There are only five or six couples to a class, so there wouldn't be loads of people there – if that's what you're worried about."

"Who said I was worried?" He took a step forward and stood over her. "I'm not worried. Sounds to me like you're the one doing all the worrying."

"I think we should *both* be worrying. We should be doing more, now that I'm so far on."

"Yeah, that's coming across loud and clear."

"In these classes, we can watch films about births and take part in discussions. We'll have a chance to ask questions. I've heard it's an opportunity to make friends, too. I want you to come with me." She looked at him. "Will you?"

"You want to sit watching films of women giving birth?" He laughed and shook his head. "I don't believe this."

"It's not funny, Billy."

"No, it's not. And as far as making friends goes – is that really what you want, to meet a bunch of strangers, have them coming around the house at all hours? They'd be a pain in the arse. Asking to meet up and talk about all sorts of guff." He checked the clock on the wall. "Listen. I'm gonna be late for work, we'll have to go into this later."

"We're running out of time to go into it."

He put on his jacket. "Just stop flapping, for Christ's sake. It won't do you or the baby any favours, getting worked up."

Dottie stayed there on the bed for a few minutes, until she heard him leave the house. She felt like crying again, but ardently fought the urge. She stood, went to the window, and looked down over the front drive. His high-top green van backed out to the road. In a matter of seconds, he was gone, leaving only a thin haze of exhaust fumes.

"Why won't he make an effort like any other father?" she asked the empty room, touching the windowpane. If he wouldn't help her now, what was going to happen after the baby arrived? She was going to be left to raise the child alone, wasn't she?

CHAPTER 11

"There, you see? The baby's grown too large to move about freely in the womb. You can make out the head, to the left there."

"Aw, I see it," Dottie squeaked, studying the baby's image, now at thirty-four weeks. She smiled at Billy, who yawned back at her from his chair, revealing a gold tooth.

"You can also see the outline of the forehead, nose, and chin. The arms and legs are tucked in." Dr Cassidy moved the scanning head around the water-soluble oil on Dottie's belly. The dark image of a slumbering baby was transmitted to the screen of the Real-Time scanner. "And that's it. We're nearly all finished for today. I'll just have a quick word with you before you go."

As Dottie tidied herself, Dr Cassidy said to Billy, "I'll have to see her each week from here on in. It's standard procedure, just to be sure everything's as it should be. Okay?"

"You know best."

"Have a seat, Dottie," the doctor said as she reappeared from behind the curtain.

She adjusted the front of her gown and smiled at them as she sat down.

"Anything you'd like to bring up while you're here? Any concerns?"

Dottie thought a moment. "I've had bleeding gums sometimes, when I brush my teeth. And leg cramps. And backache, too."

"These are normal physical symptoms. Don't worry about them. Anything else?"

"No, I don't think so. My palms get red and itchy sometimes."

"That's not uncommon, either. You may find this happens with the soles of your feet also. It'll disappear after the delivery."

"Okay."

"Well, everything seems to be going fine. The results of the glucose screening test were normal."

"What was that for?" Billy asked.

"Routine, that's all. I had Dottie drink a quantity of juice, and we drew a little blood. It's a simple test to ensure the mother is producing enough insulin to process the extra glucose in her system. Gestational diabetes occurs in maybe one to two percent of expectant mothers. But even then, it's easily managed. Usually, any abnormalities clear up after the birth. In Dottie's case, the results were fine, so there's no need to worry."

"Sometimes I have dreams about the baby," Dottie said, looking sheepish. "Does that mean anything?"

"It's good," he told her. "Practice parenting, a kind of bonding with the child, prior to birth."

"That's normal, too?"

"Very." He smiled reassuringly. "As for the backache, it's just your body preparing to give birth. Try not to stand for long periods of time. In the kitchen, a small rug is handy for a hard-surfaced floor, just to ease the pressure. If you have to lift things, make sure you're positioned properly, bending the knees and not the waist. Even better, Billy here will do any lifting for you. I was just after saying to him that I'll want to see you every week from now on. And that's it. We're done for today."

71

"Thank you," Dottie said. "Ready, Billy?"

"Ready when you are," he said, jangling the van keys. "Thanks again, Doc."

Dr Cassidy lifted a hand as they left. "Take care out there."

Alone, Nick Cassidy shrugged off his jacket and spun in his chair thoughtfully. He felt concerned that Dottie was not getting the necessary support from her husband. Anyone with eyes and ears could determine that. Whenever Billy accompanied her here, he whiled away the time tapping his fingers, or checking his watch, looking thoroughly bored. In fact, the man's nervous tics and inability to stay still made Nick wonder if he was using. He certainly displayed little interest in his wife and child's welfare, from what Nick could see.

Having lately emerged from a gruelling separation from his girlfriend, Nick knew how precarious the search was to find someone with whom you really belonged. He would give anything to have a woman like Dottie in his life. Sweet, kind, and cute as hell. She had the most amazing green eyes, almost feline. Plenty of women offered him subliminal openings, and he dated periodically, but seldom did he feel a *connection*. Dottie was fun and upbeat and radiated sunshine with her presence. She didn't rely on materialism to make her happy – and women able to make such a claim were becoming rarer than ... Well, *damned* rare.

Dottie's baby – a girl, though she didn't want to know – would be loved like no other. Dottie would cope with the new family member admirably, taking this journey in her petite stride. He had seen enough new mothers to know.

Still, the husband was clearly problematic. With Dottie's parents overseas, her man should be bestowing unflinching support, being the wall on which she leaned. With the baby yet growing, Dottie and Billy should be spending as much time together as possible, although Nick doubted this was happening. Billy didn't appear prepared for the demanding life changes of a new baby. Rather than involving himself, he seemed content to watch from the sidelines, to let Dottie cope alone. Nick had attempted to include him in the discussions, to make him feel part of things, but Billy only shrugged or mumbled, as if he didn't need a doctor's help, as if everything was in hand. Furthermore, Nick had the distinct impression that Billy disliked him, disliked him because of the time he spent with Dottie. This, of course, was madness, as any time he spent with Dottie was in a professional capacity and to benefit the baby – Billy's baby.

But you do like her, don't you, Nick?

He sat forward and prodded at the plastic model spine on his desk, flicking at the yellow nerves and red discs between the vertebrae.

His concerns for Dottie were probably excessive and misguided; still, he couldn't help his perception of the situation. Whenever she came into the hospital, he wanted to embrace her, wanted to support her, to be part of her life. God knows she deserved better than the guy she was with.

He loathed feeling this way. Dottie was his patient, and he was her doctor, and she was carrying her husband's child. There it was. Three indubitably sound reasons to put her out of his mind. It was morally and ethically wrong to even harbour such feelings for her. Was he crossing professional boundaries purely by thinking this way? Were his thoughts tantamount to malpractice? No, that was ridiculous. He wanted just for her to be healthy and happy.

"She'll be fine," Nick said to the empty room.

But as he went about his business, he thought only of seeing Dottie again.

*****

When Billy arrived home, he put his feet up in front of the television and began working his way through a couple of Millers. He had the rest of the day off, which felt fine.

There was racing on TV, which was better than those bloody soap-opera repeats. Dottie had put the dinner on – steak pie and veg, she said – and was now messing around upstairs, sorting the washing or putting away the ironing, or whatever it was she'd said she was doing. Every so often, he heard the floorboards above groan beneath her weight.

She was forgetting a lot these days and spent more time standing scratching her head than doing anything else. Talk about scatty. The kitchen was a mess of yellow sticky notes – her new system for remembering what she had to do on any particular day. Things like watering all those plants she had the house filled with. Phone so-and-so and thank them for this, that, or the next thing. Get Billy to collect this or that from the store…

It was not lost on him that her due date was closing in, and he'd be a liar if he said he wasn't a trifle worried. What exactly was cooking in her oven up there? Dottie wanted to wait for the surprise, but he had the feeling the baby was a boy. He *wanted* a boy, although he knew he had to keep an open mind. It wasn't like he had a choice in the

74

matter, was it? A girl would be less troublesome, maybe, but a boy would carry his name.

Yet, what if the child – boy *or* girl – grew up with problems? What if the kid hated him, or if Billy couldn't get on with it? Jesus, his own father-son relationship was about as skewed as it gets. Would his child be the one screaming in the department store, with enough decibels to clear the place faster than a gas leak? The child whose mother always yanked it around by the arm, looking like she'd be happy to abandon it on the spot? Would his kid be the one bringing the police to the door, when he was old enough to wreak havoc in the world? Would that be his kid? It was food for thought.

Sitting there pondering this, Billy heard Dottie calling down to him, and he cranked the racing to cover the sound of her voice. She kept at it, though, and he eventually shook his head and tossed the remote on the couch.

"Billy! Will you come up here, please?"

He crumpled his empty beer can, got to his feet, and set off upstairs, heavy-limbed, a step at a time, muttering under his breath.

"Billy!"

"I'm on my way, woman, for Christ's sake. What's all the bloody noise about?"

He followed the sound of her raised voice to the bathroom and nudged open the door.

"Are you in here? What is it?"

Dottie was standing, pointing at the bathtub. "In there."

"You look like you've seen a damned ghoul, Dottie." He laughed and stepped inside the room and leaned over the tub. By the plughole

75

was a small garden spider, its legs splayed as it tried in vain to climb the side of the bath.

Billy grinned and shook his head.

"I'm sorry, Billy, but I can't get rid of it myself. You know I can't even touch those things. Can you please just put him outside? Don't hurt him, just put him out in the garden for me, okay?"

"Bloody wee spider's more afraid of you than you are of it, you know that?"

Dottie shook her head now too, keeping her distance. "I doubt it."

Billy rolled up his sleeves, leaned into the bath, and scooped the spider in his cupped hands. "You wanna see?" he said to Dottie, stepping towards her.

"No!" Dottie shuffled back into the corner, raising her arms. "Just take him outside!"

"Yeah, yeah, yeah. What a fuss about a little insect."

Billy took the spider downstairs and walked out into the garden. There, he squatted and set it loose and watched as it scuttled for its life among the green lawn.

"Better than Dottie flushing you down the plughole, huh?"

He belched and went back inside to get another beer, still amazed at how afraid someone could be of spiders.

CHAPTER 12

Dottie's labour began in her thirty-eighth week of pregnancy, at seven-fifteen p.m., on the fourteenth of September. She was standing in the garden, surrounded by colourful dwarf lupins, pinning clean towels and laundry to the clothesline, the washing billowing gently in the breeze. The contractions announced their arrival in the small of her back and crept painfully and stealthily around to her stomach.

After discarding the wash basket on the kitchen floor, Dottie shuffled into the living room, where Billy lay slumped on the couch, watching the News, working his way through a Miller. She settled herself in an armchair, trying to relax, the contractions affecting her at twenty-minute intervals. Finally, when it became clear Billy wasn't about to play the gallant husband, she said, "The baby's coming. We have to go to the hospital."

"You sure?" he asked, sipping his Miller.

"I think so. Are you okay to drive?"

"What d'you mean?"

"How many of those have you had?"

"I can drive just fine, Dottie."

"I know, but what if we get stopped? You won't be any use to me spending the night in a cell, Billy."

"I said I can drive just fine. Are you sure it's time? Aren't there ... false alarms, sometimes?"

"We'd better go," she said.

Billy collected the pre-prepared bag – which contained two nightdresses, slippers, maternity bras, pads, and toiletries – from its spot by the front door, and assisted her out to the van.

Belted in, unable to adopt a comfortable position in Billy's malodorous vehicle, Dottie ceased trying and watched the houses and streets slip by. She found herself wishing that Nick would be at the hospital, waiting to reassure her, to care for her, and to deliver her baby. After his support throughout the pregnancy, she felt oddly disappointed that he would not see the job through.

Haven't you got more important things on your mind right now, Dottie?

Halfway between the house and hospital, they ran into a stalled line of traffic on Tower Hill Road. Cars wound back from a temporary set of traffic lights. Ahead, workmen in reflective jackets and ear defenders were gathered around a hole in the road. One of them was working a pneumatic drill, deafeningly breaking ground and churning up the tarmac. Another man was standing before the traffic with a red STOP sign on a stick.

"Aw, can you believe this?" Billy complained, leaning out of the window. "Of all the days to run into these jokers."

Dottie was taking deep breaths, holding her belly. "Don't do anything silly. They're just doing their jobs."

"Hey!" Billy called over to the workmen. "Hey! Can we get the sign flipped here? I got my pregnant missus in the van. She's in labour!"

One of the men made a neck-cutting gesture to the guy with the drill, and the noise stopped. He wandered up to the van's window, his face smeared with grime and black spots.

"What's the problem here?"

"I could do with getting the traffic going," Billy told him. "We're on our way to the hospital. She's having a baby."

Dottie gave the workman a sorry-to-be-a-nuisance smile. The man removed his hard hat.

"Okay, no worries, buddy."

The workman wandered back towards his colleagues, holding his hat, making a spinning gesture with one raised finger.

"Turn it around. Let's get this side through!"

Within a moment, the cars were shifting along. Billy leaned out of the window as he drew up by the workmen. "Thanks, man."

In the obstetrical unit, the contractions intensified. Presently, Dottie implemented her learned relaxation exercises, though they did not alleviate her anxiousness. She began shivering all over, without feeling at all chilled. Her bladder and bowels felt ready to burst, threatening to unleash everywhere – and she prayed *that* wouldn't happen.

Like she didn't have enough to contend with.

Soon people bustled all around her – Billy, the midwife, the nurses – and the room was a hive of commotion. This was it. She was, at long last, going to be a mother. With her cervix open, her legs apart, Dottie was using her abdominal muscles to push the baby out.

"You're doing so well, Dottie," the midwife said, her youthful face brimming with encouragement. "That's great. I can see the

79

crown. Okay. Now, I want you to stop pushing, so we can deliver the shoulders. That's it. That's it."

Dottie let her head fall back on the pillow. She was eager to follow each command, but simultaneously exhausted and light-headed. Trickling beads of sweat made her brow itchy and nipped her eyes. Her matted hair clung to her cheeks in damp, untidy ringlets. Billy clutched her right hand, and she drew strength from the physical contact. Someone blotted a cool cloth across her forehead. She tried to breathe deeply, but her inhalations came in short, sharp bursts.

"That's it, you're doing great. Now, I need you to push again, Dottie, come on, let's go. One more time."

Dottie gripped shut her eyes, preparing to give it everything she had. Then, with a monstrous effort, she yelled and pushed with her full strength, wailing, oblivious to whatever accidental embarrassments might accompany the birth. Her pained cry reverberated around the room.

"—Come on, Dottie, keep going—"

"—Just a little more—"

"—*Push*, Dottie—"

"—Here we go—"

She emitted another pain-racked outburst, whereupon overwhelming relief swept through her body, a magical gift from the heavens after such gruelling agony. All of a sudden, the young midwife was cradling the baby in her arms. A beautiful tuft of light-coloured hair sprouted from its slick head. But there was something lingering in the midwife's eyes, something that should not be there…

Concern.

"Is everything ... What's wrong?" Dottie gripped the hand that held hers, looking to her side. "*Billy?*"

The pale-faced woman severed the umbilical cord and thrust the baby into a nurse's arms, instructing something that Dottie could not hear, did not *want* to hear.

"Where're you taking my baby? What's going on? Please ... what's going on?"

*****

Later, Dottie lay curled in the hospital bed, her face tacky with dried tears, staring at the darkness, seeing nothing, the powerful sedative in her system gradually teasing her towards sleep. Night engulfed both her room and the world beyond the walls. She was alone, accompanied only by the word lodged inside her head, branded on her brain. The word she had afforded no consideration in the past months, because it was ... unthinkable.

Stillborn.

The bond she had forged with the life inside her was gone, snuffed out before being given a chance to bloom. This revelation left her numb inside, cold, and unable to comprehend a world in which her baby could be born without life.

Stillborn.

Dottie heard the door-handle turn, ever so slowly, as if someone were trying to enter the room without disturbing her. She looked in that direction. A vertical backdrop of florescent light silhouetted the dark figure, and her eyes smarted. Although the visitor was featureless, the lean, muscular build, she knew, belonged to Billy. She had no idea how he felt about what had happened. He had so rarely opened up about becoming a father that his inner feelings were a mystery.

Footsteps sounded on the floor.

"You awake?"

The sedative coursed through her, blurring her thoughts and awareness, her perceptions and sensations. Drowsy. So Drowsy.

"Look at me when I'm talking to you."

She angled her head, though it required considerable effort. He was by the bed, partially in shadows.

"What have you got to say for yourself?"

"Billy ..." she mumbled. "I can't ..." The words would not come, and sounded like the voice of someone else, distant and meaningless.

"You're an embarrassment, you know that?" His seething voice was by her ear, and flecks of spittle touched her cheek. A dull memory of alcohol tainted his breath.

"No," she whispered.

"Yes. You're an embarrassment."

"No."

"What good are you to me? You can't even deliver a healthy baby."

She could not keep her eyes open; the drug's soporific effect was taking over, dragging her towards oblivion, away from the spiteful words in her ear.

"You sleep. You sleep well, Dottie. Then get your shit together, you hear me? I don't wanna be kickin' around this dump any longer than I have to."

She was vaguely aware of him leaving her bedside. More faint steps sounded on the room's floor. Through heavy eyelids, she saw him receding and heard the soft snick of the door closing, eliminating the light.

Everything inside shut down, and sleep claimed her.

PART TWO

STARTING OVER

CHAPTER 13

With Dottie laid up in the hospital, Billy took advantage of having the house to himself. He had been granted time off work on compassionate grounds and resolved not to waste it. Such a treat, not having her fluffing damned pillows the moment his arse left the couch. He called in pizza, bought a twelve-pack of Miller, cranked the stereo, and dug out his stashed porn DVDs. With the speakers thumping around him, he almost didn't hear the phone ringing. He stopped the DVD, turned down the Rolling Stones, and snatched up the handset. To his surprise, it was Dottie's mother.

"My God," she said, after he'd filled her in. "Oh, Billy. What happened?"

"They don't know. Nobody's fault, apparently. They're not even sure what causes it."

"Oh, I can't believe this. Is Dottie there with you now?"

"They're keeping her in for a few days, but there's nothing to worry about."

"Nothing to worry about? Billy, *she's lost her baby.*"

"I just meant that Dottie's doing okay. I'm well aware my baby girl didn't live, Maureen."

"Yes, of course, I'm sorry. Stillborn. I ... can't believe it. That poor wee thing."

"We've twenty-one days to register the death," Billy said. "The hospital's holding on to the baby until we make funeral arrangements. They've been really helpful and offered a social worker for bereavement counselling. The hospital chaplain discussed a religious service with us, but we wanted to do something ourselves."

Billy supped his beer, contemplating how to get rid of her without sounding offensive. Maybe he could rustle tinfoil in the mouthpiece, pretend there was interference. That might be fun.

"Well, I think we should come over there, Billy," she was saying. "Dottie needs the support right now. We can get a flight in the next day or two—"

"I understand you wanted to be here, Maureen, really, I do. Still, I think it'd be best to give us some time. We need to get past this in our own way."

"We'll check into a motel, then."

"I'm not telling you not to come, but I think you should just give us a little space. Dottie's very emotional, and I'm finding it difficult, too. She's been preparing for motherhood for months. I'm only asking that you wait a while, let things settle, and pop over in a month or so. You understand, don't you?"

There was silence on the line, and Billy shook his head, checking his watch.

"Well ... if you really think that's best. I don't want Dottie to think her father and I don't care."

"She knows how much you care, Maureen. And so do I. I'll tell her you called and give her your love."

After the call, Billy slammed the kitchen door, sending a picture crashing to the ground. He killed the music and switched off the television. The bloody interfering old cow had ruined the mood altogether. Now he would have to tell Dottie her mother had called and that he'd told her to stay away. But it was understandable, right? They'd just lost a baby, for Christ's sake. He didn't want her parents messing in his business, bleating on about everything he was doing wrong. And he could only handle so much of her father. Bloody know-all, with a head full of bullshit wisdom for anyone willing to listen.

He decided to take a stroll down to the Admiral, feeling he deserved a few cold ones, after what he'd been through this week. He was shrugging into his jacket when the doorbell rang.

*****

Lynette parked her BMW in the rounded cul-de-sac outside Dottie's house. In the driveway was Billy's big van with the green arrow emblazoned on its flank, so she expected he was home. She took deep breaths, mentally composing herself for what she knew would not be a pleasant experience. *You're doing the decent thing, Lynette*, she told herself. Dottie was a lifelong friend and was going through a tough time – probably the toughest of her life. This needed saying.

Lynette strode purposefully up to the house and rang the doorbell. Billy's figure soon materialised behind the diamond-frosted glass, and she swallowed.

He tugged open the door and leaned on the jamb. "She ain't here, Lynette," he said. "They're keeping her in for a bit."

Lynette fought to conceal her distaste. The mere sight of him made her skin come alive with a sensation like tiny scuttling legs. He was glaring expectantly now; the glassy, emotionless eyes and shaved head made her hesitate in saying what she'd come to say, despite her conviction not to be intimidated. He reminded her of the bald talon-nailed ghoul from the early vampire movies, the thing that cast distorted shadows wherever it went. God, all he was missing were the two jagged incisors.

"Lynette, I was on my way out," he said and shoved his hands in his unzipped bomber jacket. "Unless ... is there something I can do for you?"

"I think you should be giving Dottie more support," she blurted, and suddenly her heart was pumping harder. "Especially now, after losing the baby. She's unhappy, and you're not treating her fairly."

Something between a leer and a grin crossed his face. "That what you came here for? To give me a bleeding-heart story about my wife?"

"She needs a helping hand, Billy. She deserves—"

"Better than me?" He grinned again. "Tell me, oh wise one, what makes you so all-important, Lynette? You think your shit smells sweeter than everyone else's, don't you? Just because you write them trashy books for women to flick themselves off to. That doesn't make you better than me."

"Do you have *any* idea how ridiculous you sound? I'm here because I'm worried about my friend. *Your* wife."

"Wanna know what I think?"

Lynette shook her head. "You actually have thoughts? You amaze me."

"I think you write that smut all day 'cause your man ain't doing the business in the bedroom. You get off imagining what it'd be like making it with other guys. Of course, you'd never admit to that."

"You're one deluded screw-up, Billy. You're a bully. Dottie told me what happened with the lipstick. What kind of man says something like that to his wife? What kind of weasel threatens a pregnant woman?"

"You're welcome to come upstairs, Lynette." Billy motioned to the empty hall behind him. "No one here but us. Perfect opportunity. I bet you'd like a backdoor delivery, right? Never know, you might get some ideas for your next dirty book." Billy made a point with his tongue and wiggled it at her.

"You're disgusting, you know that? Don't you even care what she's going through?"

"Typical of you women. Can't keep out of other folks' business."

This was a waste of time. Lynette turned and stormed off back towards her car, heels clicking on the drive. She heard him wolf-whistle as she started the engine.

"Neanderthal," she growled through clenched teeth. "Bloody Neanderthal."

She looked over at him as she pulled away. He was standing in the door, laughing all the while.

*****

Propped against a pillow, Dottie stared out of the hospital room window at a white-grey sky. She could not shake the sense of disappointment and loss dwelling inside her. She should be holding her baby now, feeding her, staring into new little eyes, touching those impossibly small fingers and toes. Instead, she just felt so alone. She felt dejected, like she could not rely on her husband to help her through the worst ordeal of her life.

"Hey there."

Lost in reverie, Dottie looked up. Lynette was leaning into the room, her long black hair falling around her shoulder. From the bed, Dottie did her best to muster a smile, but it was a weak and forlorn attempt.

"Hey, Lynette. Come on in."

"You sure? I can come back later, if you'd rather."

Dottie beckoned her in.

"I brought you these," Lynette said, shaking a bunch of carnations by the stalks. "I see you've amassed quite a collection already. Look at all those beauties."

"Dr Cassidy brought them by this morning."

"That was nice of him." Lynette picked up a large sympathy card from the shelf and looked inside. "The kids at the school give you this?"

"Yeah, they've all signed it. It was sweet of them. Mr Bowden dropped it in."

Dottie took a moment to study her friend, and as a result, felt that little bit sadder. Lynette, as usual, looked great, dressed immaculately in a coffee-coloured suit and chiffon scarf. Earlier, Dottie had dared to check her own reflection in a small handheld mirror, and it wasn't pretty. The attractive woman who normally looked back had disappeared, replaced by a tired, heavy-eyed stranger.

"I'll leave these here," Lynette said, laying the flowers beside the others. "Maybe the nurse will put them in some water." She sat down in one of the two plastic chairs.

90

"Listen, Dottie, I'm really so sorry about the baby. I can't imagine how you're feeling. When I heard what happened ... God, I just felt terrible for you."

Dottie drew in her legs beneath the bedcovers, making two peaks with her knees. "It wasn't meant to be, I suppose. They let me see Emma, let me hold her. They said it would be easier to ... to get over her. I kept a lock of her hair."

"That's good, Dottie. You should have something to remember."

"Her face was so small," Dottie went on sadly. "Her tiny nose and lips. It seemed like she was asleep. She looked so at peace that it seemed impossible she wasn't breathing ..."

"I wish there was something I could do, something I could say."

"You're here, Lynette, and that's more than enough."

"Has Billy been by today?" Lynette asked, looking away.

"He said he'll come by later."

They were quiet for a time, and Dottie said, "It must be as big a shock to him as it was to me."

Lynette nodded. "Do the doctors know why it happened?"

"I haven't really spoken much to anyone about it yet. They've all been so kind, just letting me rest. One doctor did say it won't stop me from getting pregnant again. There shouldn't be any future complications."

"That's great, Dottie."

"How're Graham and the kids?"

Lynette thumbed towards the door. "He's in the waiting area with Tara. I didn't think you'd want a crowd around, so I told him to stay put. Tara's got her nose in a load of books, so she's content enough."

"Oh, Lynette, ask them in, please."

"Are you sure?"

"Mm-hmm."

Lynette opened the door, and after a few seconds, Graham was there, in jeans and a black V-neck sweater. He held Tara's hand. The little girl was dressed in a red polka-dot dress, clutching the paw of a small button-eyed bear. She looked shyly up at Dottie.

"Hello there, missy," Dottie said. "Who's your little friend?"

Graham let go of Tara's hand, and she approached the bedside. "This is Bert," she squeaked, as her mother hoisted her onto the bedcovers.

"Hello, Bert," Dottie said, scratching the bear's black nose. "He's a handsome fellow, isn't he?"

"How are you feeling, Dottie?" Graham asked. "I know it's a dumb question ..." He shrugged, looking uneasy.

"Thanks for coming in, all of you." She touched Tara's cheek as the girl played with the teddy bear. "It's great to see you. To be honest, I'm just looking forward to getting out of here. I've had as much rest as I can stand."

"Can I get you anything?" Graham asked. "I can scoot on down to that little shop out front. You need magazines, drinks, anything?"

"The cupboard there's brimming with lemonade and magazines," Dottie said. "Thanks anyway."

"Are you not feeling well, Dottie?" Tara asked.

"Well, I had some bad news, petal," Dottie told her. "I was sad, although I'm feeling better now, after seeing you and Bert here. That's cheered me up, one hundred percent."

92

Tara smiled at her, and Dottie smiled back; but inside, she had no idea how she was going to carry on another day.

CHAPTER 14

"I keep thinking I did something wrong," Dottie said, hanging her head. "Something that caused her to die."

"I assure you that no one did anything wrong, Dottie. Not you, not Billy, not the hospital staff. Stillbirths are very rare these days, but unfortunately, they do happen."

"Why?"

"There are no known causes, really, although there are factors sometimes taken into account. Diabetes in the mother, for instance. Haemorrhage. Alcohol abuse. Smoking. There may be problems involving the placenta separating too soon from the uterine wall. Sometimes the oxygen supply is blocked before the baby's ready to breathe on its own, when the umbilical cord comes from the vagina before the baby. None of these things is relevant in your case, however."

Dottie looked up at Nick's friendly face. She had been seeing him regularly since leaving the hospital and found their conversations tempered her feelings of loss. Today, he'd suggested they stroll in the park behind the maternity unit. It was mid-afternoon. The thick boughs above their heads sheltered them from much of the sunlight. The grass was mottled in a million golden shards. Beneath her skirt, Dottie felt the warm breeze on her legs.

"The funeral was horrible," she said. "It was the worst day of my life, seeing her buried like that."

"I can recommend specialist counselling, Dottie, if you'd like. It will help, I promise. They're exceptionally good at what they do."

"Can't I keep coming to see you?"

"I'll be here as long as you need me."

Their path forked to the left and rounded a pond choked with reeds. They slowed there, and Dottie scooped up a handful of small stones. She tossed them into the water one at a time, watching the ripples spread outwards. When the stones were gone, she brushed her hands together, and they moved on.

"Have you let the school know what happened?"

She nodded. "Mr Bowden has been great. The kids sent me a big card; they'd all signed the inside. That was sweet of them. I don't have to go back until next year, unless I want to, that is."

"That's good. You should accept that the baby will always have a place in your heart, Dottie. Often in these cases, the parents are advised to do something special on the anniversary, at least for the first few years. I know it feels like the world has ended, and there's no greater pain a mother can endure. I can only tell you to give yourself a chance to heal."

"I feel like crying all the time. I feel so useless."

"You should cry as much as you think you need to. Get the tears out now, or they'll just build up inside. Tell me, how's Billy handling it?"

Dottie shook her head. "He blames me."

"That's crazy, and unfair. He should be supporting you."

"That's what my friend, Lynette, keeps telling me."

"Your friend is right, Dottie."

"I don't just mean about the baby. He blames me for everything. Things he hasn't achieved, things he'll never do. He's angry *all* the time, Nick."

They walked on, Dottie ruminating on how her life had become such a convoluted web of disappointments. Every aspiration she'd harboured since leaving school – the ideal marriage, a baby to care for – had amounted to nothing.

A jogger trudged past, breathing heavily. Nick motioned towards a cast-iron bench, and they sat down.

"Sounds to me like you have some thinking to do, Dottie."

She shrugged. "Things just aren't how I thought they'd be."

"Which things, particularly?"

"My life. Marriage. Everything, I suppose."

"Marriage requires constant work, Dottie. They all have to be persevered. They need devotion and hard graft."

"I know that better than most," she said, tweaking her skirt over her exposed knees. "What if it's not worth saving?"

"Is that how you feel?"

"I had so many plans. Billy and I would travel the cities of Europe, see a bit of the world, then settle down and have a family. But he doesn't want to travel with me, he isn't interested. He doesn't want to do anything; yet he insists I'm shackling him here, married to me."

"I think your husband has some problems," Nick said, as diplomatically as he could. "The main one being his inability to see how lucky he is, having you as a wife."

Despite herself, Dottie couldn't suppress a brief smile. He looked so handsome in his scarlet shirt and black slacks, and he smelled all clean and lemony. She met his eyes and resisted the urge to take his hand. Instead, she faced front, where a woman passed with two bushy-haired Dobermans, the dogs' tongues drooping from open muzzles.

"That's a nice thing to say," she told him. "Billy never tells me things like that. He never gives me flowers anymore, compliments, nothing."

They were quiet for a minute. A large lady went by in a magenta frock with a matching handbag and hat, licking fervently at a cone.

"Do you fancy an ice cream, Dottie?"

"No, thank you."

"Sure? There's a stall right over there. My treat."

"I'm fine, really."

They sat and watched people coming and going, and Nick said, "So, which European cities have taken your fancy?"

She considered. "There're so many. Barcelona, definitely. I'd love to see Venice, and Paris too. All the romantic places, I suppose."

"I've visited Venice twice. It's amazing."

"Really?"

"Oh yeah. Once when I was young, and the last time was two years ago, give or take. I think you'd love it. A whole other world."

"Would you tell me about it, Nick? Just for a minute or two."

"Well, Venice charms everyone. It's by far the most photogenic city in the world, in my opinion. The Grand Canal, St Mark's Square, the Doge's Palace; these spots are breathtaking. But Venice has a kind of secret side too, only accessible by water. In a gondola, you discover the city as it was designed to be seen – all the secluded gardens and ancient houses. Quite remarkable. That's the real Venice."

"Sounds fantastic," Dottie remarked, wishing she had seen these things before marrying. "Were you there alone?"

"First time, yes. I did a lot of travelling when I was younger. My girlfriend Karine was with me the last time. We've since separated, however. Apparently, I'm not what she's looking for."

"Carry on, please."

"I've never met anyone so interested in my travels." He chuckled, and said, "It's a beautiful city, no question. Nothing really prepares you for it. Magical, I'd say. The spires and domes reflected in the shimmering water. The labyrinthine alleys, moored boats rocking everywhere. Waterbuses and motor launches rather than cars and taxis. In the morning, you're woken by church bells and barge hooters, all sensory spices that add to the whole experience, I suppose."

"What about restaurants?" Dottie asked. "They nice?"

"There're hundreds of them around the city. A multitude of choice, like everything else there. Garden restaurants, restaurants by the waterside. All you'd expect and more. What can I say? You have to see it to believe it. And I'm sure that one day you will, Dottie."

"I'd like to think so. But it won't be with Billy."

"That's something you'll have to decide for yourself. It won't do any good to dwell in a marriage if you're truly unhappy. These decisions must be your own, though. All I can advise is that you don't rush into anything. You've suffered a profoundly traumatic experience, and it's bound to affect your thinking. You're a plucky little thing, Dottie, and I've no doubt you'll work this out."

She smiled sheepishly, and another layer of gloom lifted from her and floated away in the breeze. Once again, she felt longing stir deep

98

within her, kicked up like the silt of a seabed. This time his warm hand closed around hers, and she wondered what kind of crazy girlfriend would let Nick Cassidy slip through her grasp.

CHAPTER 15

To keep occupied, Dottie cleaned the house when she returned from her appointment with Nick. For the first time since the baby's death, she felt quietly optimistic, having drawn resilience and self-assurance from her session with him. She kept reliving their time in the park, that electrically charged moment when their hands had touched. Nothing had ever felt so right. She had experienced real emotion, real male friendship, and had a glimpse of the happiness that had for so long eluded her.

Nick had felt something too. She had sensed this, through the enveloping warmth of his hand, in the benevolence of his words, in the caring inflection of his voice. His eyes had revealed even more to her, for the eyes were indeed the windows to the soul. But she sensed reluctance in him also, and Dottie could understand this. The situation was untenable, yet he ignited something inside her and sent her emotions dancing. Nick Cassidy quickened the beat of her heart.

Upstairs, Dottie looked in Emma's room, wondering what life would have been like had the baby lived. She imagined her lying there in the cot, gurgling happily, her little chubby legs kicking out. When these thoughts became too much, she stepped back and closed the door.

Dottie crossed to her bedroom. Billy's clothing littered the bed and floor. She scooped the garments up and dumped them in the laundry basket. As she checked the pockets of his jeans for coins and keys, her fingers brushed against something. She withdrew a piece of paper and unfolded it. Some kind of invoice from his work, dated months ago.

But something else fell from the piece of paper – something shiny – and landed on the carpet. It winked there in the sunlight. She squatted down and lifted it from the floor, turning it in her palm, frowning.

*****

Like so many nights before, Dottie sat at the dinner table, head in her hands, apprehensively awaiting the sounds of his key scraping into the lock. Tonight, Billy's absence afforded her ample time to rehearse her lines, to clarify what she needed to say. Lynette had been right, and Nick had been right. She deserved better than this. She was a decent person, and things had to change, although her heart assured her that change would be a long time coming. Billy would have to care enough about their marriage to *want* to change, but she felt he was completely lost to her now.

Everything was such a mess. Her feelings for Nick seemed to grow in proportion to the gulf widening between her and Billy. It was wrong, but she deserved some happiness, didn't she? Some manner of fulfilment?

On top of this, she missed her parents and longed to see them. She wanted to hear her mother's kind words and needed the paternal firmness of her father's embrace. Billy had told them to stay away after the birth, and she could not forgive him for that.

She decided to call them.

Her father picked up on the fifth ring. "Hi, sweetheart, how're you coping?"

"I'm okay, Dad. Just thought I'd give you a buzz, see how you both are."

"I'm so sorry about the baby, Dottie. You know we wanted to come over there."

"I know."

"Billy told your mother to give it time. Is that what *you* want, Dottie? Because we can be there, as soon as you need us."

"That's good to know, Dad. I'm doing okay, and the doctor said there shouldn't be any complications with future pregnancies."

"I'm so glad to hear that, really."

"Is Mum there?"

"She's down the shops. She'll be blathering to auld Betsy behind the counter. That's why I don't go with her anymore. Those two get gassing, and you've got one demon wait on yer hands. I'll tell her you rang. Knowing her, she'll be right back on the blower 'fore you know it."

"Just tell her I love her, and I'll call again soon. And I love you too, Dad."

After the call, Dottie began thinking about the days she spent in the hospital. Her memories were patchy at best; still, she recalled fragments of that first night, when Billy came into her room. The sedatives had been dragging her towards sleep, but she'd heard his words – enough to know they were malicious and devoid of any concern. An embarrassment, he had called her. Yet another indication that their marriage was doomed.

As the night wore on, she dozed, her head still pressed into her hands. When the front door opened, she started, sitting up straight, bleary-eyed. The clock in the hall chimed eleven.

Billy shambled into the dining room. One look at him confirmed her misgivings. His eyes were glazed. The caustic reek of drink emanated from his breath.

"Where's dinner?"

Dottie stared at him. "There isn't any," she said. "We have to talk."

"You're right." Billy walked into the kitchen and reappeared with a dishtowel in his hand. He placed it on the table, under her chin. "I've told you about wearing that crap on your face."

"It's not crap, it's make-up."

"Don't get smart. Wipe it off, now."

"No."

"What did you say?"

"This can't go on anymore."

He glared at her. "This?"

"You, drinking all the time. Treating me like garbage. Abusive names." She grabbed the dishtowel and shook it. "Threatening me over a little make-up. Surely you can see we can't go on like this."

Billy removed his jacket, draping it across the arm of the couch. "You ain't gonna see that quack anymore, either."

Dottie blinked. "What?"

"Cassidy. You're not pregnant anymore, Dottie, in case you've forgotten. So, you ain't to be running to him every other day, like a damned basket case."

"I won't stop seeing him. He helps me – he helps me more than you do."

103

Billy stopped dead, as if slapped by an invisible hand. "You got the horn for him?" He leaned into her face, breathing alcohol fumes over her. "That it, Dottie? He gets the juices flowing downstairs?"

She tossed the condom wrapper on the tablecloth, where it glinted in the lamplight like a new silver coin. "I found *that* in your jeans." Billy stared at it, and Dottie saw the guilt bleeding through his expression. "Like wearing socks in the bath, is it?" she said. "Who've you been sleeping with, Billy?"

"Me and a few guys were messing around with them at the Admiral—"

"You're a liar." Dottie got up a thumped his chest with her fist. "Liar! You're a *liar*!"

With the speed and accuracy of a lizard's tongue, Billy's arm shot out and seized her throat, silencing her. His grip immediately closed off her windpipe, slamming her body back against the wall. Dottie tried to scream, panic-stricken, her eyes bulging in their sockets. She clawed at his fingers, pried at them, and tried to scratch at his face, but he squeezed tighter and tighter, until her heart hammered, and she thought he was going to kill her.

"Not so much to say now?"

He looked into her eyes, close enough for her to see the marbled red lines in the whites of his. She continued to claw uselessly at his hand.

Have to have air ... have to breathe ...

He threw her onto the table, facedown, causing her mouth to collide against its surface. She tasted blood and broke into a series of rasping coughs, unable to draw oxygen. His hand suddenly manacled the nape of her neck, pinning her head down, and before she knew what was happening, he was flipping up the hem of her skirt with his free hand.

"No!" she cried, the word muffled as he pressed her face to the table. "No, Billy! Stop!"

"Shut your mouth."

She struggled hysterically, arms and legs thrashing about to no avail, tears dampening the tablecloth. His sharp fingernails gouged the small of her back as he yanked at her underwear – "No! Stop!" – and her words went unheard.

Frantic, Dottie heard the foreboding clink and jangle of his belt buckle, followed by the popping of his fly buttons. She fought to free herself, struggling to comprehend what he was doing. But she could not move – his fingers were fierce talons around her neck, painfully biting into her flesh like a bird of prey seizing a defenceless animal. And now he was guiding himself inside her, thrusting deep. He moaned, a repulsive, sexual sound, and pounded into her again and again, faster and faster, crashing his hips back and forth.

Dottie opened her mouth to scream, but nothing happened. Her hair was splayed across her eyes and lips, salty tears mixing with the coppery blood from her split lip. Billy's breath was hot against her shoulder, the stink of alcohol sickening as he gasped and growled behind her like an animal.

The power to fight abandoned her, and she grew limp beneath his vice-like grip, pinned there, eyes clenched shut behind her cascade of auburn hair. Billy's breathless gasps reached a crescendo, and he came inside her, twitching in spasms, groaning, and finally, he stopped moving, collapsing on top of her.

His fingers released her neck, and she felt his weight lifting off her. She couldn't move; instead she remained there, clutching the edges of the oval table. Her underwear, which dangled from one foot, slipped and dropped to the floor.

"You asked for that," he said behind her. "You start answering me back, you see what happens. Well, let that be a lesson to you, Dottie. I tell you to do something, you do it. No arguments. Now clean yourself up and fix me something to eat."

When she heard his footfalls on the stairs, Dottie slid to the floor, knees together, dragging the tablecloth down with her. She clutched at the wooden leg of the dining table, sobbing, bleeding, lengths of her long hair streaking her face like strands of seaweed.

CHAPTER 16

Lynette clicked the mouse and saved her night's work, before switching off the computer. The screen darkened and closed down. Habitually, she didn't write in the evenings, but with so many strands of her novel limping along, she had attempted to implement a few fixes. Had she not done this, the problems would keep her awake all night, careering around in her head, demanding attention until she reluctantly conceded and rose at an ungodly hour to start work again.

For Lynette, powering down her mind long enough to rest was an ongoing problem. Since childhood, she had averaged only four or five hours of sleep, which usually sufficed to see her through the day. A light sleeper, it was during the small hours that she did her deepest thinking, be it story ideas or plot issues, ruminations about her life, worry over the kids, or whatever else crept up in the dead of night.

She yawned, covering her mouth, and walked from her lamp-lit study into the living room. Netherwood House was silent, the lights turned low, creating the serene and peaceful ambience she liked. Long shadows splashed across the panelled walls and carpeted floors. Mark and Tara were upstairs, asleep. Graham was at the warehouse, working until eight a.m. when his shift change would relieve him.

She wandered through the spacious kitchen, past the marble-topped island that housed the cooker and other appliances. Rex lay snuggled in his basket, dreaming his doggy dreams. She eased open the back door and lit a cigarette, expelling smoke into the breeze. Damned fags were the bane of her life. She just couldn't quit, even after weeks of abstinence.

The night-shrouded woodland around Netherwood House was calm, breaths of wind soughing through the conifers, stirring leaves, swaying branches. Beyond those trees, over a mile away, the town of Aradale slept.

She and Graham had bought Netherwood five years ago, when sales of her second romantic novel, *Winter Blossom,* exceeded the expectations of her publisher, agent, and especially Lynette. The house purchase was well-timed, as she had become pregnant with Tara soon thereafter. Since moving in, she and Graham had renovated most of the rooms, stamping their own tastes on the old place.

She admired Netherwood House. It was the kind of location she liked to write about, and the solitude here was paramount to her creativity. Some days she craved the hurly-burly of town life, but predominately she welcomed the peace and tranquillity, the absence of traffic and people.

From as early as her primary school days, Lynette had wanted to be a writer. More, the fixation could be traced back to one particular day. Setting them a task of creating a short story, her teacher chalked a sentence on the blackboard, instructing the class to run with it in whatever direction they wished. Lynette couldn't recall the first-person sentence verbatim, but it had something to do with hearing a noise upstairs, followed by ellipses. Even at a young age, she had felt the buzz of creativity, as if this was what she was put on Earth to do. From that day forward, she had been hooked on the craft.

She drew on her cigarette, its amber tip smouldering in the darkness.

"Arsehole," she said, recalling her exchange with Billy, remembering what he had said about her husband. Graham was ten times the man that arrogant sod would ever amount to. He was hardworking, loving, caring, and great with the kids. She couldn't ask for a better partner, and it had smarted when Billy had slighted him. The sooner someone put that layabout in his place, the better. He was—

Lynette heard her mobile ringing in the kitchen and slipped back inside, where Rex was now awake, peering about, the corgi's ears pricked up.

"Relax, Rex, it's just the phone. Go to sleep." She fished in her handbag, through hankies and make-up and other detritus. "Come on, come on, where is the bloody thing?" She finally found the mobile and saw Dottie's name on the caller display.

"Hey, Dottie. I thought I was the only night owl around here?"

"Lynette? I ..."

"Hey, are you okay?" There was silence, and Lynette frowned. "Dottie? Are you there?"

"Could I stay with you for a while, Lynette? Would that be okay?"

Lynette had never heard Dottie sound so weak and hurt. And her friend had never called this late before. Crushing out her cigarette, she said, "Tell me what's happened. Has Billy done something to you?"

"We ... we had a fight. I have to get away from him."

"Did he hurt you?"

"He's upstairs now. He doesn't know ..."

"What, Dottie? What doesn't he know?"

"He doesn't know I'm calling."

"Give me ten minutes. Just sit tight, okay?"

"Thank you, Lyne. I'm so sorry about all this."

Lynette snapped shut her phone and bolted upstairs, towards Mark's room. When she eased open the bedroom door, the landing light poured across the carpet and single bed, revealing a tuft of Mark's dark hair on the pillow. He stirred as she approached, palming sleep from his eyes, wincing against the brightness.

"Mum? What's going on?"

"We're going for a little ride into town," she said, sitting on the bed. "Throw on some clothes. It won't take long."

"What time is it?"

"Just please do it, Mark. I'll be back in a minute, after I wake your sister. Hurry up now."

*****

Dottie sat in the kitchen, her hands shaking so intensely that she thought they might never stop. A dull ache throbbed between her legs. She could feel his seed inside her. She had packed a T-shirt and a pair of jeans into a carrier bag, both of which had been hanging on the line outside. Taking more clothes was out of the question, for that would necessitate going upstairs, beside him, and she could not bring herself to do that. Collecting her things was a task for another time, another day.

His steps continued above her head, in the bedroom. She prayed he would fall asleep before Lynette arrived, although the chances of such luck were doubtful. He hadn't eaten, and he rarely slept on an empty stomach. Any minute now, he would tramp downstairs, demanding food.

Hungry after all his raping.

The doorbell rang. Dottie hurried down the floral runner covering the hallway and pulled open the front door.

"Christ, Dottie," Lynette said, upon seeing her. "You look awful. What the hell's been going on?" She touched Dottie's cheek gently. "Your lip is bleeding. You're shaking, Dottie."

Dottie ran her tongue over her split lip, wincing as she brushed a chipped tooth. "Can we get out of here? I can't take another run-in with him ..."

"Where the hell d'you think you're going?"

They turned and looked up at the top of the stairs. Billy was there, bare-chested, wearing only jeans, and glowering at them. He lifted a hand and pointed at Lynette. "What's she doing here at this bloody time of night?"

Through her tangled shock of hair, Dottie looked him dead in the eye. "I'm leaving you," she said.

His face darkened, his narrow eyes going from Dottie to Lynette and back again, taking their measure. He took a breath, inflating his chest. "She's put you up to this?"

"No one's put me up to anything, Billy. We're through. I'm leaving. I can't live like this anymore."

He started slowly down the stairs. "You think I'd let you just walk outta here? You're my wife, and you'll do as I say." He thumped himself on the chest with a closed fist. "You'll only leave when I say you leave."

"You come one step further, and I'll be straight on the phone," Lynette warned, holding her mobile. "You've beaten her, big man.

111

Unless you want to spend a night in the police station, you stay the hell away from her."

Billy stopped halfway down. Dottie saw the muscles in his face tighten. He smirked, as if unable to believe someone – a *woman* – had spoken to him with such disregard.

"You cross me, you'll regret it, bitch."

"Yeah, yeah," Lynette tossed back, undaunted. "Very scary. She's been hurt and it's your fault. Come on, Dottie, let's go."

"You best reconsider, Dorothy."

Dottie vacillated for a second, staring up at him. "I have, Billy. Too many times."

That said, she allowed herself to be harried from the house, out towards Lynette's BMW. The weather had turned, the night foul and rain-swept, a blustery wind gathering. As she approached the car, Dottie gasped at the two white moon faces peering from the rear window.

"You brought the kids?" she asked, as Lynette opened the passenger door for her.

"Graham's at work. I couldn't leave them."

"Lynette, I'm so sorry about this."

"Quit apologising. Kids get too much sleep, anyhow. Now, will you get in the car, please, before Happy Larry in there decides to make another scene?"

Dottie climbed in and gave the kids a cursory smile, endeavouring to hide her split lip.

"Hi, Dottie," Tara said, peeking out from a pink hood.

"Hey, kids. Sorry about all this upheaval."

"I'm up *late!*" Tara announced proudly and clapped her hands.

Lynette got in the driver's side, gunned the engine, and began turning the BMW in the cul-de-sac. The headlights played on neighbouring houses. Rain thrummed on the car's roof. Looking out at her home, Dottie saw Billy's silhouette in the open doorway, motionless and threatening. In the darkness, she could not see the expression on his face, but he was shaking his head, side to side, as if assuring her she had just made the biggest mistake of her life.

CHAPTER 17

Belted into the BMW's spacious passenger seat, her size fours barely skimming the floor, Dottie felt like a bullied, overgrown schoolgirl being driven home by her mother, so crushed was her self-respect and confidence. The residual ache between her legs, however, reminded her that the situation far exceeded a case of simple bullying. Houses and stores gradually grew sparse as Lynette steered the car north, away from town. Dottie knew her friend had a multitude of questions, but Lynette would not voice them until they were alone.

So, Dottie said nothing. What was there to say? Here she was, twenty-eight years old, a childless rape victim, married to a husband who hated her. *Thanks a bunch, God. What did I ever do to you?*

She dabbed her lip gingerly with a paper handkerchief from the glove compartment. The bleeding had ceased, and her lip was swollen and fat. She kept her tongue away from the broken tooth, avoiding the brain-jarring sensation triggered by touching the exposed nerve. The real damage was in her overloaded mind and in her heart. How was she ever going to get past this? She could tell herself that she wasn't to blame – but that would not help. Not for long, at any rate.

Dottie had always believed, perhaps a little naively, that if the time ever came when a man tried to force her into sex, she would be able, one way or another, to fend him off. There would be a violent struggle, surely, but she'd be able to do *something* to retain her dignity, to make sure she did not become another statistic. That was exactly what she felt like now – another woman unable to defend herself when such a situation arose. She felt weak and incapable. How could she tell anyone what he'd done? What would people think?

Still, her hands trembled, although this was hidden in the car's dark interior, the red-orange instruments from the console providing the only light. The digital clock read eleven fifty. The dashboard heater, coupled with the wipers' squeegee blades arching back and forth, made her eyes heavy.

She tried to remember when her marriage had come so far off the rails, but her mind would not concentrate, the pain and heartbreak now all-encompassing. When had the decline actually begun? It was difficult to say. Whatever bond had once existed between her and Billy was dead.

Dottie closed her eyes.

Over the years, he had become less and less interested in her, irritated by her, though she constantly tried to please him, like a dippy animal too stupid to see the heavy boot coming its way. She should have heeded the signs and reacted earlier, instead of passively hoping the rift would eventually right itself. She remembered the time when he'd struck her for hoovering while he was watching TV; and his refusals to accompany her when she was invited out by her colleagues at the school. Most recently, of course, was his newly developed aversion to her make-up, as if he were afraid of her drawing unwanted male attention. The list was long and grim, and Dottie didn't want to think about it, for no good would come from doing so.

You best reconsider, Dorothy.

He always called her Dorothy when he was in a foul mood, when he meant business.

If he wanted her to know she had overstepped a mark, he called her Dorothy, not Dottie. A simple means of intimidation from his bag of tricks. God, how blind had she been?

They were leaving the main road from Aradale, bearing left up the long rise, the way becoming narrow. This lesser road was rutted and peppered with potholes, though the BMW continued along unfazed. Wind-tossed trees swayed in the headlights, the birches and firs moving behind old split-rail fences. Through the rain-filled night, Dottie glimpsed the dated sign that read: NETHERWOOD HOUSE 1 MILE.

"You okay there, Dottie?"

"I'm okay," she said, but she didn't move or say anything else. Had Lynette guessed what had happened? She certainly knew what Billy was capable of. Perhaps Lynette had seen something like this coming, all along. Maybe everyone had. Everyone except silly old Dottie.

"Awful quiet back there, you two," Lynette said, angling her head to see in the rear-view mirror. "You okay?"

Sleepy, mumbled sounds came from the rear seats.

"Well, here we are, people."

Dottie raised her eyes, as the façade of Netherwood House materialised in the darkness. The sandstone construct was clad in ivy, glistening in the rain. Dim lights burned in the downstairs latticed windows. The brass doorknocker, an open-mouthed gargoyle, shone in the headlights below the large stone pediment above the entrance. Twin square pilasters flanked the front door.

Inside, Lynette carried Tara upstairs to the child's room. Mark took a soft drink from the fridge and went off to his own bedroom, and before long, Dottie was alone. She perched on a stool and waited. The kitchen was fitted out in whites and creams and was bigger than Dottie's living room – *former* living room. Concealed bulbs glowed from beneath cupboards and units, casting the marble counters in restful light. Rex observed her from his basket, licking his chops.

"Hey, Rex," Dottie whispered. "Fancy trading lives for a while?"

Lynette reappeared with two large glasses of red wine. Dottie barely managed to steady her hand enough to accept one of them.

"Get your laughing gear around that," Lynette advised. "Watch your lip, though." She took a stool, pinching her navy slacks and crossing her legs. A black sling-back shoe dangled from her toes.

"Thanks, Lynette. I owe you for this."

"Nonsense. You owe me nothing."

"I needed help, and you were there."

"Want to tell me what went on?"

Dottie didn't reply. She looked around the kitchen. "Are you sure it's okay for me to be here? I'm not putting you and Graham out. Or the kids?"

Lynette fingered her raven-black hair from her face. "I told you, Dottie, you're welcome as long as you want to be here. We've mountains of room, and you know Graham and the kids love having you. So, stop worrying about putting people out, okay?"

Dottie smiled glumly, fingering her swollen lip.

"What happened tonight? You sounded terrified. You were shaking like a leaf when I got there."

117

Dottie quaffed wine. "This is great," she said, looking at the glass. "Blossom Hill."

Dottie took another sip. "He came home drunk again. We fought. He hit me." She rubbed at her nose. "It just scared me."

"You did the right thing, clearing out."

"He's been sleeping with someone else," Dottie said, sounding as if it required a great effort to admit this. "I found a condom wrapper in his trousers."

"Oh, Dottie, I'm sorry."

"It's probably been going on for ages, throughout the pregnancy. God knows how long. I don't suppose it matters much. I feel like such an idiot."

"Is that what started the fight?"

Dottie nodded. "I confronted him with it, and I knew he was lying, straight off. He's never really been a convincing liar, not when you pin him down about something. I've suspected it for a while, though, I just wasn't sure. He's not the kind of person you can ask such questions, is he?"

"Do you know who he's been sleeping with?"

"It doesn't matter to me. I feel nothing but disgust for him. All those times he's left the house, telling me lies, coming home late. What would've happened if the baby had been born into a mess like that? Maybe it's worked out for best, in a crazy sort of way."

"Don't think about it just now, Dottie. Just be thankful you've made a decision."

"I've realised I can't be with him. Still, what am I going to do, Lynette? I mean, we stay in the same town. Can I really live separately from him? Can I? He's going to be around all the time, isn't he?" She sighed. "My life's such a mess."

"Don't punish yourself for his faults, Dottie," Lynette told her. "And don't try to get everything straight, right away. You've got somewhere to stay in the meantime, and that's all that matters now. The rest will slot into place, you'll see. The first step is realising you can't go on living with him, living with abuse. That's half the battle."

"It took me long enough. I'm such an idiot."

Lynette drank her wine, and said, "I'll swing you by there tomorrow, so you can pick up some clothes and whatever else you need. Or you can borrow the car yourself, whatever you want."

"I haven't driven in years."

"Then I'll drive you. He'll be out, won't he?"

Dottie nodded, sipping her wine. "You don't know how lucky you are, having Graham and kids. Your life is so ... complete."

"You're kidding me? It isn't all roses here either, Dottie. Graham can be a jerk when he wants to. And those two upstairs" – she pointed at the ceiling – "they could make a monk scream sometimes."

"But the four of you make a great family."

"If it really is over with you and Billy – and I hope it is – you'll find someone else, Dottie. You're a wonderful person, and I'm glad to call you a friend."

Dottie suddenly found herself thinking about Nick Cassidy. She looked at Lynette with doleful eyes. "I must look a fright, huh?"

"Hair by Crazy Meg," Lynette said, and they both laughed.

"Hey, quit it, my face hurts enough as it is."

"The swelling dies down soon enough, and so will the situation. Give it time, everything will sort itself out. He can't hurt you while you're here." She took Dottie's glass. "Ready for a refill?"

Lynette went for more wine. Rain rattled against the windows. Dottie couldn't stop thinking about what had happened tonight. She remembered Billy standing in the doorway, shaking his head, watching her finally walk out on him.

You best reconsider, Dorothy.

This wasn't over. Not by a long chalk.

*****

Later, Dottie indulged in a hot shower, lathering her body, washing her hair, and trying to rid her mind of the evening's events. But, how could she? This was going to haunt her for the rest of her life. She remained under the spray as long as possible, trying to scrub away the memory of Billy's weight on top of her, of his hand around her neck.

Afterwards, wrapped in a robe of Lynette's, she sat on the bed in one of the house's spare rooms. She brushed her hair slowly. Rex was curled on the duvet, watching her with a careful eye as Dottie stroked his warm side.

Again and again, she contemplated talking to the police, but she and Billy were husband and wife, and it was his word against hers, wasn't it? Any evidence they looked for would undoubtedly amount to nothing. She could claim she had been raped; Billy would say it had been consensual. The police, probably up to their eyes in domestic disputes, would determine it was just one more to add to the list. She had a broken lip and scratches on her back, but this wouldn't convince anyone of rape. It would prove nothing. Only she had seen his enraged state. And still, hours later, she could not believe it.

CHAPTER 18

"Will Dottie be staying with us?" Mark asked, as his mother drew up outside the primary school the next morning.

"For a little while," Lynette said. "She's having a rough time and needs to be away from home."

"Did she and Billy have a fight?"

"Just a misunderstanding. Sorry, I had to wake you and Tara, but it was unavoidable."

"That's all right. I didn't mind."

"We were up late!" Tara called from behind her mother. She was kneeling on the BWM's upholstery, fogging the window with her breath. "Late, late, late!"

"We won't be making a habit of *that*, young lady," Lynette told her. "And I hope you're not doodling on my nice clean windows."

Mark looked out at children filing through the schoolyard gate. "Will they get divorced now?"

"I'm not sure. Listen, don't you worry about it. Go on and scoot, before you miss the bell."

Back at Netherwood House, Lynette went upstairs to check on Dottie. She was still asleep, a small mound beneath the covers of a huge bed. Lynette eased closed the door and returned downstairs. Tara had settled in front of the television, watching cartoons. In the kitchen, Lynette took two Aspirin to counteract last night's glasses of wine. She prepared black coffee and sipped it slowly. In his basket, Rex scratched behind an ear with rapid leg movements.

Around eight-thirty, Graham arrived home as she was rinsing dishes. He kissed her cheek and dropped his bag on the floor.

"How was night shift?"

"The usual. Quiet and uneventful. Sometimes I wish burglars *would* appear, just to liven things up a bit."

"You'd want to fend off burglars to pass the time?"

Graham removed a carton of milk from the fridge. "Maybe that's a bit extreme. It doesn't half get boring, though." He drank and wiped his mouth. "How'd you sleep? You look a bit done in."

Lynette sat on one of the stools. "We had trouble last night."

"Trouble? What happened? Are the kids all right?"

"Relax, everything's fine. Dottie called late and asked if she could stay here for a bit. She and Billy had a big fight, and I went around there to pick her up." She shrugged. "Mr Charm's been sleeping with someone else."

"You're kidding. That man must be a prize idiot."

"That's what I told her. Someday soon, Billy will realise he's thrown away the best thing that's ever happened to him. Dottie doesn't have a contentious bone in her body. She doesn't deserve any of this crap. She says they were rowing, but I know it got pretty hairy before I arrived."

"Physical?"

Lynette touched her mouth with a lacquered fingernail. "Her lip was bleeding when I got there. Billy tried to stop her from leaving, so I threatened to call the police. I think he saw sense in the end – if that's possible."

"Did he do anything while you were there?"

123

"No, not really, but ... you should've heard him. He's so full of himself. Standing there and mouthing off, playing the big man. He didn't even care that Dottie was hurt, you know? I mean, she was really shaking. I've never seen her like that."

"Where were the kids while all this was going on?"

"I got them up and took them with me. Don't worry, they waited in the car. I was only in the house for five minutes. She needed my help, and I couldn't think of anything else to do."

Graham sat down. "Wow. Sounds like an eventful night. Where's Dottie now?"

"Upstairs in a spare room. I'm just letting her sleep. She looks shattered, which is understandable. I can't believe that ... that *arsehole* treats her the way he does, after her losing the baby and everything."

"You know we've been over this. You can't get between them, Lynette. If they have problems – and they've *got* problems – they have to work them out for themselves. Dottie's a smart girl, she'll do the right thing."

"She's not going back to him. I've told her she could stay with us until she works out her next move. That's okay, isn't it?"

Graham nodded thoughtfully. "Of course, yeah. She's welcome here as long as she wants to stay. She always will be, after what she did for Mark in the water that day. She knows that."

Lynette began pacing the kitchen. "She just needs to get away from that man, permanently."

"That's not your call, Lyne."

She became silent. The sounds of blaring cartoons and Tara's giggling drifted in from the other room.

124

"When Dottie was in the hospital, I went around to see Billy."

Graham frowned at her.

"I thought I could make him see what he was doing to her. She needed his help, and that waster just didn't care."

"You told him that?"

"Damned right I did."

"Lynette, for God's sake ..."

"Well, it's true. Anyhow, he was more interested in dishing out verbal abuse than acknowledging what I was telling him."

"You should've known better than to expect anything else. What did he say?"

Lynette waved a hand. "Doesn't matter. I wouldn't repeat it, anyway. Suffice to say, he was rude, disgusting, and completely unwilling to listen. Nothing out of the ordinary."

Graham folded his arms, still frowning. "You know the type of guy he is. If you go around there and antagonise the man, he'll only resent you for it."

"I think he resents the human race. I really do. I can't believe she ever got entangled with him, Graham."

"Morning."

Lynette spun around and saw Dottie in the doorway. She was swathed in a stripy blue-and-white robe, which was ridiculously too big for her, like a monk's habit. Her mousy hair was tousled, her face careworn. A residual mark from last night's skirmish with Billy darkened her lip.

"I hope I'm not causing any trouble," she said, stepping into the kitchen.

125

"Not in the slightest," Graham assured her. "I hear you had quite an adventure last night. How's the lip?"

"It looks worse than it is. Lynette was great." Dottie lifted her arms, lost inside the long sleeves of her robe. "I know it's not an ideal situation."

"You ready for breakfast, before we go collect your things?"

"I'm not very hungry."

"Sit yourself down there. How do scrambled eggs sound?"

"Always best to just do as she says," Graham pointed out, smiling. "I learned that years ago. Saves a lot of time and wasted breath."

Lynette started breaking eggs into a bowl. Dottie looked down as Rex came tottering into the kitchen between them. "Good morning, Rexy," she said. "Thanks for keeping me company last night."

The corgi rubbed his muzzle against her leg.

"That dog will swear allegiance to anyone who pets him," Graham said. "He's a spoiled lump."

"He's an adorable little doggy," Dottie said.

Graham cleared his throat. "I know this is probably none of my business, but if you want to go to the police, I'd be happy to run you over there. That's clear evidence on your face, Dottie. Billy shouldn't get away with ... well, whatever happened between you."

"I just want to forget about it," she said.

"Well, if you change your mind, let me know. Okay, on that note, ladies, I'm going to grab a few hours kip, if you can bear to be without me."

"Oh, I think we'll struggle through," Lynette said, whisking up the eggs. When Graham left the room, she glanced at Dottie and asked, "You sure you're all right?"

Dottie nodded. "Fine," she said adamantly. "This is the first day of the rest of my life."

CHAPTER 19

Billy had been dog-rough and hungover at work and felt no better when he finally got home in the early evening. Despite necking water on and off since morning, he was still dehydrated. By lunchtime, he'd been close to throwing in the towel and just going home, but he had worked through killer hangovers before and had earned his stripes. Besides, he was a big boy, and by lunchtime, the shift *was* half done. Throughout the day, he'd been irascible and hardly mouthed two words to anyone, other than what was necessary when dropping his parcels. Had he been pulled over by the cops, the chances were fair he'd have exceeded the drink-drive limit. Hell, he would have probably melted the device.

He chuckled mirthlessly at this as he closed the front door. The house was quiet, which struck him as strange, despite being pre-prepared for it. No Dottie. No lights on. No scents of dinner wafting from the kitchen. No nothing.

Last night's farce lingered hazily in his mind. He recalled only snippets and flashes.

Dottie had found a rubber wrapper in his trousers. That was a rookie mistake. Things had got heated. Perhaps *that* was understatement. She had gone for him. He had taken her over the dining-room table. Then she'd left, walked right out the door. Lynette had come around and whisked her off. Adios amigo.

Unless you want to spend a night in the police station, you stay the hell away from her.

God, he hated that fucking woman. In the past, he and Lynette had tolerated each other. But Billy knew she felt the same way he did. They'd tolerated one another because she was Dottie's friend, and he was Dottie's husband. Yet he had always known she looked down on him, as if he wasn't good enough.

What did his and Dottie's lives have to do with her?

Billy lumbered upstairs and doused his face with cold water in the bathroom sink. As he did, he noticed Dottie's electric toothbrush wasn't in the pot. Her mouthwash and floss were gone too. Her conditioners and deodorants were nowhere to be seen.

In the bedroom, towelling himself dry, he discovered her clothes were gone from the closet. The plastic and metal hangers dangled there, making his meagre garments appear oddly alone. The floor space which usually housed her shoes was empty. The suitcase was absent from the shelf.

He tugged open drawers one by one. Everything was gone. Her sweaters, underwear, everything. Lynette had probably persuaded her to come here and get the stuff. Well, he wasn't fussed. Dottie would be back. She was his and would not stay gone for long. He slid the closet door shut with a thud and trudged off downstairs.

Man, he needed a drink, just something to straighten him out. He opened the fridge and found his beers were finished. He'd tanned them last night, drinking into the small hours after Dottie had left, hence the day of self-induced illness he had just suffered. There was nothing on the fridge shelves but milk and food, and he had no desire to eat.

He kicked the fridge door shut and trod through to the living room cabinet, which opened stiffly outward like a drawbridge. The bottle of

129

Smirnoff there had barely a measure left in it, nowhere near enough to fix him up. He could feel the shakes coming on and so had to have a leveller.

"Bollocks to this," he said, clutching his jacket from the door. He slipped it on and walked outside, not bothering to lock the house behind him.

*****

Ten minutes later, Billy was seated at the long mahogany bar inside MacDougal's, the live-music place on Oldwick Road. It wasn't his favourite haunt, but he didn't feel like frequenting the Admiral tonight, and the bars up on Prince Street were always heaving.

Tonight's band – a bunch of shock-haired schoolboys – were getting organised on the stage, preparing and assembling amps and leads. As Billy watched them, the barmaid approached him, a hefty Goth type with tattoos and nose rings. A lollipop stick protruded from her dark lips. She removed the glistening orb and asked what he wanted.

"Double Smirnoff an' lemonade," he told her.

"Want ice?"

He nodded, taking out his wallet.

The first drink went down a storm, never touching the sides. The second tasted even better. Billy sat and stared at his reflection in the mirror beneath the optics. By the fourth double, he felt pretty levelled out. He was not rattling any more and was beginning to feel human again – and a little smashed too. Maybe he should have eaten something after all.

By his fifth vodka, the music had started, a chaotic din of drums and thrashed chords. Billy did not recognise any of the new-fangled stuff and didn't much care for it, either. It all sounded the same to him, all equally bad. The bar had begun filling slowly, mostly with black-clad young punks gathering by the walls, lingering there like ghouls from a horror movie. Billy necked his drink and ambled off to the men's room, finding his steps and balance somewhat impaired. When he returned, he gestured to the Goth barmaid and wiggled his glass.

"Don't you think you've had enough?" she said.

"If I thought that, my arse wouldn't still be on the stool, would it? Thanks for the concern, though. Makes me feel all warm and fuzzy inside." He wiggled the glass again. "Smirnoff an' lemonade ... *lemonade*."

"We have to refuse anyone who's already drunk."

"Yeah? Who's drunk?"

"You are. You're slurring your words, and you can't even walk straight. I saw you coming back from the toilet just now. You nearly knocked a guy's drink over."

"Why don't you just do your job and save the Mary Poppins act for someone else?"

"I'm not serving you any more alcohol."

"Look, I didn't mean to be rude. Just gimme one more drink, and I'll call it a night."

"If you don't leave, I'll call the doorman."

Billy glanced to his left. A square-shouldered bouncer stood outside, arms folded. There were rolls of fat around the nape of his muscular neck. Billy sneered at the barmaid.

131

"You look like a damned panda bear with all that black shit on your eyes, you know that? You auditioning for *The Adams Family* or something?"

"Okay mister, get out."

"Pleasure."

Billy slid his empty glass at her and ambled from the bar, staggering out into the night. The air hit him straight away. Jeez, he was more wasted than he thought.

From MacDougal's, hearing the band's muffled rock music recede behind him, he made an unsteady right turn to Prince Street and then left when he reached the thoroughfare. An A-frame sign stood on the pavement outside a barbershop, and Billy kicked out at it, sending it flying across the road, where it collapsed on itself. Far off, high in the distance, barely more than pinpricks of light in the darkness, he could see the stark outline of the Mosgrove Care Home. He stared up there, sneering, wondering if the old man had dried off yet.

Billy found a quiet spot by the cemetery wall and took a piss against it. He realised the booze was making him a little horny. Alcohol created testosterone in the body, he'd heard someone say once. He stood for a moment, getting his bearings, a little wobbly on his feet. Then he decided to pay a visit to Angela Dunbar, and he shambled off in that direction.

CHAPTER 20

In her room at Netherwood House, Dottie hung her clothes in the wardrobe and folded them neatly into drawers. This done, she sat on the bed and looked out at the sliver of moon suspended above the treetops. An assortment of emotions kept firing in her mind, altering, changing, merging together. She felt confused, humiliated, let down, barren, and altogether worthless.

Regardless of how hard she tried, she could not help but feel her whole life was derailing, rushing headlong into one disaster after another. Lynette had said to give it time, that things would gradually improve, but Dottie struggled to see that far ahead. Right now, she could expect only negatives, unable to envisage a way of starting her life again. She could not picture a time when she would feel settled and loved, when she would know her life was as it should be. She appreciated Lynette's benevolence and support, the whole family's support, but still felt like a transient lodger.

After rifling through her handbag, she flipped open a little ornate mirror that her mother had bought for her birthday, years ago. The graze on her lip had faded and could now hardly be seen at all. Soon, the visible traces of that night would be gone, and she would be left with only the psychological scars. Even those might heal in time, she reflected, although the memories would prove indelible. The memories were part of her now.

She left her bedroom and walked down the hall, peeping into Tara's room. The little girl was fast asleep, her face partially concealed beneath long black hair, an arm protectively hugging a stuffed toy. Dottie closed the door and descended the carpeted staircase.

In the living room, Mark was engrossed in a loud DVD, slumped in an armchair like a puppet with its strings cut. The lights were turned low, the television's echoing surround sound cranked up, making the space feel somewhat like a small cinema theatre.

"Hey, Dottie," the boy said.

Dottie winced at the loud explosions coming from the TV. "Hi, Mark. Is your mother around?"

"I think she's working." His fingers danced on an invisible keyboard. "In the study."

Dottie crossed the living room and eased open the study door, which was ajar. Lynette was perched behind her large rosewood desk, a pair of rimless glasses on her nose. The desktop, lit with an anglepoise lamp, was awash with envelopes and correspondence. The little wicker basket by the wall was brimming with balled wads of writing paper, a few of which had spilled over to the jade carpet. Rex dozed on his belly by Lynette's feet.

"You're working late," Dottie said from the doorway.

Lynette glanced at her, a letter opener in her hand. "Oh, I'm not working – not writing – just sorting out some bits and pieces, catching up. I have a mountain of mail I haven't looked at. Keeps piling up every day. Drives me crazy. It's my own fault, though, for letting it accumulate." Lynette beckoned her forward. "Hey, don't just stand there, come on in."

"I don't want to disturb you."

"Get yourself in here and close the door. That din Mark's making is driving me crazy."

"I think he may need a hearing aid shortly," Dottie said.

"Tell me about it. I keep warning him, but it's like talking to a mannequin sometimes. He needn't come crying to me if he's deaf by the time he's twenty."

Dottie looked around, at the high ceiling and decorative plastic mouldings. The walls were dark-wood panelling. There were adjacent bookshelves, both of which were filled to capacity with hardbacks and paperbacks. On Lynette's desk, among the wealth of paper, was a copy of her second novel: *Winter Blossom*. The cover depicted two lovers holding hands in a snow-dusted setting, walking into the distance between denuded trees. Dottie wondered what it would be like to work from home, building a career without having to leave the house.

"Do you have enough space for your stuff up there?" Lynette asked. "I can hunt around and find you another set of drawers, if you need it."

"Everything's fine," Dottie said. "Plenty room."

"And the bed's all right?"

"It's all fine."

Lynette smiled, scrunched another letter, and pitched it at the bin. "Is there anything else on your mind, Dottie? Apart from the obvious, I mean. You seem a little down."

Dottie paced to the back of the study, where the sole window looked over the rear grounds and surrounding woodland. On the windowsill was a framed picture of Lynette and the family. Even Rex

135

was present in the snap, sitting proudly before them on his haunches. "I'm just a little bewildered by it all. It wasn't that long ago I had a husband and a baby. I knew what was going on in my life ..."

"Hey, come on, we talked about this. You still know what's going on. You're taking charge of things and refusing to be treated like a doormat, remember?"

Dottie shrugged half-heartedly.

"Dottie, don't feel bad because of what's happened. None of this was your fault, sweetheart. If you want my opinion, this has been brewing for a long time. I'm just glad you're seeing it for yourself." Lynette removed her glasses and steered her chair back on its castors. "People change direction all the time, Dottie. Attitudes change, and wants and need change. Friends outgrow each other because they end up as different kinds of adults. And inevitably, lots of marriages fail, but that doesn't mean *you've* failed."

"You're right, I know."

"Dottie, if things are finished with Billy, really finished, then isn't it better to be tackling this situation now? Isn't it better to get past it and leave it behind you?"

"I know I'm being silly," Dottie said resignedly. "I just don't want to impose on you."

With her fingernails, Lynette drummed a tattoo on the rosewood desk. "What am I going to do with you? Listen, this house is your home until *you* decide otherwise, Dottie. There's no time limit, there are no ... no conditions, and we all love having you. Is that clear enough?"

Dottie managed a meek nod. "Thanks, Lynette. And thanks for coming with me today to get my stuff. I don't think I could've gone into that house on my own."

Lynette spun in her chair, popped her reading glasses back on, and smiled encouragingly. "What are friends for?"

"Mummy?"

They looked around and found Tara standing by the door. Barefoot, in pink pyjamas, she was knuckling sleep from her eyes, holding a long-eared toy.

"Hey, what're you doing up, missy?" Lynette asked.

"Thirsty."

"Oh, well, let's see what we can find for you—"

"Let me," Dottie said, taking Tara's hand, and they went off to the kitchen together.

*****

The crisp night air had done nothing to clear Billy's head when he made it to King Edward Court. A rain shower had come and gone. Lights burned in the tenement flats, revealing threadbare curtains and dull interiors. In the lower apartments, blue-tinged reflections from TV sets played on the walls. Across the street, Billy ducked behind a parked lorry and undid his jeans, relieving himself over one of the vehicle's huge tyres. The damned booze was just running through him. A black Doberman passed and regarded him briefly, before loping off along the rain-slick road.

As he put himself away, Billy looked across the street and saw Angela Dunbar and someone else leaving the flats and starting down the walkway. Angela wore what looked like a sky-blue dress, although it was hard to tell exactly in the dull streetlight. Her hair hung loose, the way Billy liked it. She was laughing with a guy wearing a leather jacket and jeans. In the darkness, Billy couldn't really decipher the man, but could see he wasn't much taller than Angela. And he was built like a beanpole. A streak of piss.

Billy sidestepped back behind the lorry, watching in a crouch.

He got a better look when they stopped under a streetlight. Billy didn't recognise the dude – but then, why would he? Angela was a free agent and a fairly good-looking lassie. She did as she pleased, at least when Billy was not there. She was laughing again now, he saw, and looked happier than she ever had in his company. The guy leaned in and kissed her, and she kissed him back, her arm encircling his shoulder. They remained entwined for a time, smooching, embracing, and the guy's hand crept around and cupped her pert butt. Getting a good old grope, he was.

Billy felt something ignite inside him.

This shouldn't bother him.

But it did. Damn it, it *did*.

When they stopped kissing, Angela scuttled back up the walkway towards the flats. She waved at the guy, performing a funny little curtsey, then disappeared inside. The guy in the leather jacket set off on foot.

Out in the open, Billy crossed unsteadily to where the couple had stood. He looked at the flats, briefly contemplating going there to see her. But he decided against it and set off after the guy, increasing his pace to try to gain ground.

The beanpole was fifty yards ahead already, lurching off down a path with dense trees and undergrowth on either side. The pathway was poorly lit. Still increasing his pace, Billy removed a black beanie from his jacket and tugged it over his bald head. He turned up his collar and kept walking.

He was some thirty feet away from the guy now.

He happened upon a short fencepost lying in the ferns and grass. Its end was pointed and grimed with earth, its length machined into four equal sides, like a stake for killing vampires, Billy thought. He clutched it by the sharpened point without breaking stride, moving faster now, the makeshift weapon held behind his leg, just in case the beanpole guy looked around.

Twenty feet.

The rain came on again down through the overhead trees. The guy had his hands in his jacket pockets and was sauntering along, moving with less urgency than Billy. Probably thinking about how fine Angela's arse felt, Billy thought. Drawing closer, he half expected the guy to look back at any moment, so he kept the fencepost hidden as best he could. He maintained his pace, narrowing the distance without walking so briskly that it would draw the punk's attention.

Ten feet.

Billy's boots were squelching over sodden leaves, making more than enough noise to give him away. The guy finally angled his head slightly – aware that someone was closing in behind him. In a flash, Billy hoisted the fencepost and rushed to close the last few feet, bringing the wood down against the guy's skull. The strike connected cleanly, and the beanpole collapsed like a sawn timber.

Billy hunched over the fallen man. Curled up, the guy moaned incoherently, spots of rain rippling a puddle by his side. Billy saw blood on his neck, seeping from the headwound. The dude's eyes fluttered open and shut, as if he were semi-conscious. Billy considered hitting him again, maybe stamping on him a couple of times, but accepted it wasn't necessary.

He snatched the guy's wallet from his jeans and went through it. There were about fifty quid inside. Billy withdrew the notes and stashed them in his pocket. He rolled the guy onto his back and spotted a gold chain around his neck: Billy yanked it loose, breaking the clasp, and stuffed it in his jacket with the money.

He rummaged hastily through the wallet's compartments, ensuring he hadn't missed anything valuable. A card for the swimming club. Snooker membership. It was all dross. He tossed the wallet and launched the muddy fencepost into the darkness, where it clunked against a tree and dropped to the foliage.

The guy began moaning again, still semiconscious, trying to lift his head from the ground. Billy kicked out at his face for good measure, then started for home.

CHAPTER 21

On the first of October, Friday, Nick Cassidy returned home from a gruelling shift at the hospital, poured a glass of pomegranate juice, and peered through his living room window. The affluent scheme of pebbledash bungalows in which he lived was located in Aradale's southeast quadrant, a couple of streets behind one of the town's two secondary schools. Autumn had begun yellowing the leaves on the trees in his front garden. The day had been dry, thus far, although thunderheads marred the evening sky, threatening a downpour.

Nick tasted his drink, wincing slightly at its sweetness.

Dottie had not been to the hospital this week, nor had she called to say she would not make her appointment. This could be a positive thing, of course – indicative of her having come to terms with losing the baby, a sign she was ready to get on with her life again. It was possible, sure – but somehow, it didn't fit. Dottie had sounded particularly dejected during their last talk, and Nick found it curious that she hadn't at least called to say she could not come to see him.

He had concluded that he benefitted from their time together, just as much as she did. The more they talked and shared, the more he felt the promise of a perfect fit, a dovetailing of personalities.

Snowball, his cat, weaved lithely through his legs, stretching itself.

"What's doing, puss?" he said, squatting and bringing a hand over the animal's warm flank. Snowball's spine arched at his touch, and the cat yowled.

Nick sipped more juice. Across the street, old Mrs Brimstone was assiduously tending her lawn's borders. Her platinum hair was tied back in a bun, like Mother's wig in *Psycho*. Attired in wellingtons, she stood unsteadily from a kneeling cushion and began removing muck from the tines of her weeding fork.

Should he lift the phone and call Dottie?

That was the simple solution. He had her home and mobile number, both of which were listed in her file. There was nothing untoward about him ensuring she was okay, enquiring after her wellbeing.

That all it is, Nick?

Dottie had missed but one appointment, and this single absence had brought his feelings into focus. Lately, his emotional attachment to her had grown, little by little, and now he thought about her constantly: when he was trying to sleep; when he listened to Tchaikovsky's *Swan lake* or *The Sleeping Beauty;* when he dined alone in a house too commodious for a single occupant.

She's married, Nick. Out of bounds for you, my friend.

This was true, of course, and habitually he wouldn't dream of pursuing a married woman. But the husband didn't respect her – probably respected nothing – and Nick doubted the relationship would endure. Judging by the way Dottie spoke of her spouse, and by the man's uninterested demeanour during her hospital visits, Nick was amazed she had ever coupled with him. The man oozed arrogance like a ripe fruit oozed juice. It was a shame to see her shackled to such a type.

Moreover, something unsettling lurked in Billy Hawthorn's eyes. More than once, Nick had caught sight of the man's wanton glare, a look that instilled wariness in its recipient. Nick didn't point fingers at people (in this day and age, what was the point?), but he'd heard stories and rumours about the man. Some of them he knew to be true; others, well, he was less sure of. Certainly, Hawthorn had a capacity – maybe a proclivity – for throwing his weight around. Would his violence ever filter down to Dottie? Nick didn't know. Perhaps more love and empathy existed between Dottie and Billy than seemed evident. Perhaps he, Nick, was exaggerating their marital inadequacies because it best suited his own interests.

Because you'd like her for yourself, Nick?

He felt that moralistic twinge again, but also a growing immunity to it, as if his subconscious were trying to reassure him that his intentions were pure, regardless of the tangled circumstances. He wanted only what was best for Dottie. She deserved to be happy.

And what about Billy? What did he deserve?

Nick smiled as he pictured Dottie's face. She differed from most females he'd met, in that she had no airs and graces. Not like his former girlfriend, whom Nick had once intended to marry – difficult as that was to believe now. They had been following separate paths, pursuing mutually exclusive goals. He wanted companionship, yes, but the search for *the* right person sometimes felt like a search for the Holy Grail.

Women were indeed a mystery: this was as perfect a truth as any. One could spend one's whole life studying them, appreciating them, learning about them, and in the end, be no farther ahead. This, he supposed, was a considerable part of their allure. Each woman came with her own rules by which she gauged a potential suitor. On a date, for instance, a man auditions himself almost as he would on a job interview. The pretence is that two people are there to enjoy each other's company, but really the woman grades the man, combing for glitches, working from a checklist he hasn't even seen. Maybe he doesn't know it exists.

During the time spent gazing through candlelight, the woman will stealthily scrutinise the man's dress sense and conversation skills. She'll expect him to enquire about her, but not so doggedly it becomes an interrogation. She will judge his grooming, vigilant for protruding nose and ear hairs. She'll expect him to lead the date, certainly to pay (a given), to open doors for her, to allow her entry first, but to precede her through a crowd. All this before she sees where the poor sod lives – which introduces a whole new checklist.

Nick's smile remained. It should be enough to discourage any rational male. But Dottie didn't make him feel like that. He got the impression she was happy with a man being himself, comfortable in his own skin, and such an easy-going manner was mightily attractive in any girl.

"To hell with it," Nick finally said.

He finished his drink and went to find Dottie's number.

*****

Mumbling under his breath, Billy marched down the hallway runner and tugged open the front door. Through stewed eyes, he focussed on the ruddy man standing before him on the step. The guy

144

was a short-arse, with a ginger beard and pinstripe suit, clutching a scarlet folder under his arm.

"Good evening, sir," the man said, flashing a winsome smile. "I represent Elite Windows. If you have some time, I'd love to show you our newest ranges—"

"I got windows," Billy said and floated the door shut in the man's face.

In the living room, Billy pressed one nostril and snorted the haphazard line of cocaine from the coffee table. He lapsed against the sofa and closed his eyes, his heart thumping as the drug coursed through his system. A sour acidity burned at the back of his throat. His mind was so blocked with the stuff he couldn't think straight. He was supercharged, but also strangely drained – as if the drug's effects were battling his tiredness. His appetite had practically disappeared, and he hadn't slept properly in days.

He looked around at the mess. Barely a clean plate, glass, or pan in the house, but he'd be damned if he would tackle the disarray. Dottie would be back. Once she realised she had nowhere else to go, long term, she'd come scuttling home, asking forgiveness. She would take charge of the cleaning and cooking and suchlike. No point in him getting involved with it now.

He pressed his fingertip into the last of the cocaine and rubbed it vigorously into his teeth and gums. He plucked another Miller from the fridge and drained half its contents in one. Along with the mess, the house had begun to smell, too. Faint odours had taken up the space around him. When Dottie cleaned, a pleasant smell lingered throughout. Now, only staleness filled the rooms.

He understood her being hurt. Looking back, perhaps he had been a bit heavy-handed with her. Still, women liked that sort of thing, from time to time at least. You could be all roses and wine with them, but they tired of that too. The truth was they expected a man to be everything. Romantic. Rough. Sensitive. Manly. Caring. Supportive. Absent, when it suited them.

Bloody chameleon, that's what they wanted.

He should not have left the empty rubber packet in his jeans. That was dumb, and he had mentally kicked himself more than once since it happened. But, she couldn't *prove* he'd been cheating, and he would never admit to it. Billy sniffed and wiped at his running nose. He saw there was blood smeared on the side of his hand. Sniffed again. He tore a piece of kitchen towel from the roll and wedged it in his nostril.

He would allow Dottie time to come to her senses. Then, if she still hadn't dragged her little arse home, he would take action. Rectify the situation. She was staying out at Netherwood House, with Hobin and her husband. That bitch Lynette had a brass neck, talking down to him like he was a kid. Maybe one day, he would teach her a little respect, too. Teach her to watch what she said. He'd enjoy that.

Netherwood House. Billy had been to the property with Dottie once before, when she'd insisted he make the effort. But he hadn't been comfortable there, among the Hobins.

He drained his Miller.

He would march out there and drag Dottie home by the hair, if he had to. No use her staying away, because she would never be with another man. Not while he had breath in his lungs and blood in his heart. No other man.

146

The phone suddenly came to life beside him. Billy snatched up the receiver. "Hawthorn residence," he said, chuckling inside to himself, looking at the strewn tins and unwashed plates.

"Uh, is that Billy? Billy Hawthorn?"

"The one and only." He plucked the paper towel from his nose. The end of it shone bright red with blood.

"It's Dr Cassidy, from the hospital. I was wondering if Dottie's around. Would it be convenient to have a quick word with her?"

"She ain't here."

"Uh-huh. Should I call back later?"

Billy crumpled his empty beer and let it fall to the floor. "What's this about? Why are you calling my wife?"

"I'm concerned for her, Billy."

"I already warned her not to see you anymore. She's lost the baby, so she doesn't need you playing with her head."

"I wouldn't be doing my job if I—"

"She doesn't need you messing with her. Now I've told you once, don't be calling here no more."

"I'm afraid I can't agree to that. You should understand that she's been through a traumatic time. She needs support. Look, I know there's been a certain amount of strain on you, too, Billy. Losing a baby is a terrible ordeal for both parents, not just the mother. Dottie said you feel there's a degree of blame for what happened. I can assure you that isn't the case."

"She's got no right airing our business to you."

"You shouldn't look at it like that, Billy. It's not realistic to expect her to cope with what happened without asking for help. And there's

147

help there, for *you* as well. If you need someone to talk to, you could drop by the hospital, and I'd be more than happy to—"

"I'm sure you would. Be more than happy to play the Good Samaritan, hey?" Cassidy was still talking when Billy dropped the phone back in its mount. "Do-gooder pain in the arse."

He had never liked that guy. There was something about him. He was too friendly with Dottie. Doled out too much advice. He was too hands-on with *his* woman. Billy hadn't even liked him touching Dottie. Well, she wasn't pregnant anymore. The baby was dead, and if good old Dr Cassidy knew what was healthy for him, he'd keep his kind intentions to himself.

Billy shot to his feet, yanking up the phone and hurling it against the wall. The phone cracked, and a chunk of its plastic went flying across the room. He stood there, hunched over, heart pumping, drawing in heavy drags of air. He felt as if he was starting to lose it.

CHAPTER 22

"Aw, isn't that the prettiest?" Dottie said, accepting the drawing from Tara. "This is me, is it, sweetheart?"

Tara nodded proudly, smiling. "And Rex as well," she said, pointing a little finger at the paper.

Dottie studied the crayon drawing, which had occupied Tara for the last half-hour. It showed a round-headed, bright pink figure in a dress, with a broad grin – her, apparently – and a miniature brown blob with white paws and pointy ears, also grinning. The two subjects were liked by a slash of red ink, which Dottie supposed was Rex's lead. "That's so *good*, Tara," she said and touched the soft, plump skin of the girl's cheek. "May I keep this?"

Tara nodded again. The little girl had her mother's raven-dark hair, and Dottie could already see facial similarities that would sharpen with time. Obscenely cute in a cerise, pleated dress, and hair-ribbon, Tara chewed at her bottom lip. Dottie felt broodiness shroud her as Lynette's daughter wandered off to the kitchen.

"A budding Picasso?" Lynette said from the couch. She was revising pages from her manuscript, slashing and scoring with a Biro. She peered over her reading glasses. "The kitchen drawer's stuffed with her doodles. I haven't the heart to throw them away."

"She's such a darling," Dottie said.

"You haven't witnessed her tantrums yet. Some nights, getting her to bed is like trying to keep a beachball underwater."

They were quiet for a moment. The wind sprayed rain against the windows. Lynette chopped and rearranged words in the light cast from

149

a nearby lamp. "It's her birthday tomorrow," she said, after a while. "I can believe she's five years old already."

"Five, already?"

"Crazy, isn't it?" Lynette removed her glasses. "She'll be tottering around in heels before long. She's going to be a little madam, I just know it. Listen, I'm taking her to town tomorrow, to buy her something from the toy store. Why don't you come along?"

"She's picking something out herself?"

"I figured that's the safest way. Why don't you come with us?"

"Why not? Sounds like fun. I can just see her surrounded by all those toys."

"Hey, Mark," Lynette said, as her son trudged into the room. In jeans and a black T-shirt, he was tearing open a chocolate bar with his teeth. "How're the play rehearsals going at school?"

Mark shrugged. "It's not like I've got an important part."

"There are no small parts, my boy," Lynette said to him, holding up a long-nailed finger, "only small actors. Haven't you heard?"

"That's probably why Mrs Gilbertson picked me," he said, slumping into one of the armchairs. "Because I'm *small*."

"They're performing *Jack and the Beanstalk* at school next Wednesday night," Lynette told Dottie. "Should be a hoot. Graham and I are really looking forward to it."

"That sounds like fun, Mark," Dottie said.

Dottie thought Mark was a fine boy. He was in his final year of primary school, and Dottie often said hello to him there – when he was alone and wouldn't be embarrassed by the attention of a teacher. "What's your part?" she asked him.

150

Mark was skipping TV channels. News. Sport. "I'm playing one end of the cow," he muttered over a mouthful of chocolate.

"Fame beckons," his mother teased.

"Shut up, Mum."

"Hey, sourpuss. Someone's got to play the cow, it might as well be you."

"Ben Wilmot's the other half," Mark said, "and he stinks."

Dottie stifled a laugh. "The cow's an integral part of the story, Mark," she told him. "Without the cow, there are no magic beans, and without the beans, there's no story."

"Dottie's got the point," Lynette concurred. "It could be argued the cow's the *most* important part. Forget Jack and the Ogre."

Dottie giggled.

"As if I care," Mark said, sighing. "I've got no lines to learn, so it can't be that bad. At least I won't mess up."

"Every cloud has a silver lining," Lynette said, "if you'll pardon the cliché. But try to land the cow's front end, Mark. It could get whiffy down there." Lynette waved a hand across her nose, smiling at Dottie. "Especially if Ben's had beans for dinner – and I don't mean magic ones."

Tara came back into the room with a plastic cup of juice, and hopped onto the couch beside her mother. As she did, Graham appeared in the doorway, shrugging into a leather jacket and fixing his collar. He ruffled Mark's hair.

"How goes it there, Al Pacino?"

"Side-splitter, Dad."

"Even big Al must've started with minor roles."

151

Mark shook his head. Tara slipped down from the couch and ran towards her father, who hoisted her in a practised ritual, settling her in the crook of his arm.

"I won't be late," he said, "But if you're in bed when I get home, I'll be quiet as a mouse."

"Quiet mouse," Tara whispered, pressing a finger to her lips.

"More like a blind elephant," Lynette put in.

Dottie smiled, listening to their banter. Graham was such a nice guy, and his love for his family was obvious. Although he and Lynette goaded each other incessantly, it was all in jest. Graham was quite attractive, Dottie reflected, although not so handsome he would draw stares in the street. He stood maybe six-one from head to heel, and had thick, sandy hair. He was never through messing around, and she found it refreshing.

"Poker night tonight, Graham?" asked Dottie.

"A few hands and a few ales. I don't even like cards, but Lynette keeps forcing me out of the house. What can I do?"

Lynette, engrossed again in her manuscript, waved him away as if batting an irksome fly. "Why not try actually *winning* money for a change? You might get a taste for it."

"I couldn't do that," Graham said, with a frown. "The guys wouldn't ask me back if I started winning." He winked at Dottie, then lowered his daughter to the ground. "Hey Dottie," he said, "A dog walks into a Western saloon and says, I'm looking for the man who shot my paw."

Dottie rolled her eyes.

Lynette hurled a cushion at him.

When Graham left, Dottie sat listening to the rain, still feeling a little like part of the furniture. "Fancy tea?" she asked Lynette.

"Oh, I could murder some. And we'll crack open a bottle later on, once these two are in bed. If Graham can go out playing poker, we'll have our own fun."

In the kitchen, Dottie filled the kettle and prepared two cups. Despite how much she liked staying in Netherwood House, it also underlined her own life's shortcomings. The atmosphere here was a million miles from her dull existence with Billy. She could not go back to him. There was no percentage in turning her life backwards – not after making such a courageous change. But just what was she going to do? She could not stay with Lynette indefinitely. Right now, her future looked as bright as the inside of a coffin.

She had not told Lynette about the rape. She wanted to unburden herself – at least part of her did – yet she could not bear her friend to see her as even more of a victim. It—

Dottie's mobile brayed in her pocket. She took it out, but didn't recognise the number.

"Hello?"

"Hi, Dottie. It's Nick. Nick Cassidy."

"Nick?" She stepped away from the doorway, for more privacy. "How, uh ... how are you?"

"I'm okay. I didn't see you at the hospital this week, so I thought I'd ring and check you were all right. I tried you at home, but your other half, wasn't much help. He hung up on me." After a short pause, he said, "I was worried about you."

153

Dottie felt something tug at her heart. Then she thought about being raped over the dining room table. "I've left him. I'm staying with my friend Lynette and her family."

"Left him? Oh, Dottie, I had no idea."

"It wasn't working. I've tried really hard, but he's ... he's impossible to live with."

"Can I see you, Dottie? Can we meet sometime, just to talk?"

"I'll be okay, Nick. I appreciate all your help—"

"I don't mean as a patient. I want to see *you*, Dottie. If you've left Billy, I don't want to waste an opportunity. Something happens to me when I'm with you. If you feel the same, or if you feel anything, well, we should try it out, don't you think? You can get another doctor, and there's plenty of us around."

"I'm married, Nick. It wouldn't be right."

"Why don't we have dinner on Sunday night?"

"Oh, I don't know. I don't think ..."

"Don't feel pressured. You've been through a hell of a lot, and I just want to spend some time with you." He was silent for a few seconds. "I'd never hurt you, Dottie, you know that. You owe yourself ... you owe yourself a life, don't you? Let's give it a whirl and see what happens. What do you say?"

Dottie closed her eyes. He was putting himself on the line here, and she could not pretend it didn't ignite something in her: it felt like a Catherine Wheel spinning in her chest. She yearned to feel his embrace. She missed the playfulness of a male partner, those simple comforts she had been so long without. God, it felt like an eternity.

"Dottie?"

154

"Okay, I'll come."

"Fantastic. Now, where do I pick you up? It's Lynette Hobin's place, right? The writer?"

"Netherwood House. It's about a mile north of town."

"I know it. Big sandstone place in the woods. How does eight o'clock sound?"

"Terrifying."

Nick laughed, and she heard relief in the sound. "See you on Sunday," he confirmed.

When Dottie tucked the phone back into her jeans, the Catherine Wheel was still whirring away inside her. She looked at Rex, who was sitting in his basket in the corner of the kitchen. The stubby-legged corgi chuffed and scratched at himself, collar tinkling.

"What the hell am I doing, Rex?" she said.

CHAPTER 23

"Nick Cassidy asked you on a date? Whoa, why didn't you tell me?"

"I *am* telling you," Dottie replied, cupping her chin in her hands. "I'm beginning to think it was a mistake to agree to it."

"Are you loopy? Most women would donate an arm for a date with him."

"Well, I don't want to lose any limbs, that's for sure."

"You have to go," Lynette insisted. She was nursing a large glass of rosé on the couch. Rex was snoozing beside her, his muzzle buried in his forepaws. Every so often, the dog's ear twitched like a blown flame. "This is just the opportunity you need to start again. Leave the past behind you, go and have fun. If it was me, I wouldn't need prodding, let me tell you."

Dottie picked at a fingernail. "People will think it's too soon. You know, after the baby and everything?"

"Who's to say what's too soon? Nobody's opinion matters except your own, Dottie. Live life in accordance with what makes you happy, that's what my mother always said. But I'm dying to know – when *did* all this start with Nick Cassidy?"

"All what? I haven't done anything."

"There must have been something. An incident of some kind? Come on, Miss Secretive – spill. I'm not prying, you understand, just curious."

Dottie felt her cheeks light up like a Halloween pumpkin. "It was nothing, really. We had a nice talk, one day. Nick said we should go outside and enjoy the weather, so we walked through the park. I don't know, we just ... get on, I suppose. He's considerate. Not like Billy. Nick cares more for me than my husband, and I hardly know the man."

"So, what *else* happened?"

Dottie pictured herself and Nick sharing the bench, and a smile, unbidden, blossomed across her face. "He held my hand. I know it sounds a bit weird, but he was just trying to make me feel better, I think."

"Nothing weird about it." Lynette petted Rex, and the dog's ear twitched. "He likes you, and I can tell you like him. You go with him on Sunday and see what comes of it. It could be the romance of your life."

Dottie's smile vanished. "What if Billy finds out?"

"He's going to, eventually, Dottie. You can spend your life looking over your shoulder. Besides, it's time Billy understood just what he's missing. You deserve better than him, you always have."

Dottie's memory kicked in, and suddenly she was pinned to that table again, Billy's fingers gouging her neck, scratching her back, his fluids jetting out inside her. "Maybe you're right ..." she said.

"Can I ask you something?"

"Okay."

"Did something bad happen, the night you left him?"

Dottie looked away. "I told you, we had a fight."

"I remember. Is that all it was?"

Dottie felt the onset of tears, but resolved to stay in control. "I'd sooner not talk about it, Lyne. It was just a bad fight, really."

"You know I'm here, if you ever want to talk."

Dottie nodded. "I think I'll go to bed," she said and finished her glass of wine. She stood, and Rex lifted his head, sensing a change in the room.

"Get a good kip," said Lynette. "You'll need it for Madam Tara's shopping trip tomorrow."

*****

Alone with Rex, Lynette poured another glass of Blossom Hill and continued grooming the corgi with her long, painted nails. She knew Dottie was hiding details about that night. Her pint-sized friend wasn't herself – she hadn't been since the evening she had called for help. Lynette remembered how badly shaken Dottie had been, as if something awful had come to pass. Dottie was withdrawing, becoming reserved, though she endeavoured to conceal this. Nick Cassidy asking her on a date was perfect and could not have been better timed. Clearly, she had ingratiated herself with him, which was understandable. Dottie befriended people effortlessly. Maybe that dumpling Billy would have the sense to leave her alone now.

But Lynette could not envisage Billy leaving Dottie alone. The man was no more mature than a defiant child and would never let his wife leave quietly. No woman could stay chained to a man like that, least of all someone as sweet as Dottie.

Outside, the rain was coming down. A gale blew around the house, moaning in the eaves, whining in the trees. Lynette checked the brass clock on the mantle and contemplated going to bed. She decided against it, though. Despite revising pages from her manuscript all evening, she wasn't tired. She would sit and wait for Graham to get home. Perhaps he *had* won the poker game for a change.

158

*****

In her bedroom, on the east side of Netherwood House, Dottie undressed, removing her jeans and black halter. Carefully, she laid the garments over a high-backed velvet chair in the corner. The night was wet and blustery, but she didn't close the curtains. She didn't mind the darkness out here, away from the town. It didn't bother her. Her peach-coloured room was warm and comfortable and spacious, with a springy king-size bed she could almost get lost in.

Barefoot, she walked to the mirrored wardrobe in her black bra and panties and tugged a brush through her long auburn hair, working at the tangles. She thought about Nick and was barraged by a multitude of questions. Where would he take her on Sunday? What would they discuss? What would she wear? Would they hit it off on a date, or might it be awkward, the way friendships can get after a romantic element is involved?

Could be the romance of your life, she heard Lynette saying.

Dottie finished brushing her hair, crossed to the window, and stared out at the darkness. Then she did tug the curtains to, shutting away the night.

*****

High in an elm tree, cloaked by the darkness, his body wedged in a rough V-shaped split in the trunk, Billy peered through his Bushnell Infinity 8.5 x 5 waterproof binoculars. His rain-sodden clothes clung to his body like a second skin. A dip in a swimming pool wouldn't have made him any wetter. His toes squelched inside his boots. Droplets streamed from his ears and nose and ran down the contours of his back. The cold nipped his fingertips with the ferocity of a hungry animal. Climbing up into position here had been a laboured task, the tree bark slippery as fish scales, but he'd cracked it on the third attempt. He spat out phlegm, sniffed, and continued his reconnaissance of Netherwood House.

There were no lights on upstairs. One burned below, in the living room. The kids would likely be in bed, he thought. If he remembered rightly, Tara's bedroom was at the back of the house, next to her parent's room. Mark's was on the west side.

He directed the binoculars to the rooms at the opposite end of the property, one of which, he imagined, Dottie would be using. The curtains were open in those rooms, but their interiors were dark and he could see nothing.

A high wind stole through the trees in eerie song, fluttering the ivy clinging to the house's stone. Had he been straight-headed, this weather would have broken him ages ago. Thankfully, he was *wired* – had been for days. He was so choked on coke that he couldn't think clearly. The van was hidden in bushes nearby, and the drive home wouldn't take him long, but fuck, he was wedged in a tree in the shittiest of weather, and it wasn't much fun.

He lowered the binoculars and let them dangle from his neck. The town's lights glimmered in the distance. Dark steeples and spires rose against a moonless sky. He was a considerable distance from Netherwood House, maybe a hundred feet, so he didn't worry about anyone there seeing what he was up to. Not at night, and not in weather like this.

He didn't know if that dweeb Graham was home. The man worked nights, in security, but Billy could not recall where. His big Volvo was

160

parked next to Lynette's flashy metallic blue BMW. Rich fuckers. They—

A light snapped on upstairs.

Billy raised the lenses.

Dottie moved around soundlessly in the binoculars. She appeared clearer than he'd expected she might, as if he were right there in the room with her. She sat on the bed and began removing her clothes. The halter neck. Jeans. One leg, then the other. Socks. One. Two. Her lacy black underwear pressed into her flesh slightly.

Billy felt himself harden.

She walked to a full-length mirror and stood with her back to him, her dreamy gaze reflected in the glass. He studied the swell of her breasts and the little mole by her left kidney. Dottie reached for a hairbrush and tilted her head, just as he had seen her do a thousand times before. She started brushing with smooth, slow strokes.

He recalled the first time he had watched her do that. So long ago now, when they'd held hands and laughed and teased each other. Rolling for hours in the blankets of their bed. He used to fork his fingers through that hair. So soft it was. So fine.

Dottie spun around and suddenly headed for the window, walking towards the binoculars. She looked out from the house, as if aware of Billy's presence in the trees. He studied her body, mildly surprised by his own arousal, although the arousal had less to do with her near-naked form – which he'd seen countless times – than the voyeuristic stealth with which he watched her.

His tongue clamped between his teeth, Billy frowned. Through the lenses, as Dottie stood there before him, within touching distance, it

161

seemed, he homed in on one particular detail. Then she whipped the curtains together and was gone.

Billy shook his head. "Bitch," he said.

Dottie had removed her wedding ring.

CHAPTER 24

"Wow, it's absolutely heaving," Dottie said as they descended into the Alexandra Shopping Centre. "Chock-a-block."

"Always the same on Saturday afternoons," Lynette said, helping Tara safely off the mechanical stairs. "Careful, you," she told the little girl.

Tara looked up at her mother. "Careful me."

Dottie observed the throngs of shoppers. People milled everywhere. Fathers hoisted children on their shoulders; women and girls gazed through glass shopfronts; mannequins in fixed poses filled showcase windows, attired in scarves and current winter trends; teenagers in tracksuits and hoodies and football shirts skulked around in packs.

"We'd better tie a rope to our waists," Lynette joked, as they joined the wave of bodies. "We might get split up and never see each other again."

They passed a stall serving fruit smoothies and another selling iridescent crystals. Sunlight cascaded through the centre's glass ceiling, flashing off the stores' large windows with a fierce glare. In eateries and cafeterias, waitresses wended busily around tables. When Tara spotted an ice cream stand across the way, she started over there at pace, Dottie and Lynette trailing behind her with shared smiles.

"You get the feeling she wants a cone?" Lynette said. "God, look at the length of the queue."

"Ah, it's not so bad," Dottie replied.

When they eventually made it to the front of the line, Tara peered raptly through the glass counter at the containers of flavours, as if witnessing strange matter from another universe.

"And what would *you* like?" the white-gowned woman behind the counter asked her. "We have mint, strawberry, chocolate, chocolate *chip,* vanilla, raspberry—"

"Mint!" Tara called.

"Dottie, you fancy an ice cream?" Lynette asked.

Dottie smiled. "I could manage some mint."

Once served, they set off into the centre, licking at their cones. Before long, they arrived outside MacKay's Toy Store, and Tara began bouncing excitedly at the prospect.

"Now, Tara," Lynette said, hunkering down to the child's eye line, "be sure to have a proper look around before choosing something."

Tara stamped her little black shoes in anticipation, skipped over the threshold, and halted before a world of playthings.

"She's forever changing her mind," Lynette told Dottie. "It makes me wonder what she'll be like when it's time to find a man."

"That's when it pays to be picky," Dottie replied, as they stepped inside.

The store's interior was huge, wall-to-wall with more toys than Dottie had ever seen before. From the entrance, they were faced with remote-control cars and dolls and cuddly stuffed animals and board games and action figures...

Tara bolted for the array of dolls to their left. There were hundreds of them, blonde, dark, large, small, all in variously coloured frilly dresses, staring lifelessly from clear plastic boxes.

"Parents are really brave taking kids in here," Dottie commented. "I'm surprised they can ever get their children out again."

"She'll either find what she wants straight off, or we'll be stuck in here till doomsday. Tara, wait for us," her mother called after the girl, but Tara took no heed.

"Hey, look at that, over there," Dottie said, nudging Lynette.

By the escalator, someone was guised in a velvety green dragon costume, a long tail trailing behind it. The big cartoon beast pranced theatrically with raised arms, fake claws protruding from spongy hands and feet. The costume's mask had soft, shark-like teeth and yellow eyes, but looked friendly nonetheless. A raucous pack of kids was jumping and calling and screaming around it, pulling at its tail.

A young boy barrelled past, toting a plastic machine gun, its high-pitched sound effect drawing a wince from Lynette.

"So, you had any more thoughts about your date tomorrow?" she asked Dottie.

Dottie smiled and shrugged. "Not really. I told Nick I'd go, although I'm still unsure whether it's a good idea. I haven't been on a date in ages."

"That's because Billy never took you anywhere."

The dragon lumbered towards Lynette as she and Dottie passed, raising its cartoon claws and growling comically. The two women walked on and found Tara in a wide aisle, surrounded by brightly coloured gaming equipment: spongy balls, rackets, rubber balls, bats, skittles, and basketballs.

"See anything you like, sweetheart?" Dottie asked, stroking Tara's hair.

165

The girl gazed up at them thoughtfully. "Can we go upstairs?"

Tara charged ahead again, racing towards the escalator, taking care of the deep metal steps. Lynette stepped on next. "It's starting to look like doomsday," she whispered, rolling her eyes and smiling at Dottie. "Hey, where's your wedding ring?" she asked.

"No point in wearing it now." Dottie looked at her unadorned fingers. "The ring represents marriage, and the marriage is over. If I'm going to start again, I'm going to do it wholeheartedly."

"Amen to that."

On the upper floor, they found yet more aisles brimming with toys, children, and weary-looking parents. "God, where's she got to?" Lynette said, scanning around. "Honestly, she can disappear in seconds ..."

As they walked on, Dottie's attention was captured by an energetic little girl working a hula-hoop with her waist. Dottie smiled at her, wondering if her own daughter would have enjoyed hula-hoops, had she lived. She tried not to harbour such thoughts, tried not to let them gain ground, but sometimes they just filtered through when she least expected them.

"Any idea where Brad Pitt's taking you tomorrow, then?" Lynette asked.

"Oh, I don't know. He didn't say."

"I bet it'll be somewhere swanky. Tiny portions and huge bills."

"You're not helping, Lynette. I'm already a bag of nerves, without you cranking up the pressure."

"Well, my advice, for what it's worth, is to just relax and enjoy it. Remember, he'll be out to impress, so just let him. The woman's always in charge of the date."

They followed Tara around more aisles. When they caught up with her, Lynette asked if she had seen anything she liked, but Tara still looked overwhelmed and undecided. "Can we go and see the dolls again?" she asked.

Lynette sighed. "Downstairs?"

The escalator was choked with shoppers when they approached, and Tara had soon wriggled through them and slipped beyond sight. From up here, Dottie surveyed the colossal store as they slowly descended, getting a bird's-eye view in every direction.

"I never realised this place was so *big*," she said.

They reached the doll aisle once more, where an elderly woman was talking to two small twin girls. Of Tara, however, there was no sign.

"Do you believe this?" Lynette asked, exasperated. "Where's she gone now?"

Dottie peered around, over at the marauding dragon, along distant aisles. "I don't see her."

Lynette thumbed the handbag strap on her shoulder. "I'll check this side," she said, motioning her head. "If you find her, meet me back here, okay?"

Lynette stomped off past the dragon, into the crowds. Dottie waited by the dolls, sure that Tara would return here, the last place the girl had mentioned. But the minutes dragged by, and Tara did not appear.

Dottie stepped outside the store, checking this way and that, up and down. Soothing Muzak floated throughout the centre, annoyingly sedate. If Tara had come out here, Dottie suspected she would never see the child. There were too many people, bustling everywhere, and a small girl would be easily missed. But why would Tara have left the store? Dottie went back inside. Shortly, Lynette reappeared in the doll aisle, her cheeks flushed.

"Any sign?"

Dottie said no.

"Jeez, where the hell *is* she? What if something's happened to her?"

Dottie touched her arm. "It's only been a few minutes, she'll show up."

"What if someone's taken her?"

"Listen, I'll check upstairs again. Maybe she's gone back there, looking for us."

Lynette took a breath, blinking. "All right, okay. I'll keep looking down here."

Dottie rode the escalator and revisited the last place they had seen Tara. The girl with the hula-hoop was gone. A gathering of parents was staring at Dottie as if sensing something was wrong.

"Has anyone seen a dark-haired little girl up here?" she asked. "She's five years old, wearing jeans and trainers and a powder-blue jacket."

The only response she got was shaking heads, so Dottie rushed on. After a fruitless search of the aisles, she returned to the ground floor, where an agitated Lynette was standing by the dolls, a hand on her forehead.

"She definitely not upstairs," Dottie confirmed. "Maybe we should talk to the manager? He'll put a message over the Tannoy."

"Where do we find the manager?" Lynette asked quietly, worry inflecting her voice now. "God, she was right in front of us. I don't like this, Dottie."

"Lose something, ladies?"

They spun around in tandem.

Billy stood there, with Tara perched on his shoulders. The little girl giggled as Billy squatted to let her disembark.

Lynette grabbed her daughter's hand and brought her close. "Where on earth did you go off to, young lady?"

Tara's smile disappeared as she saw her mother's anguish. The girl's lip began to quiver. "I just—"

"We've been searching for you everywhere," Lynette snapped. "How many times have I warned you about wandering off?"

"But I was with Billy ..." Tara whined, on the verge of tears now.

"Don't blame the lassie," Billy said. "I was just passing when Tara here saw me and said hello. She showed me all these wonderful toys. She thought you two were right behind her." He placed a hand on his chest. "My fault entirely."

Dottie couldn't believe how awful Billy looked. The weight had fallen off him, and he had never been heavy, to begin with. His clothes were rumpled and stained. He was gaunt and pallid, his cheeks hollow caves in his face. His eyes were shadowed by dark crescents, occasioned, she imagined, by several nights without sleep.

169

"Tara, go and wait by the dolls," Lynette instructed the girl, her worry giving place to irritation. "I'll be one minute, sweetheart. Go on." Tara did as she was told, rubbing at her nose as she went. When the girl was beyond earshot, Lynette faced Billy, a finger raised in front of his eyes. "You stay the hell away from my daughter, understand?"

"You ought to be thankful, Lynette." A grin curled at the corners of his mouth. "The girl's unharmed. But I get why you're worried, of course, I do. You just never know who's wandering the streets these days, do you?" He sniffed and switched his attention to Dottie. "You ready to come home yet?"

"It's your home now, Billy," Dottie said to him. "Do what you want with it."

"You can rot in hell for all she cares," Lynette added and stalked off to her daughter.

Billy's grin dissolved. Dottie took a compensatory step back as he moved towards her.

"Listen to me, you little bitch," he whispered through clenched, yellowed teeth. "You'll never leave me. No matter what you do, you'll never leave. Just remember that, Dorothy."

He brushed past her, out of the store, leaving a smell of dry sweat in his wake.

Dottie turned and watched him go, until he was lost among the masses of Saturday shoppers.

CHAPTER 25

Later that day, back at Netherwood House, Dottie assisted with dinner, skinning potatoes and washing vegetables in the sink as Lynette prepared a pimply chicken. It was six-thirty and the sun was setting, the October night softly twilit. From the window, she saw Graham pottering in the little shed outside, where he went for a sneaky cigarette.

Billy's unexpected appearance still weighed on her; she hadn't thought about anything else since the unfortunate incident earlier. Though she and Lynette hadn't discussed what had happened, it hung between them, waiting for one of them to broach the subject. Tara was sitting on a stool beside Dottie, playing with her new doll, the little drama in the toy store already consigned to the past.

"Why don't you scoot next door and play with your doll, sweetheart," Lynette said to her daughter. "We'll call when dinner's ready."

"Her name's Lexi," Tara said, holding up the doll: Lexi was blonde and had a pink dress.

"Okay, take *Lexi* into the living room, huh?"

Tara hopped down from the stool and skipped off through the doorway.

"If you wash the veg anymore, it'll disintegrate," Lynette said, flipping the bagged chicken into the oven and shutting the door.

"What do you think he was doing there today?"

"Billy?"

"Do you think he followed us?"

171

Lynette frowned, as if this hadn't crossed her mind. "How could he have? We drove straight from here."

"It seems strange he was in that toy store, doesn't it?"

"He said he was passing outside, didn't he? He probably saw Tara and just seized the chance to wind us up. You know what he's like, Dottie."

Dottie did know. She knew Billy never spent his weekends in the shopping centre. He hated crowds, hated people getting in his way, hated bustle. It made more sense – to her, at least – that he'd been following them. But if that were the case, from where had he begun doing this? He obviously knew where she was staying ...

"I'm sorry about overreacting today, Dottie," Lynette said, earnestly. She settled herself on the stool Tara had vacated, her sequined top catching the light. "It just shook me up a bit. You hear so many stories these days, kids going missing and all that, you know?"

"You didn't overreact. Tara knows Billy, and I don't believe she was in any danger, but he still shouldn't have done it. It was irresponsible. He knew we were looking for her."

"This is Billy we're talking about. Irresponsibility is his forte, remember? Well, no harm done, Dottie, so don't let it upset you."

Vegetables done, Dottie drained the sink and dried her hands. "I was considering going back to work in a couple of weeks," she said. "I've got an appointment with the headmaster on Monday morning."

"You feel ready to work again?"

"It's time I got back to normal, whatever that's supposed to be. I'm going to start looking for somewhere to live, too."

172

Lynette affected hurt. "Are you fed up with the Hobin experience already?"

"I love it here, but I need my independence. And I can't stay with you forever. I was thinking about renting a place for a while."

"You know you're due half that house, Dottie. Why let Billy stay there while you have to rent somewhere? A divorce will give you what you're entitled to."

"I don't want to make any more trouble. He can have the house. I'm the one who left, who's moved out." Rex strutted into the kitchen on stubby white-pawed legs, his collar tinkling. Dottie bent to give him a scratch. "I just want to leave it at that," she said. The corgi sniffed at her hand. "No more ill feeling."

"Anyone ever tell you you're too easy-going?"

"It might be a while before I find somewhere, though. You won't be rid of me that quickly, I'm afraid."

"That room up there is yours as long as you need it, so don't feel obliged to rush into committing yourself to anything." Lynette got off the stool and walked to the fridge, opening the door. She grinned, removing a bottle of wine by the neck. "But I think we've more important things to discuss, don't you?"

Dottie gave her a puzzled look.

"Tomorrow night's hot date, of course."

*****

Stooped over the kitchen counter, Billy snorted the last line of cocaine. He threw his head back, staggering around a little. He was taking too much of the damned stuff now. Definitely, he couldn't seem to stop. Every time he tried to come off it, he felt like shit. Last

173

night, when he'd made it home, his clothes pasted to his body by the rain, he had tried to sleep and couldn't. He had just lain there, tossing, fidgeting, thinking about Dottie at the window without her wedding ring. The ring he had paid good money for.

So, sleep hadn't come, and eventually, he'd found himself wide awake in the pre-dawn silence, the birds twitting outside his window. He would have sworn there were bugs scurrying beneath his skin. The addiction was revealing its effects in the mirror too, not just in his mind. He barely recognised the wasted reflection that glared back at him lately.

He unfolded the wrap of cocaine, opened it out, and licked it clean, working his tongue into its creases and folds.

He had to have more stuff around the place somewhere. He'd bought so much of it recently that he must've surely overlooked a wrap. He searched his hiding places, the niches he used to conceal the drugs from Dottie: behind the wooden lip of the loft-hatch panel, under the flap of carpet in the corner of the bathroom. He found nothing, though. He had snorted it all.

Billy scratched at his bald scalp and began tugging out the drawers and emptying their contents onto the floor, searching through everything, hoping to come across a stray wrap. Just one, dammit. Since Dottie had taken off, he hadn't bothered hiding the drugs, he had just left them randomly lying around the place. He felt sure there had to be something left, for Christ's sake.

Ten minutes later, after emptying out the kitchen's bin bag, he sat among the mess, sifting through foul-smelling waste, trying to find old wraps that he hadn't licked clean. Maybe he had missed a bit

174

somewhere. But he found nothing. The used cocaine packets were soggy and filthy, covered in all sorts of crap, and one look was enough to know he was wasting his time. The stench from the mess was overpowering. He stood up, kicking his foot through empty milk cartons and the ready-meal trays he'd been existing on.

Ignoring the shit on the floor, he dug out his mobile and made a call.

"I need some more stuff," he said.

"Uh-huh. How much?"

"The usual. No, scratch that. Make it double."

"You sure?"

"Of course, I'm sure."

"I can manage that."

"Tonight?"

"Tomorrow. Best make it evening time."

"I need it tonight."

"That may be so, but you can't have it tonight. You want it tomorrow, or not?"

"I want it."

Billy hung up. He knew he should eat something, but food held about as much appeal as gouging out his eyeballs with a blunt pencil. Besides, he had more important things to do. Business to take care of. That's right. His wife was running around out there, trying to make a fool of him. Trying to leave him behind. Marching about without a ring on her finger.

He sniffed and wiped at his nose, which was weeping blood again. It was dark outside now, but thankfully it wasn't raining tonight. Billy snatched up the carrier bag of Millers he had bought earlier and snapped out the lights.

He left the house.

CHAPTER 26

Sunday night.

"Cheers," Nick Cassidy said, touching his wine goblet against Dottie's with a gentle clink.

He'd scrubbed up well, Dottie thought. Even better than she'd expected, in fact. In an open-collared, pressed white shirt, suede jacket, and blue jeans, he looked fresh and clean, exuding a faint scent of aftershave. Upon his arrival at Netherwood House, he had presented her with a dainty box of chocolates, decorated with a pretty lilac bow, and a bouquet of flowers that Lynette had promised to put in water.

Dottie sampled her wine. Nerves were still partying in her belly every minute that went by. Nick had taken her to the Wide Mouthed Frog, a classy restaurant off Prince Street. Its interior was lit by candlelight, glowing romantically against the dark wood panelling. A log fire roasted wooden blocks beneath a giant focal-point mirror. Patrons conversed quietly, intimately. Dottie had not been here before, but had always wanted to frequent the establishment and sample the cuisine. As Lynette had said, Billy hadn't taken her anywhere.

"Have you ever eaten here?" Dottie asked him.

"Once or twice, yeah. The menu's pretty fine. The Black Forest Gateau is something else." Nick made a circle with his thumb and index finger. "Trust me."

"I don't like cherries," she said.

"You can pick them off," he told her, smiling. "I'm glad you agreed to come, Dottie. I know this all probably feels as if it's going a bit fast."

Dottie sipped her wine.

"You see, I've learned over time that the guy who hesitates is usually the guy who comes last," Nick went on. "I'm just trying to let you know that I'm interested, Dottie. That way, I won't have to kick myself if someone else snaps you up. Listen, I won't ever pressure you into anything, I promise."

Dottie touched her neck. "It does seem a bit fast, but I'm still glad you asked me, really, I am."

"It's good to see colour in your cheeks again. You look really beautiful, by the way, in case I didn't mention it."

Dottie thanked him, and that old glow bubbled up inside her. She liked receiving compliments from him, especially concerning her looks. Such remarks gave her a much-needed spike in confidence. Tonight, she had dressed in black jeans, knee-length leather boots, and a flounced gypsy-like white top, revealing her shoulders. Her hair was loose and tumbled in auburn curls around her exposed skin. At Netherwood House, she had worked at length getting ready, applying make-up, doing her hair, nerves nibbling away at her all the while.

"Lynette seems like fun," Nick said. "I must say, it's the first time I've met a real author in the flesh. The two of you seem very close."

"She's my best friend. We were in school together, and we've never really lost touch." Dottie watched the meticulously suited maître d' greet a couple at the door. "She'd do anything to help me."

"It's good to have friends in your life." Nick glanced around and checked his gold-banded watch. "If you don't mind my saying, Dottie, your decision to leave Billy seemed, well, a bit out of the blue." He raised a hand. "If you'd rather not talk about it, just say so."

Yet again, Dottie's memory turned back to that terrible night, and a degree of her happiness ebbed away. She had no compunction discussing the separation from Billy. But she couldn't – *wouldn't* – mention the rape.

"I guess it did come out of the blue," she replied, after a time. "Still, in another way, I suppose I just opened my eyes to what I'd always known. Billy and I aren't compatible. I thought we were, for a while, but we're not. I don't know if *anyone* would be compatible with him, the way he is."

"Was it like that in the beginning? I mean, there must have been more between you, when you first married?"

"We were in love once, I think. He's changed so much. It's as if life has ... sucked the goodness out of him, you know? Billy's not the same man anymore. He's always at odds with the world and always sees the negatives in everything. And he drinks a lot, which I don't think helps. Sometimes, he drinks so much he just blacks out and can't remember things."

"Well, perhaps it's better this way, if you know there's no chance to save the marriage." He made a chopping motion. "Better to make a clean break."

"Hey, enough of the gloomy stuff," Dottie said, wrinkling her nose. "Tell me something about you."

"What would the lady care to know?"

179

"Anything. Do you have brothers and sisters?"

"One of each. Tracy's the youngest. She married a Frenchman a few years back and moved over there with him, a place called Rouen, in Northern France. She's the arty type and loves to paint. I haven't been across to visit her yet, but she emails often. She wakes to the picturesque Seine every morning."

"Sounds nice. And your brother?"

"Mike is the eldest. He's fighting in Afghanistan."

"Really?" Dottie gave a pout. "You must worry about him."

"There are soldiers being killed out there all the time, and I'm not even sure why our guys are involved." Nick weaved his fingers together. Candlelight fluttered against his cheek. "The powers that be, they reckon it's a worthy cause, but I'm not so convinced our presence there will amount to much in the long run. The Russians were there for years, and ultimately it didn't change anything."

"Do your parents live in town?"

He nodded. "My mother does. My dad died when I was quite young."

"That must have been hard for you."

"I was in my teens, so it was. But the human spirit is remarkably resilient, as you well know. You have to keep going, keep moving forward, regardless of what happens in life. My mother had a hard time raising us by herself, although she did a fine enough job, I think."

"Did you always want to become a doctor?" she asked.

Nick leaned back, considering. "I suppose I did, yeah. It felt natural to me. I've always liked helping people, so I guess it was a natural progression from there."

180

Dottie was quiet; then she said, "How come a nice-looking guy like you hasn't landed the girl of his dreams yet?"

"I'm working on it," he said and winked at her. "What about you, Dottie? Are there brothers or sisters?"

"Nope, just me. I think childbirth scared my mother – she didn't have much tolerance for pain, so she didn't want to do it again. I kind of understand now; it's not exactly a picnic."

"Well, I'd have to agree with you there. What about teaching young kids? That must be a handful, surely?"

"That's what a lot of people say, but I love it. The kids are great, mostly, so much fun. Some of them can be little tykes, of course – you'll encounter that in any classroom. I wouldn't want to do anything else, though. I feel that I fit in with them, and the kids like me too. At least, I think they do. I'm just fond of children. That's why I was so looking forward to being a mother ..."

"You're young, Dottie. There will be another time. Try to concentrate on what's going well in your life."

"That shouldn't take long."

"Hey, I'm serious. It's about keeping a healthy balance, you know? Sometimes your personal life may be having problems, so that's when you concentrate on your career and hobbies. Conversely, sometimes your work life might not be going so well, so you concentrate on things like friends and family. That way, you can reassure yourself, on any given day, that there's something worthwhile in life. It's just a case of balance. Very few people have everything going the way they want it, all the time."

"I suppose there's a lot of sense in that," she admitted. "My mother told me to remember that there's always someone worse off than me."

"It doesn't necessarily help, Dottie. Happiness is subjective, and shouldn't rely on how well or badly others around you are doing."

The waitress arrived then and set two plates of filet mignon before them. The food looked great, Dottie thought. The wine was great and so was the conversation. Her nerves were finally beginning to settle, as well. The evening was going okay. That was all that mattered. Anything else was a bonus, she assured herself.

*****

The door swung open seconds after Billy had rapped on the stained glass, almost as if the house's occupant had been waiting just beyond sight.

"C'mon, in," the suited man said, starting off down the hall.

Billy stepped inside and followed him into the sparsely furnished, modern living room. The place was something else. They say crime doesn't pay, but clearly, there were exceptions. The living area – which Billy had seen countless times now – never failed to impress him. It was decked in laminate flooring. A chandelier with crystal pendants hung from the ceiling. The walls and luxurious sofas were off-white, making Billy wonder how you might go about keeping such a pad clean. One big party and everything would be ruined. The stereo and TV were the best that ill-gotten gains could buy. A brief spark of jealousy went off inside him.

The dealer – who Billy didn't even know by name – was tall and well-groomed, dressed in a shiny grey suit that a tailor had surely

182

troubled over. Cufflinks. Fancy watch. Gold tiepin. Hair greased perfectly back, gleaming under the overhead lights. The man had the perfected, polished look that told of good fortune and was right now probably wearing more than Billy earned in three months.

One day that'll be me, he thought sourly. *One day I'll have all this too.*

The man walked past a huge aquarium, inside which swam iridescently coloured fish. He opened a unit drawer and tossed Billy a small wrap.

"Twice as much, as you asked for."

Billy emptied the notes from his wallet. "It's all there."

"No harm in counting it, in that case, is there?" the man said, his hairless hands skimming through the notes with the fluent expertise of a bank clerk. "Incidentally," he said, "this is all I can give you for a while."

Billy frowned. "Why?"

"That's my business. Just stay clear for a few weeks or so, okay? I'll let you know if and when things change. And if you don't mind an observation, I'd say you should lay off it for a bit. You really don't look so hot, friend."

"The dealer who cares?" Billy said. "Touching."

The man stopped fingering the money and flashed his perfect dentistry. "Of course, I care. If your heart explodes, I'll have to find someone else to sell this garbage to, won't I?"

Billy grinned, but he wanted to cut the bastard's throat.

*****

He drove through town in the Green Arrow van. The night was quiet, the roads clear. He pulled up at a set of traffic lights on Prince Street, a couple of cars from the front, and set the handbrake. A couple of young women sashayed down the path, one in bare legs, the other in patterned tights. They laughed, their Stiletto heels clicking and clacking like horse hooves as they passed his open window. He studied them as they moved, all prime legs and flowing hair.

Sniffing, he glanced through the window of the adjacent restaurant. It was full of loved-up couples ogling each other across candlelit tables…

Billy shot up straight, his eyes narrowing.

Jesus.

There she was. Sitting right there in that fancy-arse place, plain as day. He couldn't quite see her face, but he knew it was her. He recognised the contours of her shoulders, the texture of her hair, the way she often wore it on a night out. He even recognised the white off-she-shoulder number she was wearing. For a moment, such was his surprise, he didn't register her companion. His gaze was fixed firmly on her. But then he checked out the guy, and what do you know, he recognised him, too. Cassidy. By Christ, it was the damned doctor—

A horn brayed behind Billy. When he faced the front, the lights were green.

"Shit."

He revved off down the street and abandoned the van haphazardly in the nearest vacant parking bay. He got out and crossed the road, making his way back up Prince Street, resisting the impulse to break into a run. He stopped outside a hair salon with enlarged images of coiffed women in the window, and leant on the wall, half concealed behind a bus shelter.

Dottie was sipping wine and nodding. Her ring finger still showed no wedding band. She faced away from him, but Billy could see Cassidy, suave and slimy, clear as a bell. What did he think he was *doing*? He was her doctor. Was he banging Dottie? Banging *his* wife? Christ, that was why she had left him, wasn't it? That was why she had ditched her wedding ring. Ungrateful, lying little bitch. All the time rutting with the damned doctor. A stark image formed in his mind: Dottie writhing and rolling her hips as she screwed Cassidy, moaning…

In the restaurant, she reached out and touched Cassidy's hand, dispelling any possibility that there was an innocent explanation for this. Billy's whole body was beginning to shake, his teeth clamped together, his heart beating rapidly. *She* was touching *him*. Not much wonder Cassidy was sniffing around, if she was putting it on a plate for the man.

Billy drew a hand over the shaven dome of his head. Headlights swished past between him and the restaurant's broad window. He balled his hands into fists, grinding his teeth. The mere sight of them canoodling in candlelight made him want to steam in there and ... and *crush* that wineglass in Cassidy's smarmy face. And Dottie? Well, she was going to pay for this. They both were.

CHAPTER 27

"Fancy coming back for coffee?" Nick asked as he and Dottie left the restaurant. Spots of rain came down, dappling the flagstones. "And I *mean* just coffee," he added. "You'll have to keep your hands to yourself, hard as that may be."

Dottie giggled as they began along the street. The October night was cool, the sky starlit. "I'd love to see where you live, Nick," she said.

"It's nothing special, really."

"Oh, I'm sure it's lovely."

Nick unlocked his Audi with a zap from his key fob, setting the car's indicators flashing in the dark. He opened Dottie's door, letting her climb inside, and she tried to remember when a man had last done that for her. She smiled contentedly at him as he gently closed the door again.

The journey did not take long. They arrived in a street lined with reproduction Victorian street lamps. When Nick pulled into his driveway, she said, "Bungalow, huh? Very nice."

"It does for a lowly bachelor."

She followed him inside. At the rear of the house, the kitchen light flickered and revealed a spotless environment. Dottie blinked, looking around. The units and counters gleamed, meticulously clean and tidy. Utensils were racked, surfaces clear.

"Do you ever cook anything in here?" she asked. "It's like a show home, or something. That's a compliment, by the way."

"What can I say? I'm a clean freak." He filled the kettle and switched it on. "I admit it. Listen, why don't you take a seat in the next room? Feel free to look about, or put some music on."

Dottie moved leisurely through the bungalow, impressed by what she'd seen thus far. The living room was kitted out with classic furniture. Thick rugs and warm colours lent it a cosy, unquestionably masculine air. Lots of books in cases. The fact that Nick was educated and knowledgeable impressed her too. She approached a tall wooden CD rack and glanced at some of the cases. Mostly orchestral music, she saw. And soul, as well.

Dottie started as something shifted in the corner.

A cat, pure white, appeared from behind an armchair. Its tail raised as the animal slunk towards her, rubbing its collar against her leg, its back arched.

"Hello, puss," she said, drawing a hand over its downy side. "You gave me a fright, kitty."

"I see you've got acquainted with Snowball," Nick said, appearing in the doorway behind her.

"She's lovely. So white and *soft*. Hello, Snowball."

"She comes and goes as she pleases, but we get on well enough. She likes climbing trees and attacking your feet when you're not wearing socks." He handed her a cup, and they settled on the sofa together.

Dottie tasted her coffee, then set it down. Quick as a darting fish, Snowball scaled the armchair and slipped behind the closed curtains, stirring them slightly.

"Who's that in the photograph with you?" she asked, indicating a framed picture on the mantle. It showed Nick and a red-haired woman, sitting beneath a canopy.

"That's Karine, my ex," he said.

"You make a great couple."

"Looks can be deceiving, Dottie. Honestly, she was hard work. Karine always saw herself as the main concern in any situation. She couldn't grasp that she was only fifty percent of a relationship. I don't think she *wanted* to see that. A man has feelings and needs, too, strange as that may sound. She was a very different person to you, Dottie. I keep the picture because it's a good snap, but she's not around anymore."

After a short silence, she looked at him, into his eyes. Their faces were close. Before she could say anything, he leant in slowly, and their lips touched, melting together. Dottie kissed him – she simply couldn't help it – and a barrage of emotions detonated in her mind and body. She wanted him so much, wanted—

She pulled away and stood up.

"I'm sorry," Nick said, raising his palms. "I shouldn't have done that."

Dottie touched her neck, which felt like it was on fire. "I wanted to, but ... it doesn't feel right, Nick. I'm married to someone. It feels like I'm moving into another relationship too fast. Please don't take that the wrong way."

"No, you're spot on. That was stupid. I told you I wouldn't rush anything. I didn't ask you back here so I could kiss you, Dottie. I just ... wanted to, in the moment."

She sat down again, determined that their first kiss should not be viewed as a faux pas. "Just allow me some time, before we start down that road. Can you do that for me?"

"I can do anything you want me to, Dottie." He shrugged, smiling like a cheeky schoolboy. "You're worth the wait."

*****

Squinting in concentration, Billy watched the bungalow from across the road, behind the wide trunk of a conker tree. The Green Arrow van was parked at the far end of the street, out of sight. He couldn't see what was happening inside the house. They were probably at it right now, up there in Cassidy's bed, drooling over each other, moaning, sucking…

The bungalow's drapes were drawn, low lights burning in a couple of rooms. He had tailed the doctor's car back here from the restaurant, keeping a measured distance to avoid being sprung. He didn't have his binoculars with him, but that didn't matter, since he couldn't see inside anyway.

A white cat appeared on the windowsill, snuggling down between the curtains and glass. It stared out at night with sleepy sapphire eyes.

Billy tried, but could not dispel the image of them together. Sitting there in the restaurant. Touching hands. Walking to the car. Humping each other. Dottie's sex face. Did they really think he would let this go without retaliation? If they did, they deserved everything that was coming. Well, he wasn't going to skulk around here in the dark anymore, like a sad peeping Tom trying to catch a flash of boob. He had learned all he needed to.

189

Billy flounced away from the conker tree, jingling his van keys in his hand, grinding his teeth and sniffing, shaking his head as he went.

*****

"I had a lovely evening," Dottie said, as Nick's car crunched across the gravel in front of Netherwood House. Lights burned in the downstairs window: Lynette was still up. The interior of Nick's car was dark and cosy, the heaters blowing warm air.

"Can I call you, maybe next week sometime?"

"I'd like that, Nick."

"I won't try to kiss you again, don't worry."

Dottie unlocked her seatbelt, leant over, and pecked his cheek. "Will that suffice for now?"

"Perfectly."

"I'd better get inside," she said, regarding the large sandstone house. "Lynette will be waiting up, ready to give me the third degree."

"Women's talk, huh? How will I fare?"

"Mmm. Can't say. That's privileged information."

Nick got out, walked around the car, and opened her door. "I'll call you," he said, and Dottie set off towards the house, its clinging ivy shivering quietly in the dark. She spun about and saw Nick's rear lights disappearing along the road. His horn sounded once, and she lifted a hand in farewell.

"You fared just fine, Nick," she whispered and went on inside.

*****

At home, his brain firing with drug-induced intensity, Billy sat watching old DVDs of him and Dottie, footage recorded when they were younger. On the screen, Dottie laughed and pranced in the back garden, wearing denim cut-off shorts, waving as he followed her with the camera. The summer sun was fierce, occasionally warping the image, the garden rich with those blazing plants she cared so much about.

Billy swallowed and looked away.

He felt the house's heavy silence surround him. Everything was so damned quiet. The whole place was going to the dogs. He knew he should wash the pots and pans, empty the laundry basket, buy food, hoover the rooms – he knew he should do these chores, but had also accepted that it wasn't going to happen. He knew too that Dottie wasn't going to come back. And he didn't *want* her back, not after she had been tainted by Cassidy. Violated by him.

Lurid images of their sexual exertions filled his mind again, and he began thumping his forehead with the heel of his hand. "Bitch, bitch, bitch ..."

Dottie smiled at him from the television.

It was time to take revenge.

On Saturday, when he had spoken with Tara in the toy store, the little girl had mentioned that her brother's class was performing a play on Wednesday evening, at the school. That little runt Mark was playing a cow, or something, the girl had said. Billy had let her talk, recognising an opportunity to garner information. Tara had even asked Billy if *he* was coming along to the play, and he had found it hard not to laugh at that. Well, Billy doubted Dottie would be there. She wasn't likely to tag along on a family outing, not Dottie. She would stay home, which meant she would be alone for hours that evening. Alone

191

in the big house. So, he would pay her a visit on Wednesday night, her and the doctor both. Billy wondered if they'd still think their new friendship was such a good idea after he was finished with them.

Of course, it was possible Dottie *would* accompany the Hobins to the school play. She and Lynette did everything together. That wasn't a problem, though, not really. If he didn't catch up with her on Wednesday night, it would be another night. He was in no great hurry for revenge. He savoured the wait.

Billy trudged upstairs into his bedroom. He stood staring at the unmade double bed, knowing Dottie would never again sleep there with him. She would never be back.

He went out to the landing, before entering the spare room and flicking on the light. This space, which they'd intended to be the nursery, was empty, apart from the assembled cot positioned against the side wall. Billy's tools were still there, stored in the corner. He crossed to the window and looked out at the darkness; then, he turned and approached the cot, placing his hands on the rail. The head and foot of the cot were solid wood, and the sides were constructed from vertical wooden slats. Billy had painted it pale green, and Dottie had kitted it out in similarly coloured blankets she'd bought especially. A pink bear was situated in the cot's corner, a white ribbon around its neck.

He bent and lifted the hammer from the toolbox, hefting its weight and striking the palm of his hand with it. Billy raised the tool, freezing like that, as if picking a precise spot, and swung it down at the cot, crashing straight through the side structure. The wood splintered into kindling easily. One of the sharp edges tore his flesh, just below the thumb.

Dark blood bubbled from the wound, and he swore, bringing the hammer down again, violently hacking with the clawed end. He twisted the tool free each time and battered the cot once more, striking it repeatedly until the pieces – pale green, and the swirling brown of the grain within – were mashed together in a shapeless mess. Then he began kicking at it, growling as he trashed it with his boot, until the structure was all but flattened. The little pink bear lay among the debris, still smiling up at him, so he kicked out at it, too, sending it tumbling away across the floor.

When the rage finally passed, he stood there, gripping the hammer, breathing heavily, his fist sticky with blood, hatred yet pulsing through his body like poison. He remained in that angered position for a considerable time, glaring maniacally at the cot, which was now nothing more than a pile of trashed sticks.

CHAPTER 28

On Monday morning, Dottie left Netherwood House and walked to the Aradale Primary School, where she had been employed for the last four years. The day was unseasonably warm, but pleasantly so, and she had removed her jacket by the time she arrived there. Mr Bowden, the spry headmaster, showed her into his office and proffered Dottie a seat. There was a cursive-lettered notice on the wall that read: *It takes a big heart to teach small children.*

"So, tell me, how have you been keeping, Dorothy?"

"I'm okay," she told him, smoothing her skirt as she sat down. "Over the worst, I guess."

"You're aware you have the remainder of the year to ... come to terms with your bereavement?"

"I know, thank you. I want to return to work, because I miss teaching, and I miss the children. Being away from them isn't doing me any good, not anymore."

Bowden's pinched face adopted a sympathetic look.

Dottie was fond of the headmaster. From a first glance, most people took him for an old stick-in-the-mud – which, she supposed, was a fair reaction – but beneath his staid appearance, he was patient and understanding, and the timbre of his voice she always found reassuring.

"The children miss you, too, Dorothy," he said. "They're forever asking, when's Miss Hawthorn coming back? In all my years as headmaster here, I've never known a teacher so popular with the children."

"That's certainly reassuring to hear, Mr Bowden. I guess I must be doing something right."

Bowden removed his glasses. "More like everything right, I'd say. I'm extremely proud to have you on the staff here, Dorothy. You're a fine influence on the pupils, and clearly, they view you affectionately. Please allow me this opportunity to say that it's such a shame about your baby girl. Life can be terribly cruel sometimes. Who can fathom it? I often think the worst things happen to the best people." He sat back in his chair and smiled at her. "I don't think I've ever met a woman who'd make a better mother than you. The baby's name was Emma, is that correct?"

Dottie nodded. "I try not to think about it too much. It still hurts a great deal."

"Naturally. It'll be that way for a time, Dorothy. Losing a child is a terrible ordeal, for any mother. That's why I want to be doubly sure that you're in the right frame of mind for teaching, you understand? It really hasn't been very long since the birth. And I've heard there are a few problems with your husband ... if you don't mind my saying."

Dottie nodded again. It didn't take much for the word to get around. She could just imagine what was being said in the staffroom. She would be the topic of the moment. Did you hear Dottie Hawthorn's marriage has broken down? She knew how they talked, because she had heard it firsthand enough times over the years. They wouldn't say anything in front of her, but that didn't make it any easier. She wondered what they would say if they knew what had happened the night she left home.

"I've separated from my husband," she said. "We've had difficulties, yes, and now I'm living with my friend, Lynette – Mark Hobin's mother?"

"Yes, I know both Lynette and Mark."

"My current accommodation is only temporary, Mr Bowden. I'll have a place of my own before long. I understand your concern, but I'd not let anything jeopardise the kids' education or welfare. I wouldn't be here in your office if I hadn't given it all a lot of thought. The best place for me is at the school, with the children." She gave him a soft smile. "And you said yourself that they miss me."

Mr Bowden's head bobbed up and down thoughtfully. He placed his glasses back on. "I'd say you're a very brave young lady, Dorothy. And we're lucky to have you. How does next Monday sound – one week from today?"

"Next Monday sounds perfect."

When she left Mr Bowden's office, Dottie could hear distant shouts and calls emanating from the gymnasium, along with the screech of running shoes against the buffed floor. She turned for the exit and paused, glancing along the corridor at her classroom. She didn't want to run into any of her colleagues – not while she was the subject of staffroom gossip – but she couldn't resist a peek at the children. She started down there, past the area where the kids hung their coats and anoraks, and approached the classroom door. Through the vertical glass pane, she surreptitiously looked inside.

Most of the kids were engrossed in their work, noses in their textbooks, pencils scribbling flat out. The stand-in teacher, a young woman with a blonde bob haircut and green turtleneck sweater, was reading at the front desk. Two or three kids, as always, were gazing out of the window. Like most primary school classes, Dottie's was a generally mixed bunch. Large and small, fair and dark, hefty and thin. She loved them all dearly and believed – yes, she *did* believe, especially after what Mr Bowden had said – that they felt the same about her.

"See you next week, kids," she said, and retreated away down the corridor.

*****

After leaving the school, Dottie felt better, as if life matters were slowly beginning to right themselves again. Her marriage was a lost cause, but that did not stop her from pressing on with other avenues. As Lynette had said, she would have to take it one step at a time. She felt somewhat disheartened that talk of her separation was doing the rounds with her fellow teachers. Still, what else did she expect? Perhaps it was better that her colleagues were devouring her private life now; the gossip might fizzle out by the time she returned to work, next week.

Last night's date had gone well, though. As she walked, Dottie cast her memory back, trying to recall snippets of her and Nick's conversation, the topics they had discussed, and the looks that had passed between them. She had gone over these very things last night, as she lay in bed, waiting for sleep to come, though slumber had eluded her for a long while. Without fail, her mind would wander to that instant when their lips had touched. She'd probably relived those few seconds more than a hundred times already.

Enjoying the sunshine, carrying her jacket on her shoulder, Dottie made a short detour, stopping at Brickfield Road and the terraced house where she had been raised. She came by here less and less as she grew older, but today she felt something akin to a calling, a physical draw to visit this place, to be close to her roots. Seeing the house made her think of her mother and father: right now, she missed them more than ever.

She stood outside her former home, the last house on the street, looking up at the eaves. Her short-form cast a misshapen shadow across the gable wall. The house appeared much the same as she remembered it. Through the slats of the high fence, she saw the small shed in the back garden, inside which her father had kept his tools (tools he rarely used, she thought, with an inward smile). Someone else's washing billowed on the line now, and the little bikes on the lawn belonged to somebody else's children. Around the front, the wrought-iron fencing and gate remained, but the owners had changed its colour from black to a bright post-box red. The modest garden blazed with potted plants.

She had felt completely loved here by both parents. Her childhood had been filled with fun and activity, and she'd had lots of friends her own age living nearby. Two streets away, there had been a park with a carousel and swings, but it was long since gone, and more houses now stood in its place.

Dottie smiled, recalling her father teaching her to ride a bike during the bright, hot evenings when the summer days seemed to last forever. She closed her eyes and heard her mother calling her home, before the darkness came down. *Dottie, come inside! It's getting late!*

During those interminable summers, she had been a whirlwind, in and out of the house a hundred times a day (maybe a *hundred* was an exaggeration, but that's what it had seemed like). By the time she'd had to return to school after the holidays, it had felt like years had passed rather than a matter of weeks.

"Hello there," said a voice to her side, breaking her concentration.

Dottie opened her eyes, seeing a man standing by the rear gate, a young boy in the crook of his arm. The little boy was eating something raspberry-coloured, most of it smeared around his mouth.

"Oh, hello," Dottie said, almost apologetically. "I used to live here, when I was young. I just had a quick look on my way past. A trip down memory lane, I suppose."

The man's smile was amiable. "Well, my wife and I are very happy here."

"So was I," Dottie said and went on her way.

CHAPTER 29

Billy was on his way out that evening when the phone rang. Amazingly, the receiver still worked after he'd hurled it against the wall, following Cassidy's call. He stood staring at it, indecisive, then cursed and snatched it up. "Billy Hawthorn."

"Oh, uh, hello there, Mr Hawthorn. This is Mrs Granger, from the Mosgrove Care Home."

"Who?"

"Mrs Granger. We spoke briefly the day you visited your father?"

Billy's memory was shot to pieces, much the same as his appetite and sleeping pattern. He closed his eyes and tried to think, touching his forehead. Granger. Granger. Suddenly, he had her. Nice tits. Dyed hair. Good body. She had walked him to his father's room that day.

"I remember," he told her. "I was actually on my way out."

"I felt I should get in touch ... There's been some rather bad news about your father, Mr Hawthorn ..."

"Oh?"

"Grady suffered a severe stroke this morning and lost consciousness soon after. He was rushed straight to intensive care, I'm afraid. I'm very sorry, but your father's paralysed almost completely on his left side, and he's very confused and depressed right now. I thought you might want to pay him a visit—"

"You thought wrong, lady."

"Excuse me?"

"I'm happy he's in pain. It's no more than he deserves."

"Mr Hawthorn, there's no need for—"

"Save it. Do you want my advice, lady? Roll him onto the floor and use him as a draught excluder. Give the bed to someone worthwhile."

Billy drove to the Admiral pub and parked in one of the bays facing the side elevation. Inside, the little bar was quiet, which was usual for the beginning of the week. Bandit machines flashed, blipped, and bleeped. The jukebox was on, but turned down low. Most of the tables were empty. One old guy nursed a half bitter. Another read the paper. The slouched bartender was watching football on TV, a remote control in his hand. Billy tossed him a courteous nod; then he clocked the guy he was looking for, sitting in a corner booth with a beer. He strutted over there and slid in beside him.

"Billy Hawthorn," the man said. "It's been a while."

"It sure has."

Just as Billy recalled, Boomer was built like a tree trunk, his bulk barely squeezed between the table and booth seat. Boomer had always had a strange habit of changing his appearance, as if afraid of being easily spotted in a crowd. As if a human tank like him could blend in anywhere, Billy thought. In his latest guise, a thick black beard hid the bottom of his face, and his hair was long and unruly. He looked like an extra from *Braveheart*. The man's expression betrayed no emotion. As far as Billy could remember, Boomer only smiled when someone was being hurt – and some things never changed. Once, during a violent barfight, Billy had seen Boomer carry two men in a fireman's lift, simultaneously. He had freakish strength, for sure, but there wasn't much going on upstairs.

"You look like shit, Billy."

"I've been hitting the stuff a little hard, that's all."

Boomer drew a hand over his tattoo-bright forearm. He stared at Billy with big, dark eyes. "You look half starved to death, man. I don't know why you fill your body with that shit." He motioned to the bar. "Want something to drink?"

"No time," Billy said, sniffing. "I'm due somewhere shortly."

"How's the little woman? Dorothy, isn't it?"

Billy thought about Dottie and Cassidy in the candlelit restaurant and struggled to contain his temper. "We're having a bit of a rough patch, as it happens."

"Ain't that what every marriage becomes, after a time – one long rough patch? When the sex grows stale and the words dry up, there's nothing left to do but tear strips off each other, right?"

Billy pointed to Boomer's hand, which was wrapped in a bandage. "What happened there?"

"This," the big man said, lifting his arm, "is the result of a small dispute between me and three loudmouth arseholes I ran into last week. I was putting the moves on this foxy thing in that new club, down on Baldovie Street? Proper little goer, she looked. We were having a few aperitifs and a few laughs. I was playing it cool, because I reckoned I'd get a bit by the end of the night, you know? Just had to play my cards smart. She was giving out the signals, no question about it.

"Well, these three peckers were sitting at a table, kind of scoping us. But I was keeping an eye trained on them, too. I got a nose for trouble, Billy. I know when it's brewing, sure as shite's brown, right? They weren't doing any harm, though, so there was no problem, fair

202

enough, you know? But I think they could see me and the lass wasn't a couple, that I was just chatting with her, trying my hand, like. Well, after a while, they mosey on over and start asking her if she'd like a drink. Getting really close, trying to edge me out. I told them that the lady and I were having a conversation and that maybe they should excuse us.

"Anyway, they wouldn't leave well enough alone, and I wasn't about to be pushed around by nobody – least of all, a bunch of wet blankets like these fuckers. They thought 'cause there was three of 'em, that I'd just fade away. Like that would ever happen, right? So, I hit the biggest one – *bam* – and broke his nose flat. I felt it crumple under my fist, I shit you not, Billy, old son. He goes down on his back, and he ain't getting up again any time soon, I'll tell you that for nothing. Blood was running out his face like an open tap.

"Before I know what's what, the second guy – little weasel-faced runt – he takes a bottle to my napper, but luckily it didn't break – the bottle, that is. I grab him and start hitting the bastard as hard as I can, really going to town on him, you know?

"By now, the third arsehole's arm is looped around my neck, trying to pull me off the second guy, but I wasn't about to stop." Boomer grunted a short laugh. "People were screaming and shoutin', and that's when the bouncers waded in and the whole thing turned into mayhem.

"Here's me being frogmarched outside by two knuckleheads, hands behind my back. They called the fuzz, and I spent the next hour explaining how these three morons had started the trouble. All from trying to get ma leg over, huh?" Boomer took a slug from his beer. "Hey, you sure you don't want a drink, man?"

"No thanks." Billy leaned in. "I was told you could put your hands on a car."

Boomer stared at him. "It's possible."

"I need it for Wednesday night."

"I don't have a fucken forecourt, mate."

"That's when I need it."

Boomer snorted. "That's short notice."

"I understand." Billy sniffed and tapped the table. "Can it be done?"

"Something clean?"

"Has to be."

"What about disposal?"

"I'll get rid of it myself. What I need is something that won't show up on the cops' computers, if they pass me on the street. I can't risk stealing one."

Boomer drained his beer, squinting at Billy. "What's it for?"

"I'd rather not say. I'll pay you for the motor, but that's where it ends. Besides, it's better you don't know. That way, there won't be any comeback."

Boomer brushed his thumb over his upper lip. "What exactly are you after?"

Billy shrugged. "Specifics ain't overly important. Something clean. Dark, preferably. Something reliable, an engine that can move a bit."

"It's for a job, though, right?"

204

"In a manner of speaking."

Boomer glanced outside. Headlights drifted past the booth window. "Might be a squeeze for Wednesday. I'll call you and let you know what's happening."

"There's a couple of other things I need," Billy said, sliding a folded piece of paper across the table. "I thought you might be able to help me with those, too."

Boomer looked down at the paper. "That shouldn't be a problem. Still, these items will cost you extra."

"I expected they would." Billy extended his hand, but his broad-shouldered companion only stared at it.

"You know the drill here, Billy. Anything goes wrong with whatever you're doing, you never heard of me. Understand?"

"Don't even know your name."

Boomer finally reached across with his good hand, and Billy shook it, noting the man's grip was capable of crushing a small skull.

*****

After leaving the Admiral, Billy pumped the Green Arrow van with diesel and headed out of town. Before long, Aradale's amber lights were but pinpricks in his rear-view mirror. He activated full beams, lighting the way as it twisted ahead. Wooden fencing lined the roadsides, the fir trees and flat fields indistinguishable under the blanketing cover of darkness.

Tonight, he felt marginally better than he had of late, which in itself was no real improvement. Last night, after returning home, he had collapsed on his bed, exhausted, unable to think straight, due to lack of sleep – expected effects of cocaine abuse – and was soon in a deep and welcoming state of unconsciousness. The alarm had yanked him awake early this morning, and he'd have given anything to linger in bed a few hours longer. But once he began skipping work, it was a slippery slope. Next, he would be taking time off regularly, and then he would be selling household stuff to raise drug money, because he no longer had wages coming in.

He reached over and plucked a Miller from the carrier bag on the passenger seat. He cracked the seal with one hand and drained half the tin. He belched, setting it between his thighs.

Boomer had said supplying a car at short notice would be troublesome, but Billy didn't buy that. The big dumb shit could probably put his hands on *ten* cars, if need be. He was just making the point, Billy thought – the point that he didn't appreciate being rushed. Besides, Boomer would never call him back and say he couldn't supply the car. Not Boomer. That didn't make him look good. If Billy knew anything of the man, it was that he relied on his reputation. And that he liked to get paid. There would be a car ready on Wednesday – Billy would bet on that.

He swallowed more ale and wiped his mouth with his forearm.

After a while, he crunched down the gears as the road's gradient steepened. A truck came towards him, and he dipped his bright beams. Then he flipped them on again.

There's some rather bad news about your father.

He couldn't believe the nerve of that Granger woman, calling him up like that, expecting him to scurry off to the hospital, to play the devoted little son. Let the twisted bastard suffer. It didn't sound like poor Grady had long to go, anyway. First, the old man's mind had slipped, and now his body was throwing in the towel.

As far as Billy was concerned, if he searched hard enough for a link, every hurdle in his life could be traced back to the old man. Maybe his mother would have lived longer, if her life had been easier, if Grady had been a better husband – or any kind of husband at all. Maybe Billy's little brother wouldn't have skipped town, if his father had provided a life for them.

When Billy had brought his first girlfriend home, the old man had proved nothing but an embarrassment, slumped in an armchair, stewed with drink, the house stinking like a skunk. Needless to say, any female interest in Billy soon vanished when girls got a look at how he lived.

There was never a word of encouragement from his father, either. Whether it was schoolwork, football practice, or the mental preparation for adulthood and the outside world, the old man couldn't summon a single word of parental advice or assistance. Too busy playing around with all his cheap tarts. Too busy drinking money they needed for clothes, for food, bills, for school trips that Billy rarely participated in. He had never overcome the embarrassment of watching his classmates troop off on excursions, while he missed the experience again and again.

Day after day, year after year, Billy's loathing for the old man had matured, growing as surely as his mind and body. Every punch, every slap, every cigarette burn. Those abuses had marked Billy's thin, bony fame, but they had also fuelled his hatred, and the more hatred he kept inside, the more determined he'd become to escape his father. And should the day ever dawn when Grady Hawthorn needed his son ... well, there would be no reconciliation.

Billy found he had driven several miles without really concentrating. He drew a hand over his face. He finished the Miller, worked down the window, and tossed the can.

He was among high trees again. There was woodland on both sides now. He killed his speed, watching for the turning he knew was up ahead. It appeared sooner than expected, and Billy jammed on the brake, steering the van sharply into the woods. Branches scraped the vehicle's sides and windscreen, the underside clanking from the impact of loose stones.

The track through the trees was awkward and slow going, but the van's suspension was sturdy, managing to negotiate the route without any real trouble. A small animal shot across Billy's path, hind legs were pumping, running for its life as Billy's noisy, alien machine rumbled through its habitat.

Soon he slowed and killed the engine. Leaving the sidelights on, he got out, finding the night surprisingly humid for October. Billy extended his arms and stretched, his shoulders popping. There was no wind. He could hear what sounded like the quiet scurrying of nearby wildlife.

He opened the van's side door, sliding it back on its runners. The interior light came on, revealing a shovel, a long, steel digging bar, and an old wooden crate. The tools had come from his shed at home. The wooden crate, courtesy of Green Arrow, had been used to transfer an item of antique furniture, last week. Billy had set it aside for himself earlier that afternoon, its capacity just about perfect for what he had in mind.

He worked his fingers into a pair of battered leather gloves and selected the lengthy digging bar. One end of it was honed to a point, like a spear; its opposite end was angled like the wedge of a crowbar, designed for breaking tough, stony ground. Billy lumbered out in front of the van, into the area lit by the sidelights. He glanced heavenwards as a winged creature soared against the night sky. A quarter-moon shone. After a deep breath, he spread his feet, raised the steel bar high, and crashed it down, splitting the earth.

The grave would be big enough for two.

CHAPTER 30

Dottie spent that Monday night in the living room of Netherwood House, perusing local estate-agency brochures for rental accommodation. One or two advertisements held promise – for a temporary stay, at least – so she circled them with her Biro, deciding to take a look at them tomorrow. As she paged through the brochures, she ate the chocolates Nick had bought for her.

"So, how'd you get on with Bowden today?" Lynette asked. Her svelte figure lay prone on the sofa, her glass of red wine absorbing the room's light, like blood.

"He was great," Dottie said, peeping over the brochure. "He's a nice old guy, and he always tries to help."

"He didn't think it was too soon for you to be going back?"

Dottie lowered the brochure. "I suppose he did, but I've got to get things on track again, Lynette. And that means returning to work and gaining some independence."

"And what about Dr Cassidy?"

Dottie looked at her. "What about him?"

"Well, does he feature in your future plans?"

Dottie ducked behind the brochure.

"Hey, come on, I'm interested. Has he called?"

The brochure lowered. "No, but he *will*."

"It certainly sounds like the date went swimmingly. And back to his place afterwards? Come on, what's his house like?"

Dottie squirmed. "I told you about it last night."

"Humour me."

"Nick's place is ... nice, you know. Clean, and masculine. Very tidy. He has a cat called Snowball. She's *so* beautiful, so white and soft. She has the cutest little face. I could've squeezed her to death."

"I love cats," Lynette said, "but Graham's allergic. Trust him."

"Someone wearing out my name?"

Graham appeared from the kitchen, a dishtowel draped over his shoulder. He leaned on the doorframe. "Hey, Dottie, here's a good one for you ..."

Lynette armed herself with a cushion. "Graham, we're having a conversation—"

Dottie giggled.

"—and that means no stupid jokes."

"Tom and Pete are going around the golf course, and Tom says, Your game's a little off today, Pete. Is anything wrong? It's the missus, Pete says, I think she might be dead. Might be? asks Tom. Well, can't you tell? Well, says Pete, the sex is the same, but the dishes are piling up."

Lynette hurled the cushion, and Graham darted back into the kitchen. The cushion struck the wall and dropped to the floor, billowing the beaded tassels of a lamp.

"Idiot, man. Sorry, Dottie, where were we?"

"You were fishing for details about my date."

"Right you are. Carry on."

"Lynette, there's nothing else."

"You call your first kiss with him, nothing?"

Dottie smiled and sat forward. "That *was* nice, although it felt a little too soon."

"Quite right, too, Dottie. You keep him dangling. Let him know who's in charge."

"No one's in charge of a relationship, Lynette." As soon as she said it, though, Dottie realised how wrong her statement was. Billy had been in charge of *their* relationship. He had been a dictator, a tyrant, and had done as he pleased and would have kept *on* doing it, had she not taken a stand.

"Well, you deserve all the happiness in the world," Lynette said, charging her glass from the nearby bottle.

Graham ventured gingerly back into the room, grinning mischievously at Dottie. He sneaked up behind Lynette with raised arms, in a parody of a cartoon villain, leant over, and kissed her cheek.

"Get off," Lynette protested, craning her neck in a squirmy rebuff.

"Hey, here's one I bet you haven't heard ..." he said.

Lynette grabbed another cushion, and Dottie laughed.

*****

Billy finished digging the grave several gruelling hours after he had begun. A chill sweat coated his brow and body. His face was smeared with grime and dirt, and he could even taste the stuff in his mouth.

It was into the small hours when he finally had the hole deep and wide enough to accommodate the wooden crate. He dragged it from the van and let it fall into the grave, where it settled at a skewed angle. Not a bad fit, considering he had gauged the dimensions purely by eye. The crate needed gentle manoeuvring and persuasion. Several times, when the damned thing had become wedged, he jammed the shovel's head against the grave's walls, shaving dirt and stones, allowing the box to descend a little farther. Eventually, after much grunting and muttering, the crate came to rest on the bottom, and Billy dropped to his knees in exhausted satisfaction, pulling in deep breaths of air.

He stashed the crate's lid in the trees, away from the grave but close enough to retrieve when the time came. He dragged out a sheet of old plywood from the van, which he positioned over the grave's surface, concealing the fruit of his labours. He scattered dirt and bracken and sticks across the plywood, working until the whole thing looked undisturbed – not that anyone would be out here before Wednesday night. Better safe than sorry, though. Don't leave anything to chance. That was how things went sour.

After he returned his tools to the van, he snorted a line of coke and gave the area another once-over. A mild sense of achievement filled him. God, it would be perfect. All he had to do was keep his head and everything would work out fine.

Years ago, Billy had read a book about premature burial, and the dark images it conjured had stayed with him. In centuries past, burying people alive was not an uncommon occurrence. Before the process of certifying death had been ... perfected, for want of a better word, many such mistakes were made. As a result, coffins were sometimes exhumed to check whether the poor bastards inside had been left to die in that unimaginable confinement.

It had transpired that people were indeed buried prior to death. According to various old accounts, what had been revealed inside these open coffins, once their lids were pried open ... well, suffice to say it was a scene straight from the darkest corners of hell. There was no doubt in Billy's mind that this perishing, awful death was beyond anyone's ability to imagine. According to the book, these corpses were a nightmarish vision of horrific anguish and desperation, their fingernails were worn down after clawing uselessly at the inside of the coffin. Billy guessed that this was about the worst death a person could endure. Burning to death would be bad, but being buried alive would be ... lingering, claustrophobic; and no matter how long you managed to keep panic at bay, it would not be far away. It would be right there, waiting to strike. The limited air would eventually dwindle, and the realisation that nobody could hear your oxygen-wasting screams would tip anyone over the edge, into the abyss of insanity.

And what about the death itself? When the final moments came, it would probably prove a relief. The panic and fear would have consumed the strongest of minds by this point, because there was no other possibility. Hell, a victim would be reduced to a screaming, simpering wreck.

Billy grinned, looking at the concealed grave. And what if someone else lingered down there with you? A second person would stoke the boiler of fear, steal the last of the air, and mirror your own horror. Far from providing comfort during this darkest of hours, Billy expected it would crank up the horror tenfold. And it would all take place in the blackest confinement. More than the human psyche could withstand.

He wiped at his nose and ground his teeth, wondering how the good doctor and that bitch would enjoy the experience, clinging to each other as life slowly ebbed…

Billy got in the van and gunned the engine, which was sluggish after powering the sidelights. It caught, though, and he pumped the accelerator a few times. He turned the van cautiously, the diesel engine rumbling as he manoeuvred around. Seconds later, he was rolling away from the concealed grave, the radio playing, pleased with his night's work.

CHAPTER 31

Tuesday morning.

As part of her daily ritual, Lynette surfaced early. Each day, before breakfast, she slipped on rubber boots and traipsed in the woods with Rex. This, she found, built her appetite and cleared her head for the day's writing. The first draft of her current novel was nearing completion, and another week would see it finished.

Since childhood, she had been an alfresco person at heart, drawing both exhilaration and equanimity from nature's great surroundings. As an adult, early morning was her favourite time of the day, and she never wasted it lying in bed – not unless she had severely overindulged the evening before. She felt comforted in the woods, hearing the chirping and trilling from high above, breathing the sharp, crisp air. It made her feel glad to be alive.

She trailed behind Rex as he sniffed and inspected the birches and conifers, his stubby tail and hindlegs moving comically across the woodland floor. The morning light was slowly replacing the night. A pale purple hue stretched the extent of the sky like an artist's brushstroke. To her right, at the far side of the embankment, she could hear the soft babbling of the brook.

As she walked, Lynette reflected how satisfying it was to see Dottie finally taking control of her life, finally escaping from beneath the thumb of a husband who didn't care for her. With Nick Cassidy, Dottie had an opportunity to be happy, to know what it was to be in a real relationship.

Since the night Dottie had left Billy – following whatever altercation had happened – Lynette had half-expected some manner of retaliation from him. Whether it was phone calls, begging Dottie to come home, or his unannounced arrival at Netherwood House, she expected *something* from the man. Now, after a time with no such retaliation, she wondered if Billy really had accepted the end of his marriage. It went against the grain for Lynette to believe it, but perhaps Billy had realised he had been a poor partner and that his efforts as a husband had been found wanting. Perhaps he had accepted that Dottie deserved someone better – which opened the floor to just about every man outside prison walls, she thought.

Lynette paused as Rex cocked a leg and relieved himself on a fallen tree. The tawny dog shook itself down, tinkling its collar, and strutted purposefully on.

Still, Lynette could not quite convince herself there wasn't trouble on the cards. She could be wrong, but something in her gut told her otherwise. It was possible that Billy wasn't all bad, she supposed. Dottie had loved him once, although such devotion was just incomprehensible to Lynette. In any event, Billy *had* to accept that Dottie had moved on, because there was nothing he could do to stop it.

Before long, Rex was nosing and scraping at the foot of a robust elm tree. When Lynette gained on him, trudging through fallen leaves, snapping twigs underfoot, she found the corgi snuffling among a multitude of empty Miller cans.

She frowned.

It was a strange thing to come across, as kids didn't drink in these woods, as far as she knew. The cans could have been left by a tramp, she considered. But then, why would the empties all be gathered here in one spot? She sighed angrily, wondering why people thought nothing of such wanton littering. How much effort did it require to take your shit home with you?

Shaking her head, she walked on with Rex, thinking no more about it.

*****

Her hair washed, blow-dried, and tied back with a pink scrunchy, Dottie set off from Netherwood House at ten o'clock, in a knee-length white dress mottled with little yellow roses. Engrossed in the ever-progressing draft of her novel, Lynette had bid her a distracted farewell from her desk in the study.

The weather remained mild and unusually warm for October.

The first flat Dottie viewed was on the middle floor of a building on Bridge End Close, on the west side of town. It wasn't the finest of schemes, but it wasn't the worst, either. Because nobody currently occupied the one-bedroom apartment, the landlord, a squat and slightly pushy man with a moustache and sour expression, allowed her to look around at her leisure, on condition she returned the keys afterwards.

When she arrived outside, Dottie used a key to open the security door, and the other to open the apartment door, after ascending the flight of stairs to number Twenty-Eight.

The apartment was pokey and pretty much what she had expected.

The sofas and armchairs were threadbare, but she could replace these things, in time. The bedroom was an acceptable size, with an insipid view of a car park and its overgrown shrubbery. The bedroom walls had been whitewashed, providing any potential tenant with a blank canvas to flavour in line with personal taste. Judging by the odd patch of colour showing through the white emulsion, the walls had been robin's egg blue in a previous life.

Dottie brought a finger across the walnut bureau's surface, creating a streak through the patina of dust.

The casement windows were double-glazed. Storage heaters were situated in each room and appeared well-maintained. The wooden doors and skirtings had been treated with a dark stain, but had begun to fade over time.

She entered the living area for another look. It was bright, with sunlight flooding in from the east. The walls were magnolia. A few plants and pictures would combat the blandness, she thought. Maybe a rug and some flowers. A round table was situated in the corner, with a telephone atop it.

She pushed open the bathroom door and flicked on the light. The bath was small, but so was she. The sink and toilet were cream-coloured. The white shower curtain looked new, with no encroaching mould. The bath was clean, at least. Linoleum covered the floor. A tiny cabinet was fixed to the wall. She opened it and found the lonely head of a nasal-hair trimmer someone had left behind. A perished bug lay withered on the windowsill.

In the living room again, Dottie sat in an armchair and set her handbag on the floor. After years of marriage, and years of working, was this what it came down to? Setting up alone in a one-bedroom apartment?

Well, it wasn't so bad. She could make it work.

Plenty of people around the world endured worse situations. Some had to drink filthy water just to survive; some existed in housing that had nothing more than corrugated iron for walls. People had lost entire families to war and genocide. Dottie's mother had instilled in her the need to be thankful for what she had, because someone somewhere always had less.

As long as you have your health, Dottie, you have all you need. When your health goes, then you have real concerns. Until then, embrace every single day.

Dottie smiled sadly. She wished her mother were here with her, offering counsel and reassurance, hugging her, and assuring her everything would be all right. And she thought longingly about Nick, and the softness of that kiss. Somehow, regardless of the setbacks along the way, she knew a future awaited her.

*****

At twelve forty, during his dinner hour, Billy sat in his van on Ferntower Place, outside the pizza joint where Angela Dunbar worked as a waitress. He studied her from behind his sunglasses. Today, Angela looked grim, with dark rings under her eyes. She was thin as a racetrack hound, too. Through the massive livery-clad window, he saw her serve a deep-crust to an absurdly fat man. The place was heaving, punters coming and going all the while.

Billy flicked peanuts into his mouth from a bag on the dashboard.

His muscles *ached* from the previous night's exertions. His arms, hamstrings, and shoulders were tender, complaining painfully with every movement. This discomfort was a fair price to pay, though, and was nothing compared to what Dottie and Cassidy were in for, tomorrow night.

It was not too late to abandon the idea, but each time he thought about them together, that old red mist descended. He would not be able to live with himself if he didn't set this right. No sooner had Dottie left him than she was rutting with another man. And the good doctor? Well, Cassidy should have known better. He should have recognised Billy as a worthy enemy. Instead, he thought *nothing* of moving in on Billy's wife, taking what he clearly wasn't entitled to.

Billy dusted and licked the salt from his fingers, then got out and walked inside the restaurant. A young waitress escorted him to a table set for two and scooped away the spare cutlery. She handed Billy an open menu.

"Would you like something to drink?" she asked.

"I'd love an orange juice," he told her. His mouth was dry as a camel's arse after all those peanuts. He watched Angela from the corner of his eye. She hadn't yet noticed him.

"Small, medium, or large?"

She was carrying a load of empty pizza pans and disappeared through a doorway, bumping it open with her backside.

"Sir?"

"What?"

"Your orange juice. Small, medium, or large?"

"Best make it a large one."

"Thank you."

The waitress spun away, Billy watching her rump wiggle inside the tight black skirt. She returned promptly with his orange juice and placed it down.

"Thanks, sweetheart."

The place was crammed with families, hungrily transferring floppy slices of pizza from pans to plates, from plates to mouths. Quiet music played from somewhere, but it was drowned out by the chatter. There was a baby screeching in a highchair, distressed and red-faced, sounding as if it had just been dunked in boiling fat. Jesus. These people should be told to leave, Billy thought. Silence the rug rat or get out.

After a few minutes, Angela reappeared, laden with plates of pasta and garlic bread. She whisked them over to a family table in the corner. As Billy waited, he concentrated on the fat man situated across the floor from him, who was ramming pizza into his mouth as if time were running out.

On her return, Angela caught Billy's eye and came to a stop. He smiled at her, enjoying the uneasiness he saw on her face. He beckoned her to him with one finger.

"Well, Angela. How goes it?"

She tucked her hands into the pouch of her apron and shrugged. "Busy."

"So I see, very busy. You're working really hard." Billy stared at her. He took a mouthful of orange juice and smacked his lips.

"I can't really talk, Billy. We're flat out, you know." She poked an errant strand of hair behind her ear. "It's lunchtime."

"When do you finish?"

"Six o'clock," she said, avoiding his eyes.

"Well, I'll see you outside at six, then. Give you a ride home. There's something I need your help with."

She looked at him warily. "My help?"

"That's right. An important job I have to do. I need someone I can trust. So, I'll see you at six, and tell you all about it." He drained his orange juice and rattled the ice cubes in the glass. "Off you go," he said. "Busy, busy."

Angela began clearing tables, glancing back at him now and then. Billy left some money to cover the drink, and a moment later, he was out the door and gone.

CHAPTER 32

After his lunch break, Billy reverse-parked on Castle Hill Avenue, leaning out of the window, guiding the steering wheel with the palm of one hand. When he had the vehicle positioned, he climbed down and slid open the side door. He had a bunch of parcels to drop inside the old Victorian market: a few for the florist, one for the health-food place – he hated going in there because it stank like a damned birdcage – and a couple for Carroll's Pet Store, which smelled worse than the health-food place.

Checking the labels, he gathered the smallest parcels first and slid closed the van's door with his foot.

"You can't leave that there, sir."

Clutching the boxes under his chin, Billy spun around and saw an elderly traffic warden bearing down on him. The guy wore a black peaked cap and was kitted out in the usual black and yellow threads. His weathered face was a mass of loose skin, like a St Bernard.

"I've got drops to make in the market there," Billy said reasonably, nodding sideways. "Gimme a break, huh?"

"There's an appropriate loading bay at the end of the street, sir," the warden said, pointing past Billy's head with a pen. "As I'm sure you're well aware."

"I'll be five minutes. Can't you look the other way while I deliver a few boxes?"

"Look the other way?" The warden couldn't appear more surprised, Billy thought, if he had been asked to take a dump on the street. "If we started doing that, where would it end? No, no. I suggest you park in the designated area before you commence unloading these items. Otherwise, I'll have to write you a ticket, sir."

"God forbid you to do another human being a favour, huh?" Billy shook his head. "Well, you wanna get the door for me there?"

"Be glad to assist, sir," the warden told him and slid open the van's side door.

Billy dumped the boxes inside again and slammed the door shut. In the driver's seat, cursing under his breath, he waited for a break in traffic, indicated out, and headed on down the street. The warden was there on the path, guiding him into the loading bay, as if Billy were a retard who couldn't park without help. He gave the warden a quick salute as he shut off the engine once more. The warden gave him a thumbs-up in return.

"Cocksucker," Billy muttered.

Inside, the market was cool, and dark, making Billy grateful to be in the shade. Damned warm October. He weaved through the warren of shops, stands, and stalls. A busker, accompanied by a faithful blanket-covered hound, strummed through a version of 'Mr Tambourine Man.' His open guitar case was peppered with coins, barely enough for a pot of tea.

The market enclosure was a heady mix of smells, most of which Billy found unfavourable. High above, birds' webbed feet paced over the transparent ceiling. Many of the businesses he passed were dated and had been here since Billy was a kid. The shoe-fixing/key-cutting place. The fishmonger's, with its display window full of tentacled deep-sea life, like creatures from another world. The fusty charity shops with their merchandise on a show out front. The grubby

225

cafeterias, occupied by old women, nursing teas and coffees. He passed a window filled with kilts and sporrans and ducked through the florist's doorway, a bell sounding overhead.

The store's shelves and floor space were crammed with flowers, leaving barely enough room to walk. Billy had made drops here many times, but didn't recognise the woman behind the counter. She was blonde and buxom, wearing an apron, attractive. Mid-twenties, or thereabouts.

"Got a few parcels here for you," Billy said.

"Could you leave them by the door there?" she replied politely, pointing to the floor.

"No sweat." He laid them down and produced a delivery slip from his back pocket. "Just need a quick signature," he said and slid it across the counter. "Just there, at the bottom."

She tucked loose hair behind her ear and scribbled her name. Left-hander. Funny writer. Held the pen all twisted and weird. She smiled, showing nice teeth, and handed him back the slip.

"I haven't seen you in here before," he said, tearing off the yellow copy for her.

"I just started last week."

"Is that so? Well, this place needed a pretty face to go with all these flowers. Listen, how'd you fancy coming out for a drink with me sometime?"

She glanced down and pointed at his hand. "You're wearing a wedding ring."

"Oh, that." Billy raised his fingers and wiggled them. "Well, I ain't got around to getting rid of it yet. We're not together anymore, don't worry about it. So, what do you say?"

The woman shook her head, looking uneasy. Her hands sought each other. "No, I don't think so."

"Come on, you'll have fun, I promise. I know a quiet little place we can try out."

She shook her head again. "I'm sorry, but I'd rather not. I've only just—"

"Don't sweat it," Billy said, snatching his delivery slip from the counter. "What are you – a damned wallflower? You fit right in here, don't you?"

Following a trip back to the van, he dropped a parcel at the health-food place, in and out as quick as possible, holding his breath for as long as he could. All those seedy and herby whiffs made him want to puke. Finally, he was in Carroll's Pet Store, placing two boxes on the counter.

Billy palmed the bell. After a minute, a guy appeared from the back and ducked in behind the till, slipping on a pair of horn-rimmed spectacles.

"One of the girls called in sick this morning," he said. "We've got deliveries arriving, and I'm supposed to be everywhere at once. Working the till, stacking shelves, doing paperwork." He took a calming breath and sighed. "Right, that's my rant over for the day. You need a signature for these boxes, son?"

"That'd be great," Billy said. "At the bottom."

Outside again, Billy looked at the large clock above the market's exit: a couple of minutes after two. He glanced at the expansive pet-store window, which was filled with colourful hand-written notices and signs. ALL KINDS OF PETS INSIDE read one. ALL YOUR PET SUPPLIES stated another. He was about to move on when his eye caught a sign below the rest. NEW IN! TARANTULAS! ASK INSIDE!

Billy stood staring at those words for a time, and a wicked smile crept across his face. Then he went back into the store.

CHAPTER 33

Dottie viewed another apartment that afternoon, but the two-bedroom place had been neglected by the previous tenant, and it took her only a minute to decide she didn't want it. She made a show of looking around, in any case, ostensibly neutral because the landlord was shadowing her every step.

"The place needs some touching up," the old man kept saying, as if it were Dottie's job to decorate for him.

She was amazed that he could show the property without hanging his head in shame. She wasn't averse to investing effort in a place, but its condition should at least be decent, if someone expected to be paid rent.

"Needs touching up there, too," he said, patting his pot belly.

Once they had toured each room, and Dottie had done her best to feign interest, she said she had other apartments to see and politely left.

"Don't leave it too long," he advised. "Another lady is quite interested."

Does she have a white stick? Dottie thought.

Later, on the trek back to Netherwood House, she felt glad to be free of the stuffy apartment. She carried with her a handcrafted Tiana porcelain vase, which she'd purchased on impulse in a department store. The magenta ornament was beautiful, with textured swirls and a lacquered finish. It was a gift for Lynette, a small thank you for putting her up in her hour of need. As she walked, surrounded by the elongated, jagged shadows of tall trees, her mobile rang, so she set down the vase to take the call.

"Thought I'd check in and see how you're doing," Nick Cassidy said.

"I've been looking at a couple of apartments."

"Oh yeah? Anything catches your eye?"

"Hmm. The first one wasn't too bad. The second – I wouldn't let an animal stay there. It looked as if the last tenants were squatters."

"Need a woman's touch, does it?"

"It needs fumigating."

"Maybe you could haggle, bump down the rent?"

"Nick, I wouldn't stay there if *he* paid *me*."

"Wow, that *is* bad."

"Yeah, it was. Afterwards, I took a walk out to the cemetery and laid flowers for Emma."

"That's nice, Dottie. You okay?"

"It was hard, but I just wanted to visit her grave. She's all alone out there. I started filling up as soon as I arrived, though."

"That's a healthy reaction, don't worry."

"What about you?" she asked. "What's doing in the fast lane of the medical world?"

"Ah, you know, pregnant women, ailments, obscure complaints. Nothing glamorous."

"Hey, I was one of those pregnant women, remember?"

"I remember," Nick said. "And I'm glad you were. Listen, Dottie, how're you fixed for the weekend? You doing anything?"

"I'm not sure. What did you have in mind?"

230

"Okay, prepare yourself now. For starters, I'd let you sample the world's greatest spaghetti Bolognese – that's *my* Bolognese, by the way. We could have a glass of plonk or two. Then maybe a movie, and another drink afterwards. Somewhere intimate, and quiet. Does any of this sound in the least bit tempting, at all?"

"Possibly," Dottie said, playing along. She laughed. "What's on at the movies?"

"I haven't got a Scooby, but I can find out. You can choose. Anything you like. Romance, horror, weepy – I can sit through them all."

"Well, in that case, you have a deal."

"Great. I'll call you on Friday."

Feeling suddenly brighter, bathed in October sunlight, clutching the flowery vase, Dottie continued down the road towards Netherwood House.

*****

At six o'clock, Billy was back outside the pizza restaurant, waiting for Angela to finish her shift.

He had met her almost a year ago, at a house where he had been buying coke. The first time he saw Angela, she'd been flaked out on a battered old couch, wired to the eyeballs on something. She had looked so young and helpless that day, so vulnerable. After a while, when she had come around, and they'd begun talking, he played the nice guy, turning on the smarm. He got the impression that she liked him, that she would probably be game for some fun. If he played his cards right, he knew he could have his way with her, maybe on a regular basis. She was gullible, and suggestible, a perfect combo.

231

From that first day, he had made sure he could get her some gear whenever she needed it, and would appear at her place now and again, just to let her know he was keeping an eye on her. Before long, they'd ended up sleeping together, getting high together, and soon he had Angela exactly where he wanted her. She gave him anything he asked for, anytime he asked for it. She was shit-scared of him; that was the truth. It was a damned handy position to have her in, especially now, when he had something particular he needed from her.

He didn't know where her folks were. Her mother didn't live in town, and her father, Billy had heard, was doing a stretch for assault and battery. She had a younger brother somewhere, although Angela hadn't seen him for years, apparently. All things considered, she was on her own. Billy had clubbed her lover with a fencepost, and he doubted that guy would be sniffing around her anymore. Angela was a decent girl, and he really didn't enjoy taking advantage of her. Still, it was necessary. If he had a conscience, he just might turn her loose. But she was too good a thing to give up; that was the problem.

Angela appeared from the restaurant doorway, looking across the street at him. She was still in uniform – black skirt, canary-yellow shirt – with a denim jacket over her shoulder.

Billy flashed his lights at her, although she had clearly seen him.

He leaned in and opened the passenger door, and she climbed in.

"Had a productive day?" he asked, drawing a hand across her bare knee. He guided his fingers beneath her skirt, caressing her cool thigh.

"What's this all about, Billy?"

"Aren't you glad to see me?"

232

She tried for a smile, but it faltered and died. "You said ... you said you needed my help with something? I don't want to get involved with anything funny."

"Hey," he said, drawing his roaming hand towards her crotch. "Listen, I don't need you to *do* anything, okay? I just need you as ... an insurance policy, so to speak."

"Insurance policy?"

"That's all." The tips of his fingers found the elastic rim of her underwear and brushed against her wiry hair. "If anyone comes around asking questions about tomorrow, just remember, I was in your apartment all night."

"I don't understand, Billy."

He withdrew his hand and took her fingers in his. "It's simple. Tomorrow night. Anyone asks, I was with you all night. I didn't leave until morning."

"Who'll ask?"

"That's not important. I'll leave this van outside your place, tomorrow evening. Right outside, so people will see it. You just have to stay inside, all night. Don't go out anywhere, even for a pint of milk, understand? Maybe play music, let folk know that you're home."

She nodded, her eyes downcast. He squeezed her hand a little.

"And that's it. So, there's nothing complicated about that, is there?"

"What are you going to do?"

"Well, that part doesn't concern you, Angie. Just concentrate on *your* part, and everything will work out fine. Now, let me hear it back."

"I understand, Billy."

He squeezed her fingers, crushing them in his own. Angela doubled over, letting out a *yip* of pain. Billy slackened his grip, but did not release her hand.

"Let me hear it back, Angie."

"Tomorrow n-night," she said nervily. "You'll leave the van at my p-place ..."

"Good. What else?"

"I'll stay home. If ... if anyone asks, you w-were with me all night."

"What else?"

"You didn't leave until morning."

"That's good, sweetheart. I knew I could count on you."

Billy released her hand and kissed her tear-damp cheek. Angie clutched her fingers to her chest, as if she'd been burned.

"Now, we'll take a drive over to your place," Billy said. "I've got some sweet gear in my pocket here. We can have a little party, just you and me. You look like you could use a little toot. Would you like that?"

Angela nodded.

"Say it."

"I'd like that."

Billy started the engine. "Good girl."

CHAPTER 34

That Tuesday night, after dark, Nick was unloading crockery and cutlery from the dishwasher in his kitchen, whistling tunefully. He had showered and had a towel secured around his trim waist. Snowball was perched on the worktop, purring, and observing him through sleepy eyes.

"So, what d'you think of Dottie, then?" he asked the cat. "Pretty special, huh?"

Snowball stared at him.

"If all goes according to plan, we'll be seeing a lot more of that little lady. I've got a good feeling, puss. Really good. There's something ... something great about her, but it's hard to put your finger on, you know?" He crossed his arms and considered. "She's funny. So easy to get on with. I feel that I've known her for ages – that old cliché is so true. No matter what life hurls at her, she always manages to muster a smile. That's a rarity, in my book. That's a special ingredient."

Snowball stretched her jaws in a yawn.

"That little gal's been through a hard time, but she's a tough cookie." Nick smiled. "We're seeing each other again on Friday night." He shut the dishwasher door and faced the cat, his hands on his hips. "Isn't that positive news, Snowy, huh?"

Snowball dropped lithely and silently from the counter and receded down the hall, tail high. Nick stood there, staring after the cat as she approached the door flap and insinuated her body through the small hatch, disappearing outside.

"Thanks for the feedback," he said and resumed his whistling.

He had to admit he was on a high. Here he was, a man of medicine, and Dottie had reduced him to feel like a giddy youngster, like a teenage kid thinking about a first date. He couldn't wait for Friday, if he were being honest. Couldn't wait to see her again. Things had gone great on their previous date, better than he'd expected them to, and it bode well for the future.

He had been nervous that perhaps he'd acted too hastily in asking her out. Following a recent separation and losing a baby, she might've thought him insensitive and been disinclined to get involved with anyone else so soon. But he was pretty sure that Dottie knew he respected her. On their date, he'd been as much of a gentleman as he knew how and believed it had paid off. They'd had fun and were at ease with each other, which was more important than most folk realised, Nick reflected. He had sat through one-sided dinner dates before, and they were hard work.

Nick poured himself a glass of wine and wandered into the living room.

The kiss – which had happened right here – well, it was a mistake, but he still didn't regret doing it. He had wanted to show her he cared, and he knew it had worked. When they'd kissed, he'd felt a firing of his emotions – at the softness of her small lips, at the intoxicating power of her scent, and at the slightest hint of her breath on his cheek. They had hit him at once in a delicious, simultaneous sensation.

The feeling had been over in seconds, but its smouldering effect had remained with him throughout that night, long after he had taken her home. All told, he liked her, and she liked him, and one kiss wasn't going to harm anyone, was it?

*****

Billy stood across the road from Cassidy's bungalow, obscured by shadows. Moonbeams lit the scheme here and there, enhancing and deepening the solid pools of darkness along the street. He had to prepare himself for what was to come. He was charged up on cocaine again, but his mind was surprisingly clear, like the first time he'd tried the stuff. He felt wired and able to conquer the world.

"I have the element of surprise," Billy said to himself. "And this gives me the advantage."

If the doctor had any real sense, he would be aware that a threat was in the offing. What idiot would steal another man's woman and not be prepared for the consequences? And what kind of man would Billy be, if he didn't make an example of Cassidy? If he didn't seek retribution?

Occasionally, Cassidy's form passed the window, although Billy couldn't decipher anything more than a shadow behind the drawn curtains. For the last few minutes, however, there had been no such signs of movement. It—

A quiet squeak drew Billy's attention to the door. He looked there, his eyes narrowing. He sniffed and ground his teeth.

The doc's white cat appeared through a flap – an opening that Billy hadn't even noticed. The animal came noiselessly down the drive, past Cassidy's shiny silver Audi. Its feline eyes glowed like jewels in the dark. The cat paused at the kerb, as if trained to scout for passing traffic, its flawless coat stark in the moonlight. After a

237

moment, it padded across the road, the white body headed almost directly for Billy.

He stepped out from the shadows, and the cat stopped in mud-strut, angled its neck, and yowled at him.

"Evening, puss," Billy said, squatting, rubbing his thumb and forefinger together, as if presenting a tasty morsel. "Can't stand the company in there, huh?" He glanced at the bungalow. "Well, I can't say I blame you for that."

The cat approached, displaying both caution and interest, sniffing at Billy's hand. A small, rough tongue licked at his fingertips, and the feline purred softly. Billy stroked the smooth white head, coaxing another purr, the cat working its neck playfully against him.

He scooped the animal up and stood with it in his arms.

"I suppose the humane thing is to put you out of your misery, huh? From tomorrow, you won't have anybody lookin' after you anyway. You'll starve in there, puss. You'll spend the rest of your days chasing dumb birds for your dinner."

The cat purred contentedly, comfortable in his embrace.

As he watched the bungalow, Billy's grip on the animal slowly increased. Tighter and tighter. Soon the furry body began wriggling in his arms, bucking frantically, trying to get away. Billy held on, applying more pressure.

"That's it, you struggle there ..."

The cat began hissing and writhing, trying to claw at him, but Billy's grip was uncompromising, and he kept his face clear of harm's way. As he wrung the life from the animal, he kept watch on the bungalow: Cassidy's shadow passed up there once again.

"Almost done, puss ... almost done."

Before long, the cat's frantic protests gradually subsided and came to a weakened stop.

"Catch you tomorrow, Dr Cassidy," Billy said. He discarded the cat's limp body by the roadside and went off into the night.

CHAPTER 35

At nine-thirty, Nick was watching an old Eastwood movie on TV. He loved Eastwood playing the no-nonsense copper; Clint did it better than anyone else and often threw in a laugh or two to boot. In front of the television, Nick was having a beer and eating cold chicken wings drenched in barbeque sauce. He licked noisily at his fingers. Snowball wasn't around, but that was par for the course: she was a night creature and sometimes didn't wander back until very late.

The phone rang as he was nibbling the last pieces of flesh from a rich-tasting wing. He wiped at his hands, reached from his armchair, and grabbed the handset. When he heard a familiar female voice, he sat up straight, almost capsizing his bottle of beer.

"Karine?"

"Hi, Nick. How have you been?"

He scratched at his cheek, clumsily switching the phone to his other ear. "Uh, where – where are you calling from?"

"I'm back in town. Got in this morning."

"Really? So, uh, where are you staying?"

"My sister's place. She said I could bunk with her until, well, until I talked to you."

"Talk to me?" Nick frowned. "About what?"

"Maybe I was a little hasty in leaving," she said.

"Karine, you sold your house and left town. You said you were going for good. What are you doing back here so soon?"

"Can I see you, Nick? Can we talk?"

He blew out a breath.

240

"Talk about what, Karine? You ended things. You said I wasn't what you were looking for. You said you didn't want to be saddled in Aradale all your life."

"I know, but I've had time to think ... Sometimes you need perspective. It's a woman's prerogative to change her mind, right?"

"Karine, this is—"

"I don't want to go into it now, Nick, not over the phone. Can I see you? Could we get together, just for a talk?"

Nick was shaking his head in disbelief. Truthfully, he believed he'd heard the last of her. Was *sure* he had. Karine had abandoned their relationship without a second thought, without looking back, and had made no bones about expressing her feelings. She could be a feisty mare, when she wanted to. This town wasn't for her, she'd said. Nick wasn't what she wanted, not anymore. There was a big world out there, she had said, and she was going to be part of it. He could remember the exchange with surprising clarity. It had taken place right here, in his bungalow. In this self-same room. Hell, hadn't he been sitting in this very chair? She had paced around in front of him, her long, white shiny legs on full display, tapering down from one of those revealing skirts she invariably wore.

"Nick, are you still there?"

"I'm here."

"I know you're probably surprised to hear from me. Are you free tomorrow, sometime?"

"Karine, I'll be honest with you, because I think that's always best. I don't reckon it would be a good idea."

"Hey, just hear me out, huh? Surely, I deserve that, after all the time we were together."

Nick pinched the bridge of his nose. "We're not together anymore, Karine."

"Hey, I'm trying to extend an olive branch here. I just want to talk to you."

"Come by the house tomorrow evening. I won't be home until then. I take it you can remember the way?"

"Of course I do," she said, emitting a silly little laugh. "Tomorrow evening sounds perfect, Nicky."

He said a brief goodbye and hung up. He muted the television. He shook his head and took another swig from his beer. What was *she* doing back here?

I've had time to think.

He didn't like the sound of that.

His relationship with Karine, which had lasted more than three years, was fun at first. They had travelled and holidayed together, but over the weeks and months, strains had appeared. The more time he spent with her, the more Nick realised they were very different people. Still, they *had* been together for years, so he had persevered when things became difficult, willing to make an effort to overcome the problems. But Karine had wanted out. This town had nothing to offer someone like her. She didn't want to be stuck here all her life.

Well, she had come back, and so expected him to drop everything and pick up where they left off. This supercilious element of her nature was one of her most unattractive qualities. It was too ingrained, too much a part of who she was. She couldn't change it any more than she could change the chestnut brown of her eyes. It they got back together, the problems – the same problems – would resurface. He was sure of that.

Judging by the sound of her voice, Nick believed that Karine wanted to get things restarted with him, but he was unwilling to accommodate her. She wouldn't like to hear it; but that was no longer his problem. He had tried with her before. And, of course, there were other considerations now.

There was Dottie to consider now.

*****

Billy sat at home, sniffing and coughing, with a Miller in his hand. His nose was bleeding again, and he had a kitchen towel stuffed up there to staunch the flow. The TV was on mute, showing Dottie on the screen. She ran and laughed soundlessly in the sunlight, her auburn hair flowing out behind her. He kept jabbing at the DVD remote, rewinding it over, and as he did, the darkness inside him grew deeper and deeper.

Tomorrow he would rectify everything, the whole thing. Tomorrow, Dottie and her man would realise that they shouldn't have wronged Billy. Shouldn't have tried to make him look like a fool, like a loser.

Tomorrow.

He looked at the unit on his left.

The plastic container was there, which he'd bought at the pet store that afternoon. The big spider was inside, all lumpy and hairy. Bits of rock and stones were in there with it. The thing barely moved. Its body was a strange-looking orange and black. Every now and then, it shifted

243

a little, sometimes touching a leg against the plastic container. He didn't mind spiders, on the whole, but even he had to admit it was a pretty ghastly-looking beastie. It would be a companion for Dottie and her fancy man, when they went into their grave. He'd be sure to show the spider to Dottie beforehand.

"You'll stop her little heart," he said, and swallowed the last of his beer.

CHAPTER 36

Dottie and Tara were eating breakfast – Frosties and Sugar Puffs – on Wednesday morning, when Lynette returned to Netherwood House after walking Rex. The little corgi whined, shaking off the early chill, and crossed the large kitchen to the comfort of his basket. Graham, not long home from night shift, stood by the sink, drinking a glass of milk.

Lynette shut the back door, shivered all over, and began undoing her waterproof jacket. Her cheeks were florid with cold.

"God, it's *freezing* out there today," she complained, hunching her shoulders.

"Brass monkeys," Graham concurred. "And what about that mist? I had to drive through town following the guy's lights in front. Then I practically trundled the last mile through the woods to get home."

Lynette peered out of the kitchen window, at the drab, fogbound morning. Dense mist hung in the air, obscuring the woodland and everything around it. "I could hardly see ten feet in front of me out there," she said. "It seemed to get worse as we were coming back to the house. I was half expecting to bump into the Jack the Ripper."

Graham smiled. "Bit far from Whitechapel, isn't he?"

"Who's Jack Ripper?" Tara whispered to Dottie.

Dottie touched the little girl's glossy black hair. "He was a very bad man who lived long ago, sweetheart."

"I'm serious," Lynette went on, unfurling the woollen scarf from her neck. "I had to put Rex on the leash, in case he disappeared and was never seen again. Typical Scotland. Heatwave, one minute, foggy as hell the next."

Mark entered the kitchen, yawning, and put his schoolbag on the floor. He was wearing his school uniform, his hair gelled in messy, random spikes. "Morning," he said, offering them all a half-hearted wave.

"Looking forward to the play tonight?" Lynette asked her son.

"Can't wait," Mark told her. "I always wanted to play a cow's bum."

Tara giggled, covering her mouth with her hand. Dottie laughed too, as much at Tara's reaction as what Mark had said.

"Are you going to join us tonight, for the grand opening of *Jack and the Beanstalk*?" Graham asked Dottie, placing his empty glass in the sink. "Fancy seeing Mark's acting debut as a cow's rear-end?"

"I think I'll stay here," Dottie replied. "You guys enjoy the show, though."

"Come along, Dottie," Lynette said, toeing off her rubber boots. "You're more than welcome. It should be a laugh, if Graham can stop talking long enough to let us hear the play."

"I'm sure it'll be great," Dottie said. "But I have to go back to school on Monday morning. I don't want the teachers to think I'm unable to work yet I can still go out and enjoy myself. They'll all be there tonight, so I'd better give it a miss."

"Dottie, that's crazy," Lynette said. "They know why you've been off work."

"I know, but I'd sooner just see them on Monday. You can record part of the play for me, and I'll watch it tomorrow."

246

"Oh, you can count on that," Graham said, mussing Mark's hair. "We can't pass up the chance to get this performance on film. I'll have my mobile primed and ready." He turned to Mark. "Want a lift to school, son?"

"You go to bed, mister," Lynette told her husband. "You've been working all night. I'll drive Mark to school. He's had enough of your jibes, anyway."

"You sure?" Graham asked. "It's like pea soup out there."

Lynette tilted her head sarcastically. "Men aren't the *only* ones who can navigate in heavy fog, Graham."

He held his arms up in defeat. "That's what a man gets for being considerate."

"You want to be considerate," Lynette said, gently pinching his cheek. "Stop telling crap jokes."

*****

Once astir that morning, Nick was instantly aware that Snowball wasn't around. It was unusual for the cat to absent herself at this hour. She was normally curled at the foot of his bed when he woke, sleeping soundly. It was more unusual still that she wasn't downstairs, either perched on the windowsill or dozing in her favourite armchair. She may have ventured outside, although early excursions were out of character for the cat. Like Nick, Snowball wasn't much of a morning lover.

He walked barefoot into the kitchen, his hands tucked into the pockets of his robe. He switched on the portable TV by the fridge, and news materialised on the screen. A glance out of the window showed

247

him – well, nothing really. The world was lost in heavy, impenetrable fog.

Nick began preparing breakfast, breaking eggs, whisking them, and pouring the mix into an omelette pan. As he was doing this, a knock sounded at his front door.

"Great timing, whoever you are ..." He took the eggs off the heat.

The caller was Mrs Brimstone from across the street. The old woman stood swaddled in a heavy duffel jacket with knobbly buttons. Behind her, every detail of the backdrop was lost in swirling tendrils of mist.

"Good morning, Mrs Brimstone," he said. "I hope you dropped breadcrumbs on your way over here."

She frowned. "Breadcrumbs?"

Nick shrugged. "A small joke. The weather, you know?"

"Oh, I see."

"Is something wrong?" he asked.

"I'm afraid I have some bad news, Nick. When I was on my way for my morning rolls, I found Snowball by the roadside." She motioned behind her at the fogbank.

"Snowball? Is she hurt?"

"I think she's dead," Mrs Brimstone said, sadly. "I'm so very sorry. She's cold, you see. Well, I thought I'd better come straight over and let you know. It seems she's been hit by a car, or something ..."

Nick scratched at his head, feeling sadness swell inside him. Snowball had been a gift from Karine and was the only pet he'd ever had. The house wouldn't be quite the same without her. "Uh, okay, thanks for letting me know. I'll get dressed and go take a look."

"She was a beautiful cat," the old woman said. "So friendly. She would come and see me when I was doing the garden. Always used to pop over and say hello." She smiled consolably and stepped away from the door, shuffling back into the mist, her huddled form instantly swallowed by the weather. In mere seconds, Nick couldn't see her any more.

The eggs went in the bin. His appetite had vanished. He trudged upstairs, showered quickly, and got dressed.

Outside, carrying a roll of black refuse sacks, he was taken aback by how little he could see, and how disoriented he was by the fog. Mrs Brimstone had said the cat was by the roadside, and so he had presumed he would locate Snowball without any trouble. But as he traced along the kerbside in the poor early-morning light, Nick found no sign of the cat's body. Indeed, after he had covered both sides of the road more than once, he had spotted no sign of his pet at all. At intervals, headlights passed slowly, almost sinisterly, through the thick fog, illuminating the surrounding haze.

Nick was beginning to feel frustrated when he finally came across her. Snowball's body lay three feet in from the road, on the dew-damp grass, and Nick didn't require a veterinary degree to know she was dead. He sighed, and squatted. He couldn't see any blood, but the cat's eyes were closed tightly, and the fixed rictus expression indicated a painful death.

He swallowed, forcing down a lump in his throat.

He hated that she had likely lain out here all night, exposed to the elements and alone. Only now, looking at the cat's broken body, did Nick realise how much he had loved the animal, and how much he would miss having her around. He shook open a couple of the black refuse bags and lifted Snowball's cold body from the grass.

CHAPTER 37

Before leaving for work, Nick pulled on a pair of old jeans and boots and dug a grave between his two cherry-blossom trees. The refuse bags containing the departed cat lay on the lawn beside him. Fog swirled around as he shovelled the dirt, augmenting the impromptu funeral's air of sombreness.

It was during the process of digging that he contemplated what might have brought about Snowball's unfortunate demise. The cat had known the roads and the area, known to be careful around passing traffic. It didn't make much sense that she'd been struck by a vehicle, as only residents passed through the scheme with any regularity, locals who rarely drove at excessive speeds. On the other hand, accidents did happen, and animals died on the roads every day. Moreover, the fog would definitely encumber a driver's sight and reaction time, increasing the likelihood of mishaps.

Had a driver killed the cat, however, wouldn't he or she have come and let Nick know? Nick's address was clearly engraved on the cat's collar, and his neighbours knew where Snowball belonged, in any case. Still, not everyone was blessed with a sense of honesty and morality. Had the impact taken place after dark – which it must have done, because Snowball had been alive last night – it would be all too easy for a driver to just carry on regardless.

Nick stopped shovelling and wiped the sweat from his brow.

Maybe someone had struck the cat without being aware of it. In such poor visibility, it was a conceivable scenario.

But Nick couldn't ignore the other possibility – the one he really didn't want to acknowledge. What if someone had purposefully hurt the cat? These days, malicious kids think nothing of torturing defenceless animals. Yet he didn't think such rogues roamed the streets in this area. The scheme was quiet, dull even, its inhabitants respectable.

What if someone had killed the cat because she was his?

As far as he was aware, he had no enemies. Or had he? From nowhere, Billy Hawthorn's face materialised in his mind's eye. Since Dottie left Billy, Nick had heard nothing of the man. And Dottie hadn't mentioned her husband making waves, or causing problems in the time since she had walked out. That in itself meant nothing, though. Maybe there was good reason for caution.

He remembered the hostile look in Hawthorn's eyes and the apathy he'd exuded throughout Dottie's trimesters. It had sometimes felt as if Billy resented the attention Nick gave Dottie, the circumstances notwithstanding.

He stood there in the fog, a hand resting on the shovel's handle.

Was Hawthorn aware that Nick and Dottie were on the cusp of a potentially fulfilling relationship? If not, Nick's ruminations were probably meaningless, and a touch paranoid. Alternatively, if Billy *did* know, then perhaps Nick should be watching his back – and Dottie's too. Billy Hawthorn didn't strike Nick as being blessed with an understanding nature; he struck him as the type of man incapable of forbearance. Nick wondered if he should call Dottie, just to check on her wellbeing.

Concealed in drifting fog, he lifted the black bag, gently lowered Snowball's body into the grave, and began shovelling the dirt in.

*****

Billy was driving – all but crawling – through Aradale, going about the humdrum motions of delivering his parcels. The job felt less humdrum today, though, because he was brimming with apprehension, adrenaline, and excitement. He sniffed repeatedly, still coked-up, enjoying the rock music that filled the van. Today was the day. Today was *the* day that Dottie and her fancy man would learn their biggest lesson. They would learn not to treat Billy Hawthorn as a nonentity.

Those pedestrians walking the streets were reduced to ghoulish spectres. He drove past the town church. Tall stained-glass windows and an arched entranceway loomed through the fog, the grounds cordoned by pointed black staves.

Billy's mobile rang. It was a few minutes after ten o'clock. He steered into a bus stop to take the call.

"The car's in a lockup on Candleberry Road," Boomer's deep voice informed him. "The farthest one from the right-hand side. Number Thirty-Nine. There's a black Ford Mondeo inside, a two-litre Zetec."

"That's great," Billy said. "I'll—"

"Just shut up and listen. The garage is unlocked, so all you have to do is lift the door and drop it when you leave. The keys are in the driver's visor. There's a full tank and another canister under the passenger seat. The items you specified are in the boot, in a black holdall. The car won't draw attention, but I'd advise you to get rid of it, once you finish whatever you're doing."

"I appreciate the help," Billy said.

"Remember what I said. Anything goes tits-up, and you're on your own. We never talked. We don't know each other. You hear what I'm saying?"

"I hear you," Billy said. "When do you want your money?"

"I'll be in touch," Boomer told him, and the line went dead.

Billy tossed the phone on the passenger seat. "Neanderthal prick."

He stared out at the fog, which crept and rolled in the van's headlights. The weather was perfect. It would conceal his comings and goings tonight, better than he could have ever hoped for. Like it was meant to be.

*****

Dottie was watching television in the living room with Tara and Rex. Lynette was in the study, tapping at her keyboard, lost in her world of romantic fiction. Graham was asleep upstairs, catching up on rest after his night shift. When Dottie's mobile jangled to life, she looked at the caller display, and smiled.

"I wasn't expecting to hear from you until the weekend," she said.

"Are you all right, Dottie?" Nick asked.

"Me? I'm great. Tara and I are watching *The Lion King*. Is something wrong?"

"No, nothing's wrong, really. I was wondering ... have you heard anything from Billy since you left him?"

Dottie stood and walked over to the bay window. "Why are you asking me that?"

"When I was making breakfast earlier, the old lady across the street, Mrs Brimstone, knocked at the door. She found Snowball dead by the side of the road."

"Oh no," Dottie said, drawing a concerned look from Tara. "Oh, the poor little cat. What happened to her?"

"I'm not sure. Maybe she was hit by a car, but the streets around my place are so quiet, you know? It doesn't feel right."

"Do you think Billy had something to do with it?"

Dottie heard him take a deep breath and let it out. "Truthfully, no, I don't. Hell, I don't know what I think. Does Billy know about us, Dottie? Is he aware we've been spending time together?"

"I don't know. It's none of his business, not anymore."

"Look, I'm sorry I bothered you with this. It was just a silly notion. I thought Billy might've been upset that we've seen a bit of each other. I'm letting my imagination run riot."

Dottie worried at her lip with her teeth. Not only did it all sound possible, it sounded disquietingly likely. Billy wouldn't want her to be with someone else: she had always known this, but had tried not to face it. Still, would he go so far as to kill an innocent animal? Someone's pet? She imagined that a man capable of violently raping his wife, that man would be capable of almost anything.

You best reconsider, Dorothy.

"I don't know what to say, Nick. Should I call him, do you think?"

"No, Dottie. No. He'll only feel like we're pointing fingers. And if he had nothing to do with it – which he probably didn't – then it would just stir trouble. There's no use irritating the man. Listen, don't worry about any of this. I just wanted to check you were okay, that's all. I'll see you Friday, and we'll talk some more."

"Are *you* all right?" she asked.

"Tough as old boots. I was just thinking out loud, but the more I think on it, the more unlikely it seems. The cat was probably just run down in the fog. It makes sense."

"I'm sorry, Nick. She was a lovely animal."

"She was," he said. "I'll call you Friday."

Dottie stood at the bay window, wondering again if Billy was capable of murdering Nick's cat. That would mean he knew where Nick lived – which, in turn, would probably mean Billy had been following him. Maybe Billy had been watching her, too. Was it possible that Billy was stalking them?

"Come on, Dottie," Tara said, kicking her legs impatiently and clapping her hands. "Come and see the movie."

"Coming, sweetheart," Dottie said. But she remained where she was, looking out at the mist-shrouded woodland.

CHAPTER 38

"He thinks Billy might've killed his cat?" Lynette asked, incredulously.

Finished with her daily stint at the word processor, she was attired in charcoal trousers and a mauve silk blouse, her black hair falling alluringly down her back. The morning had given way to afternoon and, from the windows of Netherwood House, the enveloping fog seemed to have deepened, intensified, pressing creepily against the glass panes.

"It sounded unlikely at first," Dottie replied, "but then I got to thinking."

Lynette raised a brow. "And?"

"Well, what if Nick's right?"

"Dottie, cats do get killed by cars, it happens all the time."

Dottie crossed to the living room door, which let into the kitchen. Tara was busy colouring a picture in there, with Rex dozing companionably at her feet. Dottie eased closed the door to ensure their conversation was not overheard.

"Does Billy even know about you and Nick?" Lynette asked, moving away from the window, rubbing the sides of her arms.

"I don't think so. I haven't tried to hide anything, but maybe he's seen us around. Or maybe ..."

"Maybe what?"

"After I talked to Nick, I thought about what he'd said. If Billy did this – and I know there's no proof or anything – then he must have followed Nick home, don't you think?"

Lynette shrugged, considering. "Not necessarily. He could've found his address in the phone book. That would be easier than following Nick home."

Dottie sat down. "God, I never thought of that."

"Dottie, if Billy was complicit in this, it really makes no difference how he discovered Nick's address."

"It doesn't?"

"No, it doesn't. What matters is that he's aware you're seeing another man, and he's reacting dangerously – to put it mildly." Lynette joined Dottie on the sofa and crossed her legs. "You know Billy better than anyone else, Dottie. Think about it. Would he really resort to murdering a cat because you left him? Can you see him doing that?"

Dottie touched her forehead. A throbbing migraine was setting up camp behind her eyes.

"Billy once told me of this dog he had, when he was young," she said. "It was a golden retriever called Alfred. He loved that dog. I could tell by the way he talked about it, how much he cared. I've seen old photos of him and the dog – pictures his mother took, probably. When I think about those photographs, part of me knows he would never hurt an animal. Part of me knows I'm being totally unfair, even thinking he'd do this. I mean, I haven't seen or heard from him since Tara's birthday. He deserves the benefit of the doubt, doesn't he?"

"And the other part of you?" Lynette urged.

Dottie recalled Billy's fingers biting into the back of her neck as he raped her, humiliated her, and took her dignity. She heard his gasping breaths as he thrust himself in and out of her on the dining-room table.

"The other part of me knows he's not that boy in the photos anymore. He's not the same man that I married. It's like everything inside him has corroded and rotted away. And what he's become ... what he's become is more than capable of killing Nick's cat."

*****

After work, Billy drove the Green Arrow van across town to King Edward Court. Today, in the soupy fog, the tenement flats appeared more dilapidated and ramshackle than ever. The high building stood sombre and grey. Protruding overflow pipes leaked water, which ran down the structure's concrete front to the weed-choked forecourt below.

It was just past five thirty and daylight was ebbing, the sky a sunless, colourless expanse of nothing. Billy fidgeted in the van's seat, watching the fog-shrouded shapes of the handful of people who passed by.

After twenty minutes, a woman left the flats and started down the walkway. Billy couldn't really see what she looked like, or what she was wearing – the fog was too thick – but the click-clack of bootheels and the confident strut told of a female, he was sure.

The woman unlocked a blue car by the roadside and got in. Billy gunned the van's engine. He gripped the wheel and waited, watching the blue car's rear lights come on, like two evil red eyes illuminating the gloom. The reverse lights activated next, and the woman's car began backing up, moving away from the vehicle parked in front. Across the street, about twenty yards back, Billy pulled the van out and started trundling along the road, mentally preparing himself. When the woman's blue car pulled out from the kerbside, he pressed the accelerator, increasing his speed.

Billy steered the Green Arrow van into the blue car's rear end, creating a heavy impact, and the car – he could now see it was a Volkswagen – was nudged forward.

The VW's brake lights flashed on, the driver's door swung open, and the woman was out like a shot, marching up to his window.

"What the hell are you doing? Are you *blind*?" she barked at him. "I was pulling out, and you rammed straight into me!"

Jesus, Billy thought, trying to keep a straight face. The woman had buck teeth, big specs, and was about three stone overweight. "Jeez, I'm terribly sorry," he said. "I was coming along here, and I didn't see you at all."

"Are you serious?"

Billy opened his door and stepped down from the van. He and the woman checked the back of her car, which had a broken light and indicator. Red and orange shards of plastic littered the road. Billy's bumper looked unscathed.

The woman put her hands on her waist and shook her head. "Were you even looking where you were going?"

"I'm so sorry," Billy said again, biting his tongue for the greater good. "It's difficult to see in this fog."

"Well, I'm not responsible for this," she pointed out adamantly, folding her arms.

Billy ducked into the van and reappeared with a pen and notebook. He scribbled down his details and indicated the Green Arrow logo embossed on the vehicle's flank. "You can see the side of the van there, so you know my details are legit." He tore off the notebook page and offered it to her. "My work insurance will cover any repairs to your car. I really am sorry about all this, believe me."

The woman's standoffishness seemed to wilt at Billy's niceties. Hell, he was starting to be pretty impressed with his own performance.

"Well, I suppose there's no real damage done," she conceded with a sigh, toeing the broken shards with her boot. "But you should really watch where you're going, especially in this weather. You could have flattened a child, you know."

"You're right, I know," Billy agreed. "I'll pay more attention. I'm usually such a conscientious driver. God, sometimes it takes an incident like this to sharpen you up."

She looked at him. "What's your name?"

"Billy. Billy Hawthorn." He indicated the piece of paper he'd given her. "Says just there, see?"

Billy couldn't believe it when she actually smiled at him.

"Okay, Billy. I'll get the damage repaired, and my insurance company will contact your employer." She shrugged, and her expression became almost apologetic. "I'm sorry I snapped at you. It's been quite a long day."

"Hey, don't say sorry. I'm the one in the wrong, remember?"

She smiled again, revealing those crooked teeth. Then she got back in her VW, the suspension dipping under her weight. The engine fired, and she drove off into the fog.

"What a stupid fucking sow," Billy said, settling himself in the van again.

He manoeuvred into the space vacated by the woman's VW and got out, locking the van doors. He glanced at the tenement flats. Angela Dunbar's high window was barely decipherable in the thick fog. She'd be waiting up there for him. He considered going to see her, just to make sure everything was all right. But that would only entail leaving her apartment again, and someone might remember that.

"Oh, almost forgot," he said, reopening the van one more time. From underneath the passenger seat, he slid out an old shoebox fastened with two elastic bands. "Better not forget the special guest."

He set off on foot, away from King Edward Court. As he moved through the fog, like a dark phantom in the descending evening, he replayed the altercation with the woman in the Volkswagen. He'd wanted to slap her – slap her hard – but that wouldn't do. Not today. The little charade wasn't about violence.

It was about being remembered.

CHAPTER 39

When Billy arrived at Candleberry Road, he ducked towards a high wooden fence, and squeezed through a space created by a missing plank. The defaced lockups were many, two adjacent rows of garages stretching into the distance. The metal doors had long been subjected to graffiti – crude depictions of male and female genitalia, and some pretty colourful language, too. At the far end, he found number Thirty-Nine, which, as Boomer had said, was indeed the last garage.

He lifted open the door, which swung upwards and folded away into the roof space. The caustic reek of petrol pervaded the enclosure. Billy noticed a light cord and pulled it, illuminating a florescent above his head. The garage floor was heavily marred in dark stains. A few old canisters and boxes were lined on a shelf. As Boomer had promised, the black Mondeo was there, sleek and polished.

Billy stepped around and opened the car's boot, where he found the black holdall. He unzipped it, looked inside, and nodded appreciatively. He placed the shoebox in the holdall and zipped it closed again.

Behind the wheel, he folded down the visor, and the keys dropped into his lap. They were attached to a ring, adorned with a little plastic axe. Billy grinned, wondering if Boomer had been trying to make a joke, but decided he probably hadn't: Boomer had about as much humour in him as Dracula.

He slotted the key into the ignition, and the engine fired effortlessly. The flick of a switch lit the interior's dials. The petrol gauge indicated a full tank. He checked beneath the passenger seat, finding a small canister of fuel. He was unsure why Boomer had thought it necessary to supply such a thing. Then again, it would come in handy when disposing of the car and burning his clothes.

He edged the Mondeo from the garage, went back to put out the light, and lowered the door. Then he was accelerating away, grinning broadly. The wheels are in motion, he thought, climbing through the gears. The goddamned wheels are in motion...

*****

Cassidy wasn't home when Billy parked the Mondeo down the street from the doctor's bungalow. The place was in darkness. No car in the drive. The night was closing in, and fog still hung suspended in the air like some manner of a chemical leak. He had no idea when Cassidy was due to return, but was content to wait it out a while. If it grew late, and the doc had not appeared, Billy would have to consider postponing the whole thing,

His eyes heavy, Billy began dozing and snapping awake. To counterbalance his tiredness, he arranged two lines of cocaine on a roadmap from the glove compartment and snorted them through a five-pound note.

He tipped his head back, coughing.

Sitting there watching Cassidy's home, Billy eventually started thinking about his father. Alzheimer's and a stroke. It didn't sound like the old man had much time left before he shuffled off his mortal coil. He was probably close to it now, lying in the hospital, helpless and incapable. It might be more humane to put him out of his misery. A syringe filled with – well, whatever poison they used on death row would do just fine, he reckoned. It wouldn't require much to end a withered fool like him.

One summer evening, when he was eight or nine years old, Billy had watched his father working his way through a bottle of vodka. Billy's little brother had been out playing with friends. Billy was worried that night, because he could always tell when the old man was reaching a tipping point. His father would grow silent and start staring, although when he was in such a state, it looked as if the man wasn't really seeing anything. His beady eyes would roll around in their sockets as comprehension ebbed away. His scarce words would emerge as little more than angry slurs. He would typically miss his mouth with the glass and slop booze over himself.

That particular evening, his father had been enraged because he'd lost money on bets, a fairly common occurrence. Oiled beyond any control, his father had decided to make something to eat. Billy had watched him try this many times, and it never ended well. Some of the food would invariably make it into the pan, but a lot would land on the floor and be running down the cupboard doors. That night, once he'd tossed whatever he could find into the pan, he succeeded in tipping the lot across the kitchen linoleum, the frying pan as well. When Billy had tried to help clean it up, his father had seized his wrist and pressed Billy's palm against the red-hot cooker ring. Pain screamed through Billy's young mind as the heat seared his skin. The kitchen filled with the awful stink of burnt flesh. Man, talk about agony ... He had never felt pain like that. Before or since.

It had been utter lunacy, trying to live with such a man. If he had been a little older, Billy could have stood up to him more. He could

265

have protected his brother more. He could have escaped the old man's clutches sooner. But what does a kid of that age know about going it alone? Without his mother there in his corner, how could a child under ten deal with abuse on that level? What sort of beast would subject a child to that kind of torture, for no reason?

Now, Billy raised his right hand and looked at it, back and front. He flexed his fingers, amazed that the hand hadn't just withered and disintegrated, leaving him with a shapeless stump.

It was nearing seven p.m. when Cassidy's Audi swept into the street and ascended the driveway. Billy sat up, squinting, pinching at his nose with his fingers. The doctor stepped out of the car in a midnight-blue suit. He opened the bungalow's door before returning to the Audi and popping the boot.

Billy's eyes narrowed, struggling to focus on the poor visibility. He rubbed at them with the heels of his hands. Cassidy was lugging several shopping bags into the bungalow. He came back and made a second trip. When he'd emptied the boot, he locked the car from his keyring, the indicators flashing in the thick fog, and Cassidy went inside.

Lights went on in one room. Then another.

Billy was out of the Mondeo quickly, slipping his hands into latex gloves. He grabbed the holdall from the boot and walked casually along the misty street, up the drive towards the bungalow's front door.

The frosted, leaf-pattern glass revealed dim light from inside. He was prepared to break in, if need be – he had what he needed to do this in the holdall – but he was banking on Cassidy's door being unlocked: the man had just arrived home, after all, and he likely wouldn't lock up until later.

Taking a last cursory glance around, Billy reached out and tried the door handle, slowly. He eased it down to its limit and applied gentle pressure with the weight of his shoulder. For a second, nothing happened, and he was poised to let go – then the door yielded, opening an inch inwards. It *was* unlocked, just snug in its frame. Billy pressed his eye to the open space, peering between the door and jamb.

An unlit, lemon-coloured hallway. A decoratively carved three-legged table stood about four feet from the door. Light bled from the end of the hall, where Billy presumed the kitchen was situated. A door lay partially open; the sounds of Cassidy's movements were clear: cupboards being opened and closed.

The doc was putting his groceries away.

Billy opened the door wide enough to slip through with the holdall and quietly shut it again. He hesitated in the dull hallway, adrenaline surging through his body. He could feel his heartbeat, feel a pulse in his inner ear. If Cassidy were to open the kitchen door and glance into the hall right now, Billy would be seen, and any attempt at surprise would be lost.

He sidestepped through a white-panelled door, into a room to his left. It was dark inside, and Billy could decipher the outline of a single bed and headboard. Presumably this was a spare bedroom. A shadow-draped wardrobe stood against one wall. Tall mirrored doors concealed a closet by his side. Billy's stealthy movements reflected eerily in the silvery glass. Cassidy likely slept elsewhere, he thought. Billy wondered if Dottie had given herself to him in this house.

267

Distant sounds continued from the kitchen. These noises calmed him a little; they assured him that Cassidy was busy and not on his way into this bedroom. Not that it would matter to Billy if he was sprung, not really. It would make everything a little more complicated and violent, sure, but the outcome would be the same.

Billy squatted and unzipped the holdall, feeling blindly among the tools. His fingers found the circular suction cup and diamond cutter. Eventually, he located the weighty steel of the crowbar and removed it. The coldness of the bar seeped through his latex gloves as he closed his fingers around it. Billy felt powerful toting the weapon. Powerful, and in control.

He slid the holdall against the wall with his foot. He would come back for it, once he had taken care of the doctor.

Billy eased his head past the bedroom doorway, peering into the hall. The kitchen door remained ajar. Cassidy passed by the narrow opening. Billy's heart drummed frantically, the cocaine and adrenaline combining in one supercharged hit. He gripped the crowbar and began creeping sure-footedly down the hallway.

Then he heard two sharp knocks at the front door.

CHAPTER 40

Nick ceased putting his groceries in the cupboards, walked down the hall, and opened the door. Karine stood there before him, all tumbling red hair and long, luscious legs.

"Hello, Nick," she said, spreading her arms. "Here I am."

"There you are."

"You look well," she told him. "Hey, this fog is something else, huh? The taxi driver could hardly see where he was going. He took about a *thousand* years to drive across town."

Nick looked past her and saw the taxi's headlights drawing off from the kerb.

He stepped aside, and she slinked past him with a smile, trailing a rich scent into the hallway. Nick remembered that aroma well – it had lured him in many times – but he couldn't recall the name. No doubt she had selected it especially, trying to trigger old memories.

"I was just putting the groceries away," he explained.

"No sweat," she said. "So, where's that adorable little cat of yours?"

They entered the kitchen.

"She died. A neighbour found her this morning, as it happens. We think she might have been run over. In the fog, you know?"

"Oh, Nick." She placed her painted fingers on his chest, and pouted. "I'm so *sorry*."

"Me too. Do you want something to drink? White wine, right?" He opened the fridge, poured a glass, and handed it to her by the stem.

"Aren't you going to join me?"

He shook his head. "No, thanks. I was about to make something to eat, actually."

"Well, don't let me stop you."

Nick regarded her. The denim skirt left little to the imagination. Her shapely thighs were any man's dream, and looked as good as ever, tapering all the way to her open-toed high heels. A little leather handbag – worth a small fortune, if he knew Karine – was looped over one shoulder. Her mouth, as usual, worked incessantly on chewing gum. Her false eyelashes were long and dark, her scarlet lips glistening and attractive. Like the handbag, the chocolate-coloured leather jacket probably set her back a pretty penny. For Karine, money was no concern when it came to clothes. Clearly, she had made an effort tonight; but then she always did. It you've got it, flaunt it: that was her mantra.

"What are you doing here, Karine?"

She looked expectantly at him. "Aren't you glad to see me?"

"I'm just asking what you want."

Her mouth stopped working on the gum. "Well, maybe I was a little hasty when I left. Let's give it another chance, Nick. I want to give *us* another chance."

Despite himself, Nick smiled. "You wanted to end the relationship, so it ends. Now you want to start over, so we start over. Just like that?"

"I made a mistake," she said. "I shouldn't have walked out the way I did." She sipped the wine and set down the glass, then stepped towards him and laid her hand on his chest again. "I know I was a bitch to you, Nick, but I want to make it up. Can't we just pretend it never happened?"

"What's changed?" he asked, genuinely interested.

"Well, you know ... I've had time to think, and I realised that we were a good thing. I can see you've no intentions of making this easy on me. I suppose I deserve that?"

"It's not about making anything easy or hard, Karine. Things aren't the same. When you left, I assumed you were gone for good. That's what you told me, remember?" Nick moved away from her. "Besides, there were too many problems. You had no tolerance for my working hours. I can't just drop everything whenever you snap your fingers. That's not the kind of work I do."

"I know, and I understand."

"But anyway, as I said, things aren't the same anymore."

Karine folded her arms. He saw a glisten of moisture in her eyes. God, he hoped she didn't turn on the waterworks.

"What things aren't the same?" she asked, suspiciously. "Is there someone else?"

"Yes."

Karine finished her wine in an uncouth mouthful and looked down at the floor. "Well, if you'd said *that* in the first place, it would have saved me making a fool of myself."

"You haven't made a fool of yourself. Telling someone you care about them doesn't make you a fool."

She pursed her lips and delved into her bag, removing a Kleenex. "Who is she?"

"I didn't go looking for someone after you left, Karine. This other person, it just happened. It has nothing to do with you."

"Do you love her?"

Nick was taken aback. Strangely, he hadn't considered it before, not in black and white, anyway. He slotted his hands in his trouser pockets and shrugged. "Yeah, I think maybe I do."

"In that case, I should go. I'm obviously wasting my time here."

"Karine, I—"

"Save it, Nick." She pushed past him, dabbing at her nose with the tissue. "I get the picture. I'm sorry I bothered you."

"Can I call you another taxi? I could give you a lift, if you want?"

"I don't *want* a lift."

She marched down the hallway towards the door. "See you around," she tossed back, almost spitefully, before opening the door and stepping outside. It closed with a slam – hard enough to rock one of the pictures on the wall – and Nick winced.

"See you around," he said.

He took a few steps and straightened the sailboat seascape. Her perfume lingered in the air. He wondered whether he should have handled that with a little more tact, but decided it was for the best. Rip off the band-aid.

In the kitchen, feeling somewhat weary, he filled a pan with baby potatoes and cut them in half with a steak knife. He topped the pan with water and set it to boil. After checking the fridge's shelves, he opened a packet of chicken breasts and laid two succulent pieces on a tinfoil-covered baking tray. He wasn't too hungry – hadn't been all day – but he had to eat, regardless. The chicken went into the oven's top shelf, and he screwed on the heat.

He couldn't believe the nerve of that woman.

Did she really think she could waltz in and out of his life at will, trampling on his feelings? As long as Karine was happy, she didn't give a damn about other people. Sure, she was an attractive woman – nobody would dispute that – but when he weighed everything together, she didn't have many more commendable traits. In fact, now that he had considered it, he realised she wasn't even a particularly nice person. Looks alone weren't enough to sustain a relationship, especially when the relationship was strained to the point of snapping.

He looked down at Snowball's litter tray in the corner. It was still hard to believe the cat wasn't going to come wandering back. The house felt curiously deserted without her. Whenever Nick glanced at the windowsills or armchairs, he expected to see her white face there, watching him.

He grabbed a beer from the fridge. Hell, he deserved one tonight. He would nurse it while his dinner cooked. After twisting off the cap, he took a long swallow—

—and felt a shadow pass over the room.

Nick froze with the bottle to his lips, sensing the presence of someone behind him. He whirled around instinctively, but had time only to confirm his suspicions. A black-clad figure loomed before him, and Nick felt something hard crash down on his forehead. His fingers opened, and the beer bottle dropped. The shooting pain was intense – followed by a blinding white light.

And all his thoughts ceased.

CHAPTER 41

When Nick regained consciousness – a swirling, sickly sensation – his mind felt scrambled, as if he was recovering from a near-death or out-of-body experience. He did not know where he was, just that his head was in a world of pain. His eyes still closed, his initial thoughts were that he'd been in an accident – a car wreck, maybe. Behind the pain, he tried to think, tried to recall the last thing he had been doing, but only further pain registered.

The ache in his head morphed from a dull throb to a sharp intensity. Something was seriously wrong. Piecemeal, his bearings woozily returned, and he realised he was sitting in a chair.

Reflexively, he attempted to touch the headwound – was that blood seeping down his face? – but his hands were fettered securely behind him. His ankles were also bound. He could barely move at all.

He opened his eyes to a blurred view of his kitchen. He tasted the distinctive coppery flavour of blood. He felt a nauseated, sick feeling in his stomach, and the urge to throw up was almost overwhelming. When his vision focused, he saw a figure pacing back and forth before him. A man – the assailant – was dressed in black jeans and a black top, and was repeatedly sniffing. The moment of the attack gradually returned to Nick. He had been preparing dinner. Having a beer. Someone behind him…

"I switched your cooker off," a voice said. "I know the condemned man is usually entitled to the last meal, but in this case, it isn't really practical."

Nick blinked twice, squinting. "Billy? Is that ... is that you?"

274

"No flies on you, Doc. I had a look around your place while you were napping. Very nice. You do all right for yourself."

Nick squinted again, seeing Billy's hateful face swim into focus. He looked bad, very gaunt and pale. His bald head caught the light from the ceiling. By his feet was a black holdall bag.

"What the hell's going on?" Nick asked groggily.

"That was one of my questions."

"What?"

"Who's the redhead that just left?"

Nick had to think. "An old ... just an old friend."

"Uh-huh. You got them throwing themselves at you from every angle, hey? Well, she didn't sound too friendly to me. She sounded a bit pissed at you."

"What ... what do you want, Billy?"

"You've been doing my wife. That's not good, Nicky boy. Not good at all."

Nick felt his concentration fading again. His head constantly wanted to drop. He heard the rushing of a tap, and cold water was flung in his face, snapping him awake. He shook off the excess liquid, his eyes wide. Trickles and chilled droplets streamed down his shirt collar and down his back.

"I said: you've been doing my wife."

Nick shook away more of the water. "She left you, Billy."

"How long's it been going on?"

Nick took a deep breath, trying to quell the urge to puke. "There's nothing going on. We're just friends."

"If you lie to me, we'll get off on the wrong foot." Billy chuckled sadistically. "I heard what you and the redhead were talking about. You told her you loved my wife. Tell me, what chance does my marriage have, when my wife's doctor starts helping himself? That's your thing, is it, Nick? Do you like to perv on patients, and seduce them? Pregnant women come to you for advice and support, and Nicky boy sees sexual opportunities? That makes you a sleaze. You should be struck off."

Nick spat away the water, settling on his lips. He tried to move, testing the restraints, but whatever bound his arms and legs, held fast.

"Billy, this is lunacy. Surely you understand that sometimes relationships fail? Sometimes they don't work out. People aren't ... aren't always compatible, and it's just time to call it a day. It doesn't" – Nick shook his head – "it doesn't mean anyone is in the wrong. It's just best to move on, maybe meet someone else."

"You don't know me. Don't make assumptions about my life."

"I'm not. Dottie told me you treated her like shit."

Nick regretted saying it immediately, but the words were out, and he could not take them back. He was bound to a chair, with his head bashed, in the company of someone clearly taking no prisoners: the situation didn't need antagonising. This man could seize a knife and hack Nick's eyes out. He could do just about anything he pleased.

"Is that what she said to you? That I treated her like shit?"

Nick looked away.

"Doesn't it bother you? I sat in your office, and you dealt with us as a couple. We were expecting a baby. Aren't you people supposed to be ... ethical?"

276

"Is *this* what you call ethical, Billy?"

"We're talking about your ethics, smart mouth. Not mine."

Nick inhaled and worked his neck a little, and even this slight movement set in motion a world of unpleasantness. "Billy, I'm bleeding. I'm hurt. I need to get my head looked at."

"You're not steering this ship, Cassidy. I am. I asked about your ethics."

Nick realised, much to his regret, that he had to talk to the man. What choice did he have?

"Whatever you think of me, I'm not in the habit of dating patients," he said. "I like Dottie, but I wouldn't have acted on it. I wouldn't have approached her, not while she was with you. You and she were separated, and Dottie and I are both adults. She can get another doctor, so there's no question of ethics."

"So you can bang her with a clear conscience? Very professional."

"You don't know what you're talking about."

Billy picked up a crowbar from the counter and tapped it against his leg. "Enlighten me."

"If you had any sense, you'd still have her in your life. Dottie's a sensitive, caring woman. She's kind, warm, and probably the most loyal individual I know. She'd do anything to help another person. You're a bully. A bully who, I suspect, gets his kicks killing animals." Nick tasted blood, and the absurdity of the situation suddenly angered him. "The lowest form of existence on earth."

Billy's face darkened. "Keep talking. It'll make the next couple of hours even sweeter."

Nick wanted to keep quiet, but damn it, this needed saying. The man was living in a fantasy world. "Look at the state of you, Billy. You're an addict, right? I can tell by looking at you. What is it – speed? Coke? You can't stop sniffing and touching your nose. You can't stand still longer than two seconds. And you wonder why Dottie doesn't want you? I'd bet you beat her too—"

"Shut up."

"I'd bet that a coward willing to choke a cat is more than capable—"

Billy punched him in the face. Nick's head lolled around on his shoulders, giving rise to another harsh burst of pain.

"Have you fucked my wife?"

Nick lowered his gaze again. He was loath to reveal how much discomfort he was in, but couldn't really hide it. "Don't be ridiculous."

"She's been here, in this house. You've been to restaurants. I've seen."

"That's what people do," Nick said resignedly. "They spend time together. They go for meals. It's called being civilised."

"You're in love with her. You've been sleeping with her."

Nick was staring into his lap. Already he could feel a bruise closing his left eye. "Is that what you do with your time? Skulk about, spying on us?" He looked up and met Billy's icy glare. "Is that what happened with my cat? Did she just happen to pass by when you were outside?"

"I throttled that little shit because she was yours, pure and simple."

Nick nodded. "Then you're a maniac."

278

"I'm settling a score with someone who's been banging my wife. Most men would understand that, Nick. And accept it. You've been busted, and you'll have to take what's coming to you."

"Don't you even know her?" Nick asked, dumbfounded. "Don't you know she wouldn't leap into bed with anybody? You're married to her, Billy. Think about it."

Billy stared at him.

"Enough," he eventually said. "I've heard all I wanna hear from you. Here's what's going to happen. I'll move your car" – Billy held up Nick's keys – "and pull my car to the house. I'll untie your feet, so you can walk outside. You'll be blindfolded, so don't think about trying anything, or I'll break your legs. You're gonna get into the boot of the car, and we'll have a little drive. Now, if you give me *any* shit, I'll bash your skull in again, and then you'll go in the boot anyway. Either method works for me."

Billy produced a long black length of cloth from his jacket and stepped behind him. Nick struggled at the restraints, but Billy grabbed the sides of his head. "I'll snap your neck right here, if you don't stay still."

Nick stopped moving. Billy secured the blindfold at the back of his head, tight and secure; and Nick's world fell into darkness.

"Just you relax, Nicky old boy. As I said, this can be done easily or hard. Makes no odds to me."

"Where the hell are you taking me?" Nick asked, unable to conceal the trepidation in his voice.

"Bottle going, huh? Well, I won't ruin the surprise, Nick. All will be revealed in good time."

"I'm claustrophobic," Nick said.

"Claustrophobic?"

"I have a phobia of enclosed spaces. I can't be locked in a car boot."

"I know what it means, dickhead."

"I'm serious, I can't be closed in there."

"If that's true," Billy said, "then you're in for a fun night, my friend."

The next sound Nick heard was a roll of tape being unwound, before Billy began wrapping it around his mouth.

PART THREE

THE HOUSE IN THE WOODS

CHAPTER 42

After forcing Cassidy into the Mondeo's boot – the idiot had barely even struggled – Billy drove away from the doctor's up-its-own-arse housing scheme.

He handled the Zetec slowly and surely, the headlights sweeping over parked vehicles, sprawling lawns, bollards, and precisely trimmed hedges, all of which quickly appeared and vanished in the mist. On both sides of the street were lighted bungalows, heavily obscured by the stagnant atmosphere. He reached the end of the road, stopped, and indicated left. There were no other cars around to heed the signal – but this wasn't a time to be tempting fate. Tonight, he would be the perfect driver. Tonight, he was Mr Careful.

No going back now. He had overstepped the line, upped the ante, crossed the threshold – and he had no choice except to go on. Everything was falling into place, though. He had assumed Cassidy would have posed a bigger problem, but the man had been tamed easily. Thanks to the element of surprise. The doctor had overlooked Billy, discounted him, as if Billy Hawthorn wasn't worth worrying about. Soon, he'd find such idle complacency would cost him his life. That would teach him to keep his pecker away from other men's wives.

Billy sniffed as he approached a junction. He indicated and turned right, onto Prince Street. Shopfronts and signs glowed dully through the fog. Those walking the streets were huddled and dark. He passed The Wide Mouthed Frog, and a fleeting glance revealed the candlelit restaurant was all but empty. There were more cars on the street here, so Billy kept the Mondeo at a steady thirty.

He drew up to traffic lights, halfway down Prince Street, three vehicles from the front. He let the engine idle quietly. A vehicle rolled to a stop behind him, and a glance in the mirror was enough to make out the word POLICE, stencilled across the bonnet.

Billy tensed and gripped the wheel. Oh, perfect.

His eyes went to the mirror again. The cop car's two occupants were pretty much indistinguishable, nothing more than dark shapes. Had they zeroed in on his Mondeo? Were they doing a radio check on his plates, right now? Boomer had said the car was clean – but what if he'd been lying? How could Billy explain a blindfolded, gagged man in the boot of a car that wasn't even his? How would he explain a holdall full of tools and a shoebox containing a big-ass spider?

Beads of sweat formed on his hairless head. His palms were clammy too. Eagerly, he studied the traffic lights, which seemed to have stalled on red. *Change, you bastards. Change, for Christ's sake, so I can get moving.*

Amber.

That's it. He wasn't doing anything to attract attention. Just driving through town, nice and easy. Seatbelt on, two hands on the wheel. That's it. No problemo.

Green.

He selected first gear, eased off the clutch, and began through the traffic lights. The police car stayed with him. Billy imagined those blue flashers coming to life, shining brilliantly through the fog. Then, that would be it. They would snoop into everything, asking for his paperwork, checking over the car – and all Cassidy would have to do is start thumping on the boot. The maggot would make as much noise as possible, if he knew the cops were there. Then, it would be curtains for Billy boy.

He indicated left, taking Oldwick Road, which curled down towards another set of traffic lights. Beyond this, the road extended out of town. If he made it through these lights, he was set. The cops wouldn't stay with him as he headed out in the direction of Netherwood House. Surely to God.

He approached the lights, praying for green, but nothing was going to be easy about this. Not a damned thing. The light was red. Bright, bold, halting red. He looked in the rear-view again, seeing the police car ease around the corner onto Oldwick Road, directly behind him. First in line at the lights now, Billy swallowed and slowed the Mondeo to another halt.

The road here was divided into two lanes. Billy was on the left, headed straight on. The right lane was for traffic bound in the opposite direction. There were no other vehicles nearby, though – just Billy and the cops. He remained stock-still as the police car inched alongside the Mondeo. They were now parked parallel to him. If he risked a glance across, he'd see the dude in the passenger seat. Shit, if he and Billy reached out their windows, they could shake hands with each other.

Do not look.

He studied the lights.

They stayed red.

Maybe he *should* look across. If he ignored the cops and kept staring straight ahead, they might assume he had something to hide. He was unsure what to do ... He certainly couldn't talk his way out of this. Say, what's that beaten-and-bound chap doing stuffed in your boot, sir? Do you mind if we have a glance inside that holdall?

Billy scratched at his cheek as nonchalantly as possible – which felt anything but – and let his head turn slowly towards the cop car. In that instant, he met the officer's gaze. The guy was staring at him.

The cop's window came down.

Christ.

Billy looked to the lights, his mouth drying up. They stayed red, as if to spite him, and two or three cars drifted across the box junction. He turned back to the cop car and saw the officer was leaning out of his window now. He was square-jawed, his hair crewcut short. Mr Authority. This was it. He was done for. With the simple wag of one finger, the officer made an unmistakable gesture for Billy to lower his window.

He pressed it down and felt the night's chill seep in.

"Maybe you'd like to turn on your fog lights?" the cop said. "This is the weather they're made for, in case you hadn't noticed."

"Right," Billy said. "I forgot all about them."

The guy's window raised smoothly again, but he kept staring through the glass.

Red changed to amber, and amber to green, and the police car headed off in the opposite direction. Billy exhaled, watching their rear lights recede into the fog. Those taillights grew blessedly weaker, until no sign of them could be seen anymore.

Billy thought he heard Cassidy banging inside the boot. He activated his fog lights and drew away, headed for Netherwood House, his heart still thumping like a triphammer.

CHAPTER 43

"Two cannibals eating a clown, one says to the other, Does this taste funny to you?"

Lynette groaned and looked over at Dottie. "Tumbleweed time again. Sometimes I can't believe I actually walked down the aisle with him."

Dottie touched Graham's arm affectionately. "Lynette! What a terrible thing to say."

"Hear! Hear!" Graham agreed, feigning hurt. "Some women just don't know how lucky they are."

Tara gazed up from inside her jacket's hood. "Why would a cannonball eat a clown?"

"*Cannibal*, sweetheart," her father said. "Not cannonball."

The little girl frowned. "What's that?"

"Never you mind, little lady," Lynette said, tying Tara's zipper and wiping something from her daughter's cheek. They were in the kitchen of Netherwood House, preparing to leave for Mark's class's rendition of *Jack and the Beanstalk*.

"Dottie, are you positive you won't come along?" Lynette asked.

"I'll get a look at it when you come back – just remember to film it for me." She smiled at them. "Do you think Mark will be in costume yet?"

"I imagine he'll wait till the last minute before climbing into that getup," Graham said. He scooped his car keys from the counter. "We all set?"

"Will Mark be dressed like a cow?" Tara asked, grinning.

"That's the plan, honey," said Lynette. "Jack swaps the cow for magic beans, and climbs the beanstalk, into the clouds. He finds the giant's castle and steals his hen, one that lays golden eggs."

Tara looked spellbound. "Golden eggs?"

"That's right." Lynette shrugged into her leather jacket, regarding the foggy night from the window. "Are you driving, Graham?"

He dangled the car keys from a finger. "Ready when you are."

"I'll leave these here, then," she said absently, placing her BMW's keys on a hook by the fridge. "Well, I think we're ready, people. What are you planning tonight, Dottie? A glass of wine and a DVD? There's plenty of plonk in the fridge there."

"I think I'll run a bath, have an early night."

Dottie accompanied them through the house, Rex bringing up the rear. At the front door, she watched them climb into Graham's Volvo. Lynette and Tara waved from inside the car. Dottie waved back at them, until the Volvo's red lights were gone. The temperature had plummeted, and she rubbed at her arms through her sweater, feeling gooseflesh pimples on her skin. Rex mewled at the dark and shook himself down, sniffing eagerly at the air.

"Not a good night to be outdoors, pooch," Dottie said to the corgi, and they went back inside together.

*****

Nick lay in the car boot, eyes covered, extremities bound, concentrating fiercely on remaining calm. He must not panic. He must not. If he did, this fiasco would worsen tenfold. He had told Billy the truth about his claustrophobia. It was a problem he'd suffered from all his days, and although it was not a major life hindrance, Nick was

288

always aware of it, and avoided situations where his tolerance might be tested. Elevators and suchlike, he could bear. They were short journeys and nothing too taxing. But this ... this situation had the potential to break him, if he didn't try to stay calm.

The punch to his head still hurt like hell. His bruised eye had swollen and was almost closed. The initial blow hurt too. If felt like there was an egg growing on his forehead. Now that he lay on his side, the need to vomit had subsided a little, but the swimmy sense of disassociation and light-headedness remained. And he was drowsy, awfully drowsy.

Hawthorn had marched him from his home and forced him into the car boot, tying Nick's feet again once he was prone inside. Then the boot lid was slammed, triggering palpitations in Nick's chest. It had felt like a coffin lid closing.

Blindfolded, he could see nothing. He felt as helpless as a child. He couldn't even call out: Hawthorn had wound tape around his mouth in a tight, ungainly mess.

The car was moving, accelerating, slowing, turning, and accelerating again. Something repeatedly clinked beside Nick's ear. The strong tang of oil emanated from close by, perhaps from an old rag or carjack. Nick wondered if he could fold down the rear seats and possibly escape that way, provided Hawthorn left the car for long enough. With his arms and legs secured, though, coupled with the impenetrable darkness, this would be next to impossible. And what if Hawthorn didn't leave the car? What if the seats didn't fold down? What if Hawthorn had envisaged this escape route and ensured the seats would not collapse?

Such negative thinking made Nick's heart pump faster. He swallowed and tried again to calm himself. As he breathed steadily through his nose, he worked his jaw and neck, attempting to slacken the tape around his mouth; but it was secure, and he didn't envision much success. He ground his face against the inside of the car's rear seats, in a bid to dislodge the blindfold. Without the use of his hands, though, it was fruitless. His shoulders ached. The ropes chaffed at his wrists. His legs were tucked in awkwardly, and the boot lid was mere inches above his head.

Hawthorn was going to kill him. What else could result from this lunacy? The madman would be aware that, should Nick escape, he would alert the police immediately. Clearly, Billy Hawthorn had no intention of letting him go. If Nick was going to get out of this, he had to think of something – and fast. But how could he possibly defend himself without being able to see? Without the use of his hands?

An image of Dottie formed in his mind's eye, and the idea of never seeing her again tugged at his heart. Was she safe? Would Hawthorn hurt her? Would he kill her? Man, he had to think of *something*.

He felt the car slowing, and heard the tyres gradually come to a stop. Hawthorn crunched the gearstick into reverse, backing up. Then the car inched forward again.

He was parking.

The engine died.

A door opened, and closed.

Alert, primed for confrontation, Nick craned his neck, listening, holding his breath. His body tensed rigidly, every sinew taut as guitar strings. Any second now, he expected the boot lid to rise…

He waited.

Eventually, Nick lowered his head again, exhaling through his nose. He listened, but could hear nothing except the ticking of the cooling engine. Tick-tick-tick. After a time, this sound also subsided, and there was only dead silence to keep him company.

*****

Billy trained his binoculars on the fog-cloaked façade of Netherwood House. There were two cars in the drive, the Volvo and the BMW. The Hobins obviously hadn't left yet. Billy waited, wondering whether Dottie would accompany them to the school. If she did, Cassidy would go in the hole alone. He'd just have to think of something else for Dottie. Actually, if he were honest, he kind of liked the idea of dumping the doctor in that grave by himself. The guy was claustrophobic. Jeez, how perfect was *that*? The man would soil himself down there in that box. Billy knew that Cassidy might be lying about his phobia – trying to appeal to Billy's sympathetic side, perhaps – but he didn't think so. The doctor had sounded sincere.

Billy had parked the Mondeo off the road, close to Netherwood but well-concealed. There was little chance of the car being spotted. It was black, and the fog rendered it just about invisible.

He sniffed, coughed, and spat out a glob of phlegm. He checked his watch, wondering how Cassidy was coping back there. His stint in the boot was a bit like a trial run for later, Billy thought, smiling.

He raised the binoculars as Netherwood's front door opened, a slash of hallway light bleeding into the darkness and mist. It was difficult, but Billy could just decipher the figures. Lynette and Graham were walking to the Volvo, Lynette escorting little Tara by the hand.

291

Dottie's half-pint frame appeared in the doorway, the small corgi sitting on its haunches by her side.

Billy grinned.

She was staying at home, after all. He'd been right. It was meant to be. This was all meant to be.

Like twin searchlights, the Volvo's beams swung over Billy's distant location, but his concealed spot in the woods provided sufficient cover. He was invisible. Untouchable.

Dottie was waving them off. She looked down at the little dog and said something. They waited there momentarily in the doorway, before retreating into the house again.

"Here we go," Billy said and slipped away, back to the car.

CHAPTER 44

The Hobins gone, and Dottie called her parents from the kitchen phone. With Rex pacing around at her feet, she told her mother all her news, talking about Nick first and foremost. Her mother was delighted that Dottie had met such a man and that her daughter sounded so happy and content. Dottie couldn't help but notice her mother's distinct lack of interest in her separation from Billy; if anything, she sounded relieved that the marriage was finished, without blatantly stating as much. Dottie then spoke briefly with her father, and before ringing off, he promised that he would book a flight soon – within the next couple of weeks – and get over there to see her.

After the call, she dialled Nick's home number, but there was no answer. She contemplated ringing his mobile, but knew he might yet be at the hospital and didn't want to disturb him. She would try him later.

Upstairs, with Rex still tottering around in her wake, Dottie drew a hot bath. She slipped on a cotton robe and tied the sash, before drizzling colourful bubble-bath mixtures and relaxation potions into the rising water level. She tested the heat with her hand as she watched the gathering froth spring up.

"Sorry, you'll have to wait outside, pooch," she told Rex, affording the dog a friendly wave. Shuffling obediently back, Rex chuffed and cocked his head quizzically as she closed the door on him. "Bye, bye."

Dottie tested the temperature again and added some cold. She disrobed and settled into the steaming heat, careful at first; then, she slipped gratefully into the enveloping warmth. She held her breath and sighed inwardly as the hot water lapped over her body. She tilted her head, soaking her long auburn hair and splashed her face a little. Submerged in fragrant bubbles, she closed her eyes. And, as if by magic, all of life's trouble and woes just melted away.

*****

Nick could hear nothing. He listened for passing traffic, or voices – any tell-tale sound that might suggest he was within reach of help. To his mounting dismay, however, he hadn't heard one solitary noise since Hawthorn left the car. Not so much as the distant bark of a dog.

He had spent several minutes knocking his knees against the boot's underside, but this achieved nothing more than panicking himself further – and sore knees – and he thus decided to conserve his energy. At any rate, he knew that Hawthorn would not have abandoned him within earshot of passers-by, so he was likely wasting his time. He—

Nick froze, hearing footsteps approach the car.

The door opened, and closed. The vehicle dipped as Hawthorn slumped into the driver's seat and gunned the engine. The car's tyres began rolling, and they were back on the move again.

As far as Nick could tell, the car wasn't travelling very fast; in fact, it was hardly moving at all. Was Hawthorn merely shifting the vehicle from one spot to another? Are we arriving at the place where he plans to kill me? Nick wondered bleakly.

Before long, the car had stopped again. The handbrake's ratchet sounded. The door opened and closed – but very quietly this time, almost as if Hawthorn were trying to conceal his presence.

Nick waited.

Surely now Hawthorn would open the boot – Nick almost wanted him to, just so he could breathe the fresh night air, just to alleviate the growing claustrophobic dread he was suffering in such unbearable confines. Again, nothing happened. Hawthorn's faint footsteps receded from the car.

Beneath the blindfold, Nick frowned.

What the hell was going on?

*****

With the Mondeo's lights off, Billy drew up to Netherwood's east gable and parked. He snapped on a fresh pair of latex gloves and, taking the holdall with him, got out. He glanced around at the stark tree branches angling through the fog.

He moved to the house's front elevation, pausing at a lighted bay window. The curtains were drawn, but an inch between them provided enough space for Billy to see through. He pressed his face close to the glass and found himself looking into the living room. He couldn't see much: a crystal chandelier suspended from a plaster moulding on the ceiling; an unoccupied sofa with a brightly coloured throw.

Billy walked by the front door, which he knew from a prior night's inspection to be fitted with a Yale lock. Well, he wouldn't be tampering with that. He decided to head around back instead.

At the rear of the house, the woodland was lost in heavy fog. Dark trunks were visible here and there, the spaces between them shrouded like sinister gateways to another realm. A small shed was situated nearby. A high washing line sagged from two poles, looking something like the masts of an old haunted ship.

His hands on the ledge, Billy peered through a quartered window, into a darkened room. There was nothing to see inside except shapeless shadows. The room's door lay partially open, providing a view of the living area from another angle. He decided he was probably looking at Lynette's study. He gave the double-glazed window a once-over, but it appeared secure, and so he moved on.

The house's back door, which led into the kitchen, was fitted with a large frosted square of glass. Its corners were dusted with stringy webs. A pair of moths fluttered against the pane, drawn by the low light burning inside. Billy tried the door. As sure as death, it was locked.

He opened the holdall, shifted the shoebox aside, and removed the suction cup and diamond cutter. He pressed the cup to the glass, close to the lock, and cut out a circular hole. Using a careful back-and-forth motion, the circular portion of glass eventually came away with the cup. Tentatively, Billy worked his hand inside and easily located the lock. He touched a protruding key, and with a deft wrist action, got his fingers around it. He repositioned his feet, dipped his shoulder down, and bit his lip as he tried to gain purchase. After a couple of failed attempts, he managed to turn the key. The door swung open, and he was in.

Voila.

He peered around the spacious, empty kitchen. At its centre, wooden stools stood by a high marble counter. Three burgundy-stained wine glasses were by the sink. Billy imagined them all standing here, quaffing their grape juice, laughing at him. Talking about how great a guy Cassidy was. How lucky Dottie was to have him.

The dog's basket was there in the corner, but Rex he saw no sign. The little shit would doubtlessly start yapping his head off as soon he saw Billy – but he would deal with that if and when it happened.

Clutching the holdall, Billy stepped inside Netherwood House and closed the door.

CHAPTER 45

Lynette was sitting between Graham and Tara in the school gymnasium, five rows from the front. Parents and children still milled in the aisles, settling themselves into seats, talking to other mums and dads before the play began. The stage, Lynette saw, was situated atop a wide flight of varnished wooden stairs, directly before the audience. For the time being, it remained concealed behind two huge, brown curtains, the material of which was decorated with white Egyptian-style figures. Occasionally, Lynette saw the curtains billow, brushed by those moving around back there. Smiling discreetly to herself, she wondered if her son was nervous, and decided he probably wasn't. Mark did not even have to show his face, after all.

Graham leaned in close to her. "Listen, what's all this I was hearing from Dottie about Nick Cassidy's cat?"

"Nothing really," she said, looking at him. "According to Dottie, Nick suspected foul play. But the cat was probably hit by a car. I mean, it's the most likely scenario, what with the heavy fog. Don't you think?"

"And does Nick really believe Billy was involved?"

"Well, he entertained the possibility, yeah."

Graham shook his head, scratching at his chin. "Surely he's not capable of stooping to something like that?"

"Maybe not. Then again, you never know. Dottie thought that Billy might have been following Nick – you know, watching his house, or something? Perhaps watching her. But I think it was Nick who put that idea in her head. Maybe he should've known better. I

298

mean, she's been through enough recently, without him scaring her with ideas like that."

"Would Billy really follow them around, do you think?"

"You know the man as well as I do," she said. "And I use the word *man* in its broadest possible sense."

"Is Billy coming to see the play?" Tara piped up, leaning over her mother's lap.

"Hey, you've got big ears, young lady."

"Have not. Is he coming, Mummy?"

"No, honey, he's not. Why would you say that?"

"We talked about it."

Lynette frowned at her. "You did?"

"At the toy store, remember?"

Lynette glanced at Graham, then back at Tara. "What did you talk about with Billy?"

Tara was chewing her lip, bobbing her head side to side. "Just that ... about the play. That we were coming here, to see Mark."

"You did, huh? And what else?"

Tara shrugged. "That's all. He asked what night."

"Billy asked you what night the play was on?"

Tara kicked her legs, looking impatiently to the front. "Think so. I can't really remember."

"I don't think there's any fear of Billy turning up here, Lynette," Graham told her. "I don't think school plays are really his style, do you? He'll be spread-eagled on his couch at home, no doubt, tanning another case of Miller."

Lynette gave him a look. "Miller?"

"Yeah, that's his tipple, isn't it? That's what we had to buy in that time Dottie took him round to our place, remember? He goes through packs of the stuff – hey, what's the matter?"

Lynette was grabbing her bag from the floor, searching inside for her mobile. "I have to call Dottie," she said.

*****

Partway across the kitchen, Billy expected the dog to appear at any second. It was possible that Rex would recognise him and react calmly, but Billy doubted it would go down like that. He was creeping through the house on his own, and the animal would probably sense as much. It would know something was wrong. Still, he didn't see too many problems arising from a confrontation with the dog. He'd come too far to let a mangy mutt hold him back. If it was unavoidable, he would kill the dog and dispose of it along with Dottie and Cassidy.

He took another step – and the wall phone beside him suddenly started trilling, unusually loud in the noiseless room. Billy's eyes fixed on it. Out in the open, as he was, he felt completely exposed. He needed to take Dottie by surprise. But if she came wandering in here now ... well, he would be seen, obviously.

He contemplated lifting the receiver and leaving it off the hook: that way, he could be sure it would not ring again. At the same time, though, it might alert the caller that something was amiss. Instead, he crossed silently to the double doors leading into the dining room and slipped behind one, hiding between it and the wall. He slid the holdall into the corner with his foot, and eased the door back as far as he could, concealing himself. The phone kept ringing, and so he waited for Dottie to appear. Why go hunting through the house for her, when she would walk right in here and answer the phone?

After a moment, the ringing ceased. Billy scowled. He peered out from behind the door, just far enough to see the kitchen clearly. Why hadn't she come and answered the phone? And where was the damned dog?

He stepped out from the corner.

Dottie was probably upstairs. That would explain why she hadn't heard the phone. She was in her bedroom, maybe. Or in the bathroom? Billy withdrew a knife from the holdall and slipped the bag back behind the door. He would return for it before he left the house; it would only hinder him while he was in the process of apprehending his wife. Dottie was petite, but he was quite positive she wouldn't go quietly. Not without an incentive.

Billy looked at the blade, turning it. Its honed edge flashed in the kitchen's ambient light, and he smiled. He slotted the knife into his belt, at the small of his back, and entered the dining room.

A large mahogany table stood before him, its polished wooden surface reflecting a perfect gleam. Silver candelabra stood at its centre. Another door by his side led into the living room, and he went there, his movements as soundless as a spider crossing a web.

The walls and units here were adorned with pictures of the Hobin family, showing the kids in various stages of growth. There were framed photographs of Lynette and that dweeb, Graham. A painting of Tara adorned the far wall. The little girl's toys and books were strewn before a big flat-screen TV. The smouldering embers of fire burned in the grate, their reflection flickering against the hearthstone. Very swanky.

To his left, an open doorway led into Lynette's study. This area was in semi-darkness, the living room's light touching her computer and the broad desk on which it sat. He saw a globe there, secured at its poles by a brass half-ring. This was where she sat and composed her tripe, he told himself. He should find her work and put a match to it. That would teach her not to meddle in his life. All those hours of work, up in smoke, gone in seconds. If it wasn't for the fact he'd be leaving behind evidence of his presence, he just might have done it.

From the living room, he entered a long hallway, which was carpeted in the same colour that evidently ran through the entire ground floor. By the stairs, a table lamp with tear-shaped frills burned softly. A varnished hat-and-coat stand stood there. Billy craned his neck and looked up at the staircase. He waited for a second, but could neither hear nor see anything from above.

He placed a latex-covered hand on the smooth newel post. The wooden handrail led upwards, towards the dim light of the landing. The house was hushed – too hushed for his liking – as if he were the only one here. The stairs were carpeted. This was good, for the carpet would muffle his footfalls. As he climbed, he kept to the outside of the treads anyway, in case a creaky step decided to betray him.

CHAPTER 46

Nick had resorted to saying silent prayers, wordless entreaties to the effect that, should he escape this nightmare alive, he would trade anything in return. Never had he been a religious man – spiritual, maybe – although now he was willing to embrace anything that might see him overcome his plight. He did not know how much longer he could last before the hands of panic seized him and wrung from him what little courage remained. When that happened, he'd be unable to endure the pressure, and he would, in modern parlance, lose it.

He could hardly move. His fettered arms and legs were numb and cramped, tingling with pins and needles. His hands and feet were starting to feel like concrete. He tried to manoeuvre himself into a position that might allow his blood to circulate, but the effort was almost useless. Breathing deeply through his nostrils, he wondered about his air supply. He assumed this confined space must be ventilated; unless, of course, Hawthorn had taken steps to seal it.

What if the man wasn't coming back?

This idea set Nick's heart fluttering again. What if this was it? What if that maniac had simply abandoned the car in the middle of nowhere, planning to just let Nick die? He tried to recall exactly what Hawthorn had said.

If that's true, then you're in for a fun night, my friend.

Nick shook his head in the inky blackness. The outlook was bleak, no question. He should have fought back when Hawthorn had forced him from the bungalow, should have tried something, *anything*. But he had been blindfolded, gagged, with his hands tied – what was he supposed to have done?

A grim image popped into Nick's mind: uniformed police officers approaching a parked car. Maybe, after a long period of time, someone had reported the vehicle abandoned. Maybe someone had reported it stolen. In any event, the officers eventually manage to open the boot – and recoil violently at the stink of death emanating from the dead body stored in there. Nick would be the source of that rancid, cloying smell. And God alone knew what he'd look like. Never had he imagined he would die a relatively young man, certainly not in the throes of agony and losing his sanity. *Man found bound and gagged,* it would say in the newspapers. *Left to perish in a car boot.*

Summoning his courage, spurred on by this most gruesome of prospects, Nick began working his jaw again, trying to dislodge the tape, ignoring that incessant voice, the one whispering that he was wasting his time and energy. He ground his face against the flat surface on which he lay, trying to free his mouth, at least. If he could scream for help, there might be a slight hope.

If anyone was there to hear him…

*****

Dottie lay in the tub, luxuriating with her eyes closed, thinking about her upcoming date with Nick on Friday. She liked the idea of him cooking for her: it somehow gave their time together an intimate, more personal dimension, as if confirming that they were serious about each other. She felt as if she were entering a new phase of her life, one that wasn't blighted and doomed to fail. She also liked the

304

idea of her and Nick going to the movies together and allowed a smile to creep across her lips. Nick was—

Dottie opened her eyes.

Was that the phone ringing?

She didn't move in the water, listening intently. Yes, she could faintly hear the phone going, downstairs. Well, whoever it was would just have to call back. She wasn't climbing from the tub to answer it. Probably it was a cold-caller, trying to sell this or that, or wanting to ask her inane questions.

She closed her eyes again and slipped further into the steamy water.

*****

"Why isn't she answering?" Lynette said, studying her mobile.

"Didn't she say she might take a bath?"

Lynette glanced at her husband. "Yeah, she did, didn't she?"

"So, there you go. She's probably soaking in it, as we speak. What's the matter, anyway? Why're you calling her?"

"I just had ... a funny feeling about something. I suppose it's nothing."

"When's it starting?" Tara asked her.

"It shouldn't be long, sweetheart. Everyone is seated, it'll be any minute now."

Graham was looking at her. "What sort of feeling?"

"What?"

"What sort of funny feeling did you have?"

"I'm going to try her mobile."

"She won't have her mobile in the bathroom with her, will she? Unless she's texting someone, possibly ..."

"I know, but maybe she didn't hear the house phone. She might hear her mobile ringing, though."

"What's this about, Lynette?" Graham asked. "Does it have something to do with Billy?"

"I don't know," she said, finding Dottie's number on the screen and jabbing CALL. "I just want to check she's all right, that's all ..."

*****

Refreshed and invigorated, Dottie opened the bathroom's casement window a crack, to allow the accumulated steam to disperse. Chill night air swirled in like a malevolent spirit. She draped her robe around her body. Bathwater gurgled and coughed, swirling and whirling down the plughole. Her hair towel-dry, she tugged open the bathroom door, half expecting to see Rex still posted there, standing sentry, looking up at her with his comical foxy expression. But as she glanced at the length of the landing, the little corgi was nowhere in sight.

Humming softly, snug now inside the robe, Dottie began along towards her bedroom. When she reached it, she crossed the threshold, barefoot, and saw her mobile flashing on the bed's counterpane. She smiled, presuming it was Nick returning her call from earlier.

Dottie advanced to the bed – and heard the door close behind her. Before she had a chance to turn around, a gloved hand had clamped over her mouth, and something sharp touched against her windpipe.

*****

From the earpiece of her phone, Lynette listened to Dottie's voicemail service, inviting her to leave a message. She waited for the tone and said, "Dottie, it's Lynette here. I just wanted to check you're okay. I was thinking over what you said about Billy, and ... well, give me a ring back if you get this message, okay?"

"No joy?" asked Graham.

Lynette shook her head. On the stage, the school headmaster, Mr Bowden, was preparing to introduce the play.

"I have to go," Lynette said, standing and shrugging on her jacket. "Can I have the keys to the Volvo?"

Graham started getting up too. "What's the matter?"

"Nothing, just stay here and record the show for me, okay? I'm sorry, but I've just got this feeling there's something wrong at home."

"Where are you going, Mummy?" Tara asked.

"Mummy has to check on something, sweetheart." Lynette took the car keys from Graham. "You stay with your dad now, hear? Go on, scoot over and sit there beside him." Lynette leant down and kissed her daughter's cheek and said to Graham, "I won't be long."

As Mr Bowden called out: "Good evening, ladies and gentlemen!", she was hurriedly leaving through the gymnasium's main exit.

CHAPTER 47

Nick had managed to fray the tape around his lips. He'd been somewhat successful in biting at it, after a fashion, feeling absurd like a dog chewing at a favourite toy. Following much perseverance, he had finally worked the tape away from his skin, just enough to breathe through his mouth. As tiny a victory as it was, a jolt of hope surged through him, as if a drug had been administered into his system.

He continued to work his cheek against the surface he lay on, pressing harder and harder at the tape, wilfully ignoring the deep grazes he was scoring into his face. Now he worked his chin, up and down, side to side, slackening the tape's adhesive hold, until he was able to speak – indeed, to shout.

"Holy Christ," he said to the utter darkness, taking deep inhalations, letting his heart rate find a level again. His voice sounded hollow and afraid, but at least he could *hear* it.

Little point in looping the loop yet, he assured himself. The chances were fair he was in the middle of nowhere. Hawthorn wouldn't be stupid enough to leave him somewhere he could be heard by other people. Or would he? Perhaps that was why Nick had been so comprehensively silenced.

Jesus, his head *hurt*.

Again, he wondered just where the hell he was, and decided that, at this very second, it was of scant importance. If there was anyone within earshot, he had a chance – didn't he? Following a moment's composure, Nick abandoned all caution and began bellowing as loud as he could.

"*HEEEELLLLP! HEEEELLLLP!*" His words were rich with panic and fear in the lightless enclosure, but to him, they sounded divine.

"*HEEEELLLLP!*"

*****

"Just you relax, Dottie, and do exactly what you're told. I'm going to take my hand away from your mouth. If you scream, I'll slash your throat. Do you understand?"

Her eyes wide with horror, Dottie nodded, and the gloved hand dropped from her face, only to settle around her neck. The knife's point remained pressed into her skin.

"Billy? Oh my God, Billy, what are you—"

"Shut up. Shut up and listen to me. We're leaving the house. I'm going to walk you outside, nice and simple. There's a car parked at the side. You're going to get in the boot."

"*What?* Billy what—"

"You feel this knife at your throat? It's real, Dottie. I'll slide it right through you, unless you shut up and do as I say."

Dottie was trembling, a hybrid effect of fear and adrenaline. She believed him. She could hear it in his voice. The man had lost it, finally. She had known it was coming, hadn't she? She had known, and she had been complacent. But how had he got into the house? She tried to think, and couldn't...

"Let's go. Open the door – easy – and we'll head downstairs. Don't make any trouble, and everything will be just fine."

Will everything be just fine? Was he serious?

Dottie reached out. With an unsteady hand, she grasped the handle and opened the bedroom door. Billy motioned her forward.

"Walk."

With his fingers still clamped around her windpipe, and the knife's tip pressed against her neck, Dottie tottered awkwardly and helplessly out to the landing.

"Go to the stairs."

"Billy, whatever you're thinking about doing—"

"I won't tell you again to *shut up*."

Her steps encumbered, and Dottie was forced to the top of the stairs. As they were about two-thirds of the way there, a low-pitched growling came from behind them. The sound quickly escalated into loud, resounding barks that echoed throughout the house. Billy whirled around, forcing Dottie to do the same, so that they faced the little corgi.

"Please, don't hurt the dog," she said.

"Stop talking!"

Rex snapped and barked, exposing sharp canines, inching nearer and backing away. Dottie saw that the animal wasn't about to cower and retreat, and so was filled with gratitude for the small dog.

Still growling, Rex's barks became even louder. The dog closed the distance between them and suddenly went for Billy's leg. Billy fumbled his footing, struggling back against the banister, keeping hold of Dottie. He kicked out, but Rex stood his ground, boldly lunging in for another attempt.

"Fuck off!" Billy snarled, kicking angrily at the dog again. Dottie sensed he couldn't do it with any conviction, though, not without turning her free. Rex went on biting and snarling at Billy's leg, and the second Dottie felt the knife drop from her neck, she closed her fingers into a fist and rammed it back, straight into his groin. She felt him double over, heard the breath leave his body, and in that instant, *she was loose*. By her side, adorning a three-legged table, was the magenta porcelain vase she had bought for Lynette. Dottie seized it and turned around.

Billy had now captured Rex by his collar, dragging the frenzied dog across the landing to an open bedroom doorway. The corgi snapped and barked at the air with bared teeth, trying to angle its muzzle to get at Billy. Dottie stood there with bated breath as her deranged husband hurled Rex inside the bedroom and yanked shut the door.

Before he had time to turn, Dottie ran to him, hoisting the vase in both hands, and crashed it against the back of Billy's head, investing all her might in the strike. The ornament fragmented into pieces, and Billy dropped to his knees, fumbling the blade, crying out as he went down. Rex continued to bark furiously, his claws scratching wildly at the bedroom door.

"*Bitch* ..." Billy said.

He staggered to his feet, swaying, clutching a hand to his skull. He emitted an outraged wail and punched at the wall, cracking the plaster with his fist. He shook his head, as if to clear it, and bent for the knife, grasping it from the floor.

Dottie took flight and made for the stairs.

CHAPTER 48

Halfway down the stairs, moving with such rapidity that she could barely control her descent, Dottie lost her footing and tumbled the remaining third of the way. She cried out as she fell to the bottom, and pain lanced through her right ankle. At the foot of the stairs, she lay on the floor with her robe pulled open and her eyes tightly closed. After a struggle, she forced herself to her feet tentatively.

Keeping her weight on her strong leg, she made it to the front door. When she opened it, however, confronted with heavy fog eerily consuming everything, she was filled with reluctance to venture out there. She could not outrun Billy, not with a twisted ankle. She could try to hide in the woods, of course – but if he caught her, he'd kill her, for sure.

From above, Rex's anguished barking continued. At the door, Dottie looked towards the top of the stairs, where Billy's distorted shadow loomed ominously into view, like something from an old horror movie. Within seconds, he'd be coming for her again.

She left the front door standing open, as if she'd decided to leave the house, hoping the timeworn ruse might prove a worthy decoy. Clutching together the lapels of her robe, Dottie headed for the living room, moving as quickly as her hindered gait allowed. Her heart thumping, she scanned for a half-decent hiding place and, seeing no better option, ducked down behind the sofa positioned against the back wall.

She crouched into the tight space and, seconds later, could hear Billy's thumping footfalls descend the stairs. He was muttering to himself and swearing. Dottie took a breath and held it. Although she did her best to ignore it, the ache in her foot was throbbing now, becoming gradually more painful.

Wedged there between the sofa and wall, she listened intently, hearing only Rex's frantic barking from upstairs. The dog – which had saved her life, she realised – sounded as if it were losing its mind. Dottie swallowed, tempted to peek over the sofa, but knowing such temerity would be risky and foolhardy.

Suddenly, the front door slammed shut: a loud *bang* that made her flinch.

She blinked, not yet daring to breathe. Had he left the house? *Please, God, say he's left the house.*

"I know you're here, Dottie," Billy said. "Come on out. I'm gonna find you anyway. That was a good shot you hit me with back there, but you should've finished the job. You hear me, you little bitch?"

Dottie covered her mouth with her hand, fearful of releasing the slightest sound. Even now, she could still feel the knife's point at her throat.

Through the arch in the wall, she could hear his steps in the dining room. She should have left the house, she thought. She should have taken her chances outside and hidden in the woods. It would have been hard for him to find her in the fog and darkness. If Billy discovered her here, however, it would be all over.

Just stay quiet, Dottie.

She had to get to Lynette's BMW. If she could make it to the car, she would have a chance to escape and to go for help. But where were the keys? She recalled Lynette hanging them in the kitchen, before leaving for the play. Damn it. In the bureau, on the other side of the living room, she knew there was a tin containing spare keys for the house and both cars. She had seen it when Lynette gave her a housekey for herself, so that Dottie could come and go as she pleased. If she could make it there without Billy spotting her and somehow sneak past him, out of the house. There was a chance—

"You in here, Dottie? Where are you, my love? Oh, but it's only doctors you go for these days, right? Well, you'll both be together very soon."

Behind the couch, Dottie stiffened. He was here, in the room with her.

"You're close, aren't you? Your heart's thumping like a little rabbit's, isn't it? I bet I could hear it, if I listen really hard."

His voice was getting nearer, closing in now. Adjusting her position ever so slightly, Dottie spotted his reflection in the glass-fronted picture of Tara on the wall. Billy wasn't more than ten feet away from the sofa.

*****

Lynette drove the Volvo through the foggy darkness as fast as she dared. This could be the world's biggest overreaction, she reflected, but a deep-seated misgiving convinced her there was something wrong. If Billy had been watching their house, there had to be a reason. He meant to do Dottie harm, obviously. Perhaps he meant *all* of them harm. The man wasn't sound in the head. Maybe Nick Cassidy had been right on the money about the dead cat. It had sounded farfetched, but those discarded Miller cans in the woods ... they told her otherwise.

314

Who else could have left them out there?

The very thought of him skulking around outside their house – in the dark, in the trees, watching them as they prepared to turn in, watching her children – it turned her blood cold.

Lynette's mobile was in the passenger seat. She snatched it up, scrolled down to the entry marked HOME, and pressed CALL.

"Please be there, Dottie," she whispered.

*****

Dottie's heart galloped as the kitchen phone began braying. Its ringtone trilled a couple of times, and Rex's agitated barks started upstairs again. Still huddled behind the sofa, Dottie's eyes were riveted to Billy's reflection in the picture glass. Would he go to the kitchen? She imagined he must, because he couldn't risk letting her answer the call.

After another couple of rings, he muttered and walked from the room.

Dottie counted to five and rose cautiously from behind the sofa, peeping over the top. The room was clear. Billy had gone. The ringing in the kitchen ceased, but Rex's distant barking continued without respite.

Go.

Like a child, Dottie scuttled across the floor on her hands and knees and eased open the bureau drawer. The black tin was exactly where it should be, surrounded by old letters and correspondence. She eased the lid off as quietly as possible. There were several sets of keys inside – house keys, car keys, and keys she didn't recognise, perhaps for the shed outside. She took the set for the BMW, which was adorned with a little book-shaped keyring. On her feet again, she hobbled out to the hallway, seizing her chance while Billy was in the kitchen.

Like a cripple, using the wall for support, she struggled down the length of the hall. At the front door, she slipped open the Yale lock and was outside, cutting awkwardly across the stony drive towards Lynette's BMW, ignoring the jabs and pricks at the soles of her bare feet. The cold night air bled beneath her robe, chilling her exposed skin.

At the car, she separated the keys, hurriedly unlocked the door, and tugged it open. As she did, Dottie froze as she saw Billy's silhouette appear in the house doorway. He had a black bag in one hand and a knife in the other. And he was coming for her.

*****

Lynette snapped shut the mobile phone and tossed it back on the passenger seat. Was Dottie even in the house? God, she hoped Billy hadn't harmed her. This was probably a false alarm; she would likely find Dottie relaxing in the bath, wondering what all the fuss was about. Yet she just couldn't take the chance, could she?

Thumping the steering wheel, she directed the Volvo off the main road, onto the twisting, narrow track that led to her home. The flanking woodland was lost in wreathing fog. Potholes caused the car to dip and jounce. Her fog lights struggled to show the way, but she knew the road well and did not compromise her speed, hurtling past the old sandblasted sign that read: NETHERWOOD HOUSE 1 MILE.

CHAPTER 49

Billy was out of the house and coming for her.

Her short legs barely brushing the pedals, Dottie started the BMW, activated the lights, and shoved the gearstick into first. She stamped on the accelerator, and the wheels spun, churning gravel, before the car shot forward. The effort of working the pedals brought fresh pain to her ankle.

She directed the car straight for Billy's knife-wielding silhouette, intent now on ramming him – maiming him, if she had to. When he saw the car hurtling straight for him, Billy slowed ... then stopped dead in his tracks. His startled face and hairless head were illuminated in the headlights, stark against the backdrop of night, and he leapt clear as Dottie sped past.

Headed for the road leading away from the house, Dottie pulled at the wheel, steering the BMW in a wild semicircle, tugging loose the seatbelt and strapping it across her front. A nervous glance in the rear-view mirror revealed Billy's dark shape, running towards the side of the house. It was then that she remembered he'd said he had a car. And she knew this wasn't over yet.

*****

"HEEEELLLLP!"

His throat raw, Nick was still screaming when he heard a commotion happening, somewhere nearby. He abruptly silenced his cries for assistance and froze, the reverberation of his hoarse pleas ringing in his ears. The subdued noises of footsteps scampering across stones were followed by the closing of a car door nearby.

317

He swallowed, frowning.

It all sounded very close by, but it was hard to be sure. His bearings and sense of direction were confused, and distorted, possibly due to the earlier blows to his head. He heard a car engine start and wheels spinning off in a hurry…

More footsteps now, running towards *this* car. The door was yanked open, and slammed shut, followed by the ignition firing. Among these sounds, he could hear Hawthorn shouting something – shouting, or swearing. Whichever it was, the words were too muffled to understand. But Nick got the impression that something was going wrong.

The engine roared to life, and the vehicle lurched forward, throwing him against the boot's interior. He struck his already aching head on an unseen metal protrusion and winced beneath the blindfold. Something was happening, undoubtedly – but a small part of him was glad to know he hadn't been abandoned.

Hawthorn was crunching through the gears, revving the engine, seemingly trying to extract everything the motor had to give. He was chasing somebody, Nick thought, or trying to escape something ... Maybe someone had realised what was going on. Maybe he had a chance of living through this fiasco, after all.

But as he thought this, Nick was acutely aware of the car clocking up more speed, and it didn't feel as if Hawthorn had any intention of slowing down.

*****

As Dottie had anticipated, bright headlights soon flared in her rear-view mirror: Billy was motoring after her. She pressed the

318

accelerator and sped through the evergreens, hurtling along the dark, tree-lined road, the speedometer creeping to the fifty-miles-per-hour mark. The glare of headlights shone oppressively in her mirror as Billy gained ground.

He was right *there*, and she expected he would start ramming her, trying to force her from the road. She gripped the wheel, telling herself, *You will not die in this situation.* At such excessive speed, she struggled to retain control as the BMW dipped and rocked, encountering pits and holes—

And suddenly, another car was heading straight for her.

Blinding lights filled her vision. Dottie cried out as she stamped on the brake, trying to kill the BMW's speed. The oncoming car swerved at the last minute, barely avoiding a collision with her. From behind, the high-pitched screeching of brakes tore through the night as Billy's car slammed into the BMW's rear.

Dottie was thrown violently forward in her seat, impacting her head on the side window. The collision was instantly followed by the unmistakable sound of breaking glass, and something else – something solid – striking the back of her car with tremendous power. She felt a terrible pain flash in her neck and cried out in agony.

When the commotion was over, when the cars had stopped moving, silence held all around. Dazed, Dottie touched the right side of her forehead, and her fingertips came away tacky with blood. As she looked out through the window, she saw somebody getting out of the other car, which had come to an angled halt next to a broad tree trunk. She recognised the Volvo. A woman with long black hair came through the fog towards her, and when that person approached the BMW's window, Dottie stared into the familiar face, dumbfounded.

"Lynette?"

Her friend tugged open the car door.

"Dottie, for Christ's sake, are you all right?"

"I ... Billy was ... he was chasing me. He has a knife."

"Come on, get out of the car," Lynette demanded. "Take it easy now, your head's bleeding."

"No, he's back there. He's—"

"He can't hurt you, Dottie."

Dottie fumbled at her seatbelt, unfastening it, and allowed Lynette to take her hand, to guide her from the car. Standing shakily, she realised her legs were rubbery, that they barely supported her weight. Her neck ached, an acute pain that stabbed at her with every movement. When she looked back, she saw a crumpled black car embedded in the rear end of the BMW. The black car's front wheels, one of which was still rotating slowly, were lifted clear off the ground, as if the vehicle had attempted to drive directly over hers. Hissing steam rose into the darkness. Billy lay prone on the bonnet, facedown, his motionless body peppered with glistening shards of laminated glass. The car's windscreen was obliterated, shattered to smithereens as he had ejected through it headlong. His face – what she could see of it – was badly cut, slick blood coursing down his cheek. Dottie found herself wondering if he were dead. It was certainly possible.

"What the hell's happening?" Lynette asked, gaping around at the carnage.

"He was – he was in the house," Dottie mouthed vacantly, as if she could not quite believe it herself. "... He was going to kill me."

Lynette seemed poised to say something, when they heard a thumping noise from somewhere nearby. Bang. Bang. Bang. The sounds were quickly punctuated by muffled shouts for help.

Lynette frowned at her.

"Do you hear that?" Dottie asked.

"It's coming from back there." Lynette walked to the rear of the caved-in Mondeo. "There's ... Dottie, there's someone in the boot."

The banging continued emphatically.

Dottie yanked open the driver's door and plucked the keys from the ignition. Limping forward, she joined Lynette and slid the key into the lock. When the boot rose, Dottie's hands went to her mouth. She started to cry.

"I'll call the police," Lynette told her.

CHAPTER 50

"I knew he was dangerous," Lynette said, pulling up outside the vast grey expanse of the hospital. "But I never thought he'd be capable of such ... *madness*. It's unbelievable." She parked the Volvo, the only one of the three vehicles involved in the accident to survive unscathed. "Do you really think he was prepared to commit murder?"

"You saw what he did to Nick," said Dottie, in the passenger seat. "The police say they're going for attempted murder. Not that it matters now. Billy's no threat to anyone anymore. When I spoke to Nick yesterday, he told me the doctors couldn't do anything about Billy's injuries. His spine is badly damaged. He can't walk. He can't even sit up."

"Don't you want to see him jailed for what he did?"

Dottie shrugged. "I just want to forget the whole thing."

Lynette looked at the hospital again. "Nick must have been pretty shaken by what happened."

Dottie stared at the rain coursing down the windscreen. The afternoon sky was overcast. "More than he's letting on, I think. He'll get over it. We both will. I won't allow Billy to ruin things between us. Not that he can now. He's finally got what was always coming to him. Perhaps this is life's way of teaching him a lesson. Karma or whatever. God knows what he was planning to do with that ... *thing* in the shoebox. It makes my skin crawl just to imagine ..."

Lynette was still staring at the hospital. "How do you feel about going in there to see him?"

"I have to leave this mess behind me, once and for all. I can't do that without letting him know that he didn't beat me, that he didn't win. I need closure, I suppose, and I won't get it until I look in his eyes."

Lynette took her hand. "Want me to come in with you?"

"No. You shouldn't wait, either, Lynette. I'm meeting Nick here in twenty minutes." Dottie was quiet for a moment, and said: "Thank you for what you did that night. If you hadn't arrived when you did ..."

"Then you'd have thought of something else," Lynette assured her.

"And I owe so much to this little guy." Dottie reached around to the back seat and petted Rex's head. The corgi yawned and scratched himself. "Well, I suppose I better get on with it."

Dottie leaned over and hugged her friend. She got out and opened her brolly. Sheltered beneath it, she waved at Lynette through the rain-smeared window. Lynette reciprocated and honked the horn twice as the Volvo drew away.

Inside the hospital, Dottie spoke to a pretty, young nurse at reception and asked for Dr. Maguire, the man Nick had told her was overseeing Billy's care.

She waited until a tall, white-bearded gentleman in a starched coat appeared beside her. His face was heavily lined and creased, his snowy hair receding in a widow's peak.

"Mrs. Hawthorn?"

Dottie nodded and did her best to smile. "Yes. Thanks for taking the time to see me."

He indicated a line of vacant seats beside them. "Let's sit down," he suggested. When they had, he slotted his fingers together and said, "I understand you endured quite a scary experience on Wednesday night."

Dottie absently touched the plaster on her head. "Billy tried to kill me. He tried to kill Dr. Cassidy, too."

"That must have been harrowing. Tell me, what exactly can I do for you?"

"I want to know what's going to happen to him. And I want to see him if that's possible."

"You can see him; that's no problem. His injuries – well, I won't lie to you. He's in about as grim a situation as you can get." Dr. Maguire smoothed his white beard with his fingers. His wedding band, inlaid with a small stone, caught the light.

"Your husband was seriously injured in the accident, Mrs. Hawthorn. His spinal cord was fractured in the neck, and there's damage to the thoracic spine – which is the back." He sighed. "You see, the spinal cord carries the nerves which control breathing, the bladder, the bowels, and limb movement. These and many of his other bodily functions may be paralysed. It's too early to be absolutely sure, but in my opinion, he'll never walk again. As I said, his injuries are extensive. The paramedics took every possible care when they arrived at the accident scene. Unfortunately, the damage was done. I would like to give you a more optimistic outlook. That's the long and short of it, I'm afraid."

"I'd like to see him."

Dr. Maguire stood. "Follow me, please."

Dottie shadowed the tall doctor until they'd walked the length of two corridors. They reached a door, and he asked if she wanted to go in alone.

"Yes, please," Dottie said. "I won't be long."

He touched her arm and left her to it. Dottie pushed open the door.

Billy lay on the single bed, his arms by his sides. His upper body was garbed in a white gown, a garment that managed to strip away much of his intimidating presence. An intravenous drip was rigged beside him, and liquid flowed from a bottle on a stand, through a tube, into his system. A brace was fixed around his neck. He stared at the ceiling, his face and arms marred by myriad cuts and scratches, more than Dottie could begin to count. He was broken, she thought. Broken beyond repair.

She approached the bed, and his eyes found hers.

"You couldn't just let us be, could you?" she said. "You couldn't just start over like I tried to. Look at you, Billy. They say you'll never walk again. Was it worth it?" She stepped a little closer to the bed. "Was it worth *this*?"

His gaze remained on her, but he said nothing. He looked too weak to even talk.

"Nick and I will still be together, Billy. I love him, and he loves me, and that's all that's important to us. You've thrown your life away, trying to destroy what we have. You failed, Billy, and now you'll be reminded of that for the rest of your life. That's what I came to say."

Dottie made to move to the door and paused. She went into her handbag, rummaging through her effects. When she had located what

325

she was looking for – a tube of lipstick – she removed the cap and slowly rolled the tip across the Cupid's bow of her pursed lips, all the while holding Billy's helpless gaze. A tear welled in his eye. It glistened, gathered, and tracked down his cheek in a clear line, soaking into the pillow.

"Goodbye, Billy," she said and left the room.

*****

Outside, the rain had ceased, though everything was soaked through from the fall. Puddles shone on walkways; beads of water shimmered on trees. Nick was waiting for her, leaning against his Audi in a plaid shirt and jeans. Dottie winced at the colourful bruise on his forehead.

"How are the wounds?" she asked, feeling in her neck her own dull memory of that night.

He smiled. "They get a little less painful every day. No permanent damage, I've been assured." He motioned his head towards the hospital. "Did you see him?"

"Yes."

"Not a pretty sight, is he?"

"Do you feel sorry for him?" Dottie asked.

"Well, considering what he's capable of and the way he'll live out the rest of his days, I suppose I do – a little, at least."

"He doesn't deserve it."

"Maybe not, Dottie, but I'm a doctor, remember? I can't just hate people because of their problems or the way they are."

"You shouldn't hate him. But you shouldn't pity him, either. He doesn't even deserve the care he's getting in there. Not really."

"He's mentally ill, Dottie."

They said nothing for a time. An ambulance went past.

"Will you take me to Venice, Nick?" she asked finally.

He looked down at her. "Venice?"

"We have to get away from here, from this place. I start work again tomorrow, but we can book something, can't we? We can have something to look forward to, right?"

Nick leant and closed his lips briefly over hers. They kissed, and for just a moment, Dottie felt like none of her recent nightmares were real.

"I'll take you anywhere in the world," he said.

Dottie put her arms around him because she knew he meant it. "Look," she said, pointing behind him.

"What is it?" Nick asked, turning about.

"A rainbow," she said. "There's a rainbow in the sky."

EPILOGUE

Billy stared at the room's ceiling, at the cracks and imperfections in its plaster. He tried to move his legs, but like each previous attempt, they stubbornly ignored him. Since waking yesterday, he'd repeatedly asked what the score was with his body, his situation. They just kept telling him that the doctors were still running tests. But he didn't need to wear a stethoscope to know he was knee-deep in shit. His body responded to none of his commands. He couldn't even move his head. He could stare at the ceiling – he had *staring* down to a fine art – and he could look at the room as far as his limited vision would roam. The clock on the wall showed ten thirty, evening hours. For the thousandth time, Billy watched the second-hand glide silently around the face.

Everything had gone wrong. Dottie was alive. Cassidy was alive. And he was stuck here, confined to a bed, unable to do a thing about it. No more capable of revenge than a brain in a jar.

He tried again to move his legs, feeling sure this whole mess must be some kind of sick nightmare. Any minute now, he'd wake at home, in his own bed, and life would be normal again. It was—

The room's door creaked open.

Billy's eyes darted in that direction. A doctor came in, a broad guy in a long white coat. It seemed late for doctors to be checking on him. Still, what the hell did he know? His body was wasted, after all: he needed every bit of help he could get.

The huge man approached the bedside, and Billy's heart somersaulted. The doctor's features were unsettlingly familiar. The

328

straggly black hair and beard were gone, revealing a face that could almost pass for friendly. But those cold eyes were unmistakable. Those eyes, deep-set and staring, showed ill intent. Even in a state of mild dread, Billy was surprised by how much the big man looked the part.

"Boomer," he whispered. The word came out dry and raspy.

"Billy boy," the man said, looking at the length of his body on the bed. "Well, you're in all sorts of bother, aren't you?"

Billy tried to move his head.

"I hear the boys in blue are pinning an attempted murder charge on you. Trying to waste the little wife and her new squeeze? That was a lame idea, Billy, even for you. If that's not bad enough, the Dunbar woman spilled her guts, too, as soon as she heard what you'd been up to. The way I hear it, she told them all about how you forced her into lying for you. It's a big mess, Billy, isn't it?"

Billy swallowed and tried to speak, but no words came.

"Seems to me it won't be long before they're badgering you about the car. Where it came from, who provided it, you know? Well, you're in no position to resist pressure, are you? No sir. You can't hold out, not in your condition. Look at you. As much use as a paper ashtray, all mashed-up there."

"No," Billy managed. "I won't ... say anything."

"Best if I take care of things myself." Boomer reached behind Billy's head and grabbed one of his pillows. "No hard feelings, amigo. I warned you about covering your tracks. You rest easy there now, and this won't take but a minute."

"Boomer, wait ..."

329

Billy's eyes rounded in panic as the pillow descended on his face. He felt Boomer's hand, huge like a baseball mitt, pressing down, the spongy material smothering his airways. The great man's weight pressed on Billy's head. Billy tried to scream, tried with everything he had, but his efforts were reduced to muffled grunts. His arms and legs managed to twitch only slightly until he finally grew calm and still. In his mind, he saw Dottie running through her garden of flowers, sunlight shining on her as he followed with their filming camera. In those last few seconds, they were young again, vibrant, laughing together.

And he knew nothing more.

Ingram Content Group UK Ltd.
Milton Keynes UK
UKHW021034140323
418553UK00015B/762